ALLY HUGHES HAS SEX SOMETIMES

ALLY HUGHES
HAS SEX
SOMETIMES

• A NOVEL •

JULES MOULIN

DUTTON
— est. 1852 —

DUTTON
—• est. 1852 •—

An imprint of Penguin Random House LLC
375 Hudson Street
New York, New York 10014

LIBRARY OF CONGRESS CATALOGING-IN-PUBLICATION DATA
Moulin, Jules.
Ally Hughes has sex sometimes : a novel / Jules Moulin.
pages cm
ISBN 978-0-525-95521-4 (hardcover)
ISBN 978-1-101-98416-1 (international edition)
1. Women—Fiction.   I. Title.
PS3613.O847A79   2015
813'.6—dc23   2014047798

Printed in the United States of America

1   3   5   7   9   10   8   6   4   2

Book design by Alissa Rose Theodor

To Isabel, with love

THAT WEEKEND

In the end, it was Harry's fault.

Harry Goodman had promised to help Professor Hughes around the house that Friday. He'd also promised the Friday before and the Friday before that, too.

But it was New England and baseball season and 2004. The Sox were moving toward a ninety-eight, sixty-four record that spring, and five months later, that October, they'd sweep the Cardinals to win their first Series in eighty-six years.

Harry grew up in South Boston and it was a very emotional time. He said he could feel it—feel it coming: the loss of the underdog status, the triumph of victory, the shedding of the past and having to look toward an uncertain future after success . . .

So he was spending most of his days calming his nerves at Mulligan's Pub.

Ally sneaked out through the back door of Robinson, dodging her boss, Dr. Priscilla Patricia Meer.

She headed east behind Mencoff, Brackett, and Partridge, and when she hit Brown Street, she turned left, hoping to God she could get in and out of Pembroke Hall before Priscilla came by or called.

She had only one. One student: Jake Bean. He was it. Then she would go home and meet Harry.

Jake lost her after the lecture. In the throng of students and halfway downstairs, Ally went right instead of left, and Jake turned left instead of right and took the front door, walking to Brown on Waterman Street. He headed north and caught sight of her at Meeting Street. "Professor Hughes!" He broke into a jog. "Professor!"

Ally skipped steps up the Pembroke stoop, heaving her backpack, cell phone to cheek, speaking to the desk assistant at the East Providence Police Department. "So they weren't the guys? The guys you picked up? They were *other* guys?" She was confused.

"Dr. Hughes! Professor!" called Jake from down the block, gaining on her.

Ally disappeared inside. She didn't hear him. Despite the two lectures she taught each semester, the most popular campus-wide two years running, sold-out, so to speak, she didn't feel like a *doctor* of anything, much less an assistant professor.

Her grades were late. On Tuesday, Yoko had called in tears. "Professor, I'm sick!"

"Yoko? Where are you?" Yoko hadn't returned her calls.

"I can't walk!"

"Willa told me—"

"My papers are *with* me. I took them to Omaha by mistake!"

"You're—*home*?"

"I'm so sorry! So stupid! So dumb!"

"Stop. Please."

"I'm such an idiot!"

"Calm down. Please. Mail them to me. Is your mother there?"

"Mail?"

"I'll grade them for you. It's no big deal. This is your *health*."

Yoko paused. "Really?"

"Really. Can she mail them today? Express Mail? Ten, twenty bucks?"

"Mom!" Yoko yelled and then said to Ally, "Hold on." Then, "Mom!"

"Yoko?"

"Professor?"

"How many left?"

"Only—only, like . . . twenty-one?"

Ally absorbed this. Twenty-one papers meant twenty-one hours of grading, at least. She sighed. *"Are you asking me* or telling me?" Yoko always inflected upward at the end of a sentence as if she were asking a question when she wasn't. A way, Ally thought, to belie her brilliance, to seem less sure than she actually was. She had been first in her class at Yale.

Yoko then said, "Twenty-one. But nine left to grade."

Ally smiled. "Nine." She could do it. "Got it. Get *well*."

"Professor!" Jake called as he flew into the building. He climbed the stairs to the second floor.

Ally shut her door and locked it. She dropped her backpack, crossed to her desk, and gathered the papers from Omaha.

She was late to meet Harry, but Harry was always late himself, and not by minutes. Harry was always two hours late. When he showed up. If he showed up. "So they're at large? Is that the right term? They're still *on the loose?*"

The story had made *The Brown Daily Herald*: "Robbery Crew Hits Nabe."

Two weeks before, a rash of break-ins beset Ally's street, two miles from campus. Three morning burglaries, three midnight robberies, three men in ski masks, all short, all armed. A neighbor had spotted the men in a pickup casing Grotto.

Ally had hired Harry to put a bolt in the back door and finish the jobs he had started in March.

"*All* the jobs, Harry," she'd said when they spoke.

This was the weekend. Harry would be at the house at one, and Ally would hole up to read and grade.

She loved the rental, the tiny Victorian, even if it was falling apart. For six years she'd paid Harry to replace shingles, empty the gutters, caulk the windows. She was sure it was rotting at its core, but did her best to keep it warm, to keep herself and Lizzie safe. It wasn't a five-star hotel, she said, when her mother complained, but it was home.

But three short men with three black masks, this was worse than leaks and mold.

Not that she owned anything to steal. The rooms were full of secondhand finds: old wooden tables, older chairs; desks and beds that Ally had bought at Goodwill, Savers, and the Salvation Army in Newport and Boston.

She hung up as Jake knocked. She turned and froze. Could it be Meer? "Yes?" she called. "Who's there?"

"Jake Bean!"

He had called Monday and booked twenty minutes of office hours to talk about his failed final paper.

She moved to the door and opened it. When she saw him, she drew back, surprised. "*You're* Jake?"

"I have an appointment."

"Yes! Okay!" She moved aside so Jake could step in. "We've never met." She closed the door. Jake turned and held out his hand. Ally shook it. "Sorry. With two hundred students—I can't always put a face to a name." Ally had thought that "Jake Bean" was the big blond guy who smiled all the time and sat down front.

She couldn't believe it. This was Jake?

Jake Bean was the boy in the back?

They hadn't talked, but the boy in the back had haunted Ally for three years.

He looked like that singer, the one from that boarding school— Exeter, it was; Andover maybe—the boy every Brown girl was drooling over: John Mayer or Meyer or Moyer, whatever it was, with that catchy little "Body Is a Wonderland" tune. Jake looked like him but much more handsome. He was the runway version of him. The rough-around-the-edges, childlike-but-tough, Hugo-Boss-model version of him.

"Professor Hughes, please. I never missed a lecture. Give me the credit. I'm begging you here."

Ally flipped through his paper. "Let's discuss it," she said kindly. Then her phone rang. She leaned in to see the incoming number. "Hold on, sorry. I have to get this." She turned and picked up. "Harry?" She listened to Harry for a moment and grew annoyed. "Really,

Harry? Seriously? Third time, Harry. Third time you canceled on me this month . . . Can you come and do the—?" She listened a moment. "No, fine. But, no, Harry. Don't call back. Good-bye, Harry." She hung up and took a deep breath.

"Everything okay?"

"No," Ally said. "I have a girl turning ten in four days and a bunk bed that needs— Harry the handyman canceled on me *three* times."

"You have a daughter?"

"Yes," she said.

"I'm sorry."

Ally laughed. "This is my life!" She was upset. Lizzie had begged for a bunk bed for years. Ally had saved and finally bought one for Lizzie's birthday. The bed had been hiding in the basement for weeks, in parts, in boxes, waiting to be built.

And she needed a lock. On the back door. She needed the downstairs windows secured.

She needed so much.

Shaking her head, she slid Jake's paper back to her lap and picked up a pen. "I'll . . . find someone else."

"What about your husband? Can't he do it?"

Ally looked up and then back down. It was a question and natural enough, but personal. "I don't have one," she said softly. "I'm a, you know . . . single . . . mom."

"I'll do it."

"What?" She focused on the page, on Jake's profile of Anaïs Nin.

"Your bed."

"Thanks." Ally looked up. "Sorry. What?"

"Me and my brother—we have a business. Bookshelves, IKEA.

Dollhouses. Do you know the *skill*—the *talent*—it takes to get that Barbie elevator going?"

Ally smiled. "I do," she said. "That elevator!" Crazy thing. Lizzie had a Dreamhouse. "But let's get back to the first part here . . . The part that sounds so . . . pseudo-academic."

Jake's gaze floated past Ally, out the window, to the trees. He was embarrassed. "I'm not a good writer," he said. "I suck."

"No, you don't. The ideas are great. Most of them. But it's too long and you change tone. At first, you use this fake formal tone." She looked up. "Why?"

Jake shrugged. "To sound smart."

"But you *are* smart. And then you change." Ally flipped to page fourteen. "Your voice changes a quarter way through. You leave Nin totally behind. You leave your subject *completely* behind and start riffing for forty pages."

"I get excited."

"You go off point: tantric sex, Britney Spears?"

"Yeah, sorry."

"This part," she said and pointed to a paragraph. She read it aloud. "'In pop culture, older women are disrespected, but I think they rock.'" She looked at him. "*Rock?*"

"They do."

"But *rock* in a term paper?"

"You said to include our opinion," he said. "That's my opinion."

"Or 'Sick sex is a fast-food burger. Sacred sex is a porterhouse steak.' Intriguing, for sure, but what does it mean?"

"There's gotta be love," Jake explained.

"There's got to be love to make the meat good?"

"Sex, like anything— Professor Hughes, if I may?"

"Go ahead, please." Ally leaned back.

Jake leaned forward. "It all exists, like, on a continuum. High cow, low cow. High sex, low sex. And Anaïs Nin, if you ask me, she was on the bottom fucking rung. Excuse my French."

"*Fuck* isn't French."

"So why this course *devoted* to her?"

"Well. I agree."

Jake was surprised. "You do?"

Ally sighed. "If a chair sent out an SOS for a popular class because the professor who normally taught it was off for the year, to research, you know, all the gender-based *leisure* habits of octogenarians in *Greece* and *Italy* . . ."

Jake smiled.

"If a low-on-the-totem-pole sucker like me—were asked to teach it, she might say yes. *Especially* if she were up for review." Ally then stopped. "Sorry," she said. "Too much caffeine. I should be quiet."

"She was an evil, evil liar."

"Who?"

"Nin. Isn't that—?"

Then, on cue, came four fast knocks on Ally's door. Meer's signature rat-a-tat-tat. Ally froze. Then four again.

"Coming!" said Ally, girding herself as she rose from the chair. Jake looked concerned. She crossed to the door and opened it. "Hi! Priscilla! Hi!"

"I left you a message," Meer said, annoyed. "Where are your *grades*?"

"Coming," said Ally. "Monday, first thing. One of my TAs had to go home."

"Who?" Meer asked, arms crossed, anchoring a thick stack of files.

"She was—"

"Who?"

"Please," Ally begged, "don't make me say."

"You have to stop babying them—"

"I'm with a student. Monday, okay?"

Meer leaned in. "Where?"

"Here—he's right . . ." She opened the door to reveal Jake. Jake waved.

"Oh," Meer said.

"I'm sorry I didn't call you back. The seniors are done. I spoke to the registrar."

"Fine," Meer said and turned and walked off, her stacked heels pounding the floorboards.

Ally stood for a moment, unmoving. She then looked at Jake and closed the door. She sat down again and looked up. "Ever had someone love you so much, you can see it in their eyes?"

Jake smiled. "Meer?"

"She wishes I was a Marxist. We approach—life—from a different . . ."

"Angle?"

"That. Sorry. Where were we?"

"The liar. Nin. Married to two guys at the same time. Cheated on both."

Ally nodded.

"*Revenge* sex with her dad? Because he left? Who does that? She was a pervert and a stuck-up sociopath."

Ally smiled. "But she was an efficient writer. Unlike you."

Jake shrugged and looked away. His cheeks flushed. "Maybe."

"Please. Don't be embarrassed. I'll give you credit, but—"

"What? You will?"

"Yes, but—"

"I love you!"

"What?"

"I love you! Thanks!"

Ally laughed. "But your writing! Jake. You can't hand in fifty-two pages when I ask for twelve." She picked up some files from her desk. "See? Look. Three years of you." She pulled the files onto her lap and opened one. She took out a midterm and a final, fifty and eighty pages, respectively. "Remember these?" She handed them to him.

He glanced down. "I—I wrote these freshman year."

"I read them all. I kept them all."

"Why?"

"None of my TAs knew what to do with them! How to grade them!" Ally laughed. "This one, on the Triangle fire, for Women and Work. *Eighty* pages."

"That was my favorite class. I was *inspired*. What can I say?"

Ally stood and pulled a paperback book from a shelf. "*Elements of Style*. All you need—to keep it short." She handed it to him, but Jake wouldn't take it. "Please," she said.

"I can buy it."

"I have another."

"You're my Sex and Gender—"

"Jake, writing—"

"I'm not coming back."

Ally stopped and quieted, surprised.

"I need the credit. In case I transfer. Ever. One day. But Brown's wicked pricey and I don't want debt. I'm not coming back."

Ally blinked. She understood. She had had luck in grad school at Brown: grants, scholarships, TA jobs, the lecturing offer from Economics. But now that her dissertation was done, she was drowning in undergrad loans. She placed the book on her desk and sat down.

"That's why I want to fix your bed. I need the cash."

"I see," she said and thought about it. She wanted the help. It wasn't that. She needed the help. "Can you do a dead bolt?"

"You have one?"

"I do."

"I hope you spent money. I like Schlage. It's got to be bump-proof."

Ally nodded. "There were robberies. On my street. Last two weeks. I need the windows—"

"Pins in the frames. Add a stopper to the ACs. Do you have ACs?"

Ally studied him as he spoke. "I do, but can you put them in?"

Jake nodded. "Tools in my trunk. Parked on Thayer."

The door to Lizzie's room squeaked too. Ally wanted to go in and out while Lizzie was sleeping and not wake her up. She knew the hinges needed that grease, whatever it was called, but she wasn't sure something wasn't wrong with the hinge.

Was he a conflict of interest? Jake? Hiring Jake? He took her classes, after all.

"Professor Hughes," Jake continued, "my mother was single. Four boys. I know how it is. You take care of everyone else, but no one's there to take care of you. Let me help. You'd be helping me, too."

"Jake," she said, "I'm not handy. Harry was supposed to do . . . a lot. He was coming the whole weekend. Saturday, Sunday . . ."

Jake begged. "Seven bucks an hour. I'll do it all."

Ally studied him.

Jake arrived to every class before Ally did, and he always left last. He lingered in the hall or just outside as if he had questions, but he never approached, never spoke up, and never once raised his hand.

Every so often, in the middle of her lecture, Ally's gaze would land on him and he'd smile in a way that made her feel breathless and leave her thoughts muddled.

His eyes caught and held hers as if he were making an assessment of something, of Ally or the lecture, she didn't know which, but he seemed amused.

At some point, she had decided to ignore him. The boy in the back, she told herself, he wasn't there to learn. Boys in back rows, they sat there in judgment. They weren't engaged. They sat back in protest.

She didn't know that the boy in the back was Jake Bean of the "love letters," as her TAs had called them—impassioned, for sure, but never ending.

"Okay," she said finally and nodded. "Let's do it."

"I'll follow you home?"

"Yes," she said and picked up the book and handed it to him.

"Fine." Jake took it.

"Thanks," she said gratefully.

"No, thank *you*."

Do I have to use it for grad school?" asked Lizzie, out of the blue.

Ally was fumbling with the remote. "What?"

It was eight o'clock, and mother and daughter were happily curled up on Ally's bed. They'd watch *The Graduate* while they ate breakfast for dinner on trays, eggs and crepes. That was the plan.

Ally wore boxers and Jake's old T-shirt, the Red Sox one, the one she had kept, and Lizzie wore pajamas.

"The money she left," Lizzie continued. Ally's mother, Lizzie's grandmother, Claire Anne Hughes, had died in March, four months before. She had left Lizzie money, meant for grad school.

"Hold on. Shoot. HD one or HD two?"

"I'm rethinking Juilliard."

"Hold on, Bug." Ally punched the remote again.

"First of all, I won't get in. We both know that. And even if I do, why spend four years memorizing Chekhov when I can be acting on TV? They say it's the golden age of—"

"My God, we've got a rover on Mars and we can't create an easier remote?" Ally was annoyed.

"Mom?"

"Yes?"

"I want Claire's money, but not for grad school. Would that be okay?"

Ally turned and looked at her tray. Her food was getting cold. "Please throw a napkin over my plate."

Lizzie arranged her mother's napkin, and her own, on top of the plate to contain the steam, to keep the food warm.

"Finally!" Ally said. The movie began. She climbed into bed and pulled the dinner tray onto her lap. "Okay, good, so everyone thinks it's about an era, but I think it's about love and lust and what it's like to grow old as a woman—"

"Mom, did you hear me? About the money?"

On the TV screen, a young Dustin Hoffman, blankly depressed, sat in an airplane on his way home after graduating from college.

"What about it?"

"Can I have it?"

"For what?"

"I can't tell you."

Ally aimed and turned up the volume. "See, to you, he's Captain Hook. To me, he's Tootsie. If you want to be an actress, honey, Dustin Hoffman— We should watch *Tootsie*! It's about acting *and* women—"

"Mother, please. Forget the movie for two seconds. Please."

"What is it? Why?" Ally turned up the volume again.

"I spoke to Cybil. You know, my agent . . . She thinks—I should do something to my nose."

"What?" Ally said, looking at Lizzie for the first time in minutes. "Like what?"

"She thinks if you're an actress and have to fix your nose, you should do it when you're young like Marilyn Monroe. When you're older—"

"Wait a sec. *What* are we discussing?"

Lizzie paused and took a deep breath. "Claire's money."

"You want a *nose job?*"

"Please. Don't freak. The whole thing costs eighteen grand, which is two thousand less than—"

"Elizabeth. Wait. I'm—wait a second." Ally pushed her tray forward, grabbed the remote, and paused the movie. She turned back around and sat up on her knees, stunned.

Lizzie's face paled in defeat. "This is *really* hard for me. To even bring this up to you . . ."

"I'm— Let me— Okay, just—give me a second to recover from the shock so we can—"

"What?" Lizzie looked at her plate. "Discuss it? My mind's made up."

"Yes, honey. *Yes,* we should discuss it—as reasonable adults—because you need to know—there is *no way* I will ever—ever, ever—give you money to do that—*ever.*"

Lizzie shook her head. "It's not vanity, Mom. It's a matter of physics."

"Physics?"

"We have two eyes. The camera has one. One lens. Without depth perception. So . . . so . . . it flattens stuff out. Whatever's in front. A lens makes everything wider and bigger."

"And?"

"*And* it puts on twelve pounds. It's why actors have to be thin to look normal and why my nose looks bigger on-screen than it does in real life."

Ally softened and inched closer to talk it through, to set her daughter straight. She took Lizzie's hand. "Sweetheart, first, your body is sacred. Second, you are a beautiful girl."

"It's not about beauty. It's about image. And how three dimensions translate to two."

"Says Cybil?"

"Yes, but—"

Ally let go of Lizzie's hand and rubbed her forehead. She scratched the back of her neck, panicked, on the verge of tears. "This Cybil? Is this the woman who—who told you—told you—to dye your hair?"

"Again. Highlights—"

"And lose thirty pounds?"

"Mother. Yes. I just explained—"

"Said you should—told *my* daughter—at five foot ten, to hover around one hundred pounds?"

"Calm down. One hundred and five."

Ally tried to stay calm. A technique she used when Lizzie was three. Instead of raising her voice when upset, she whispered. "I don't know where to start," she said softly. "The global thing or—or the fact that it's not a tattoo. You can't reverse it. Or that you're letting some surgeon slice you *open* to conform to—"

"I'm not conforming!" Lizzie interrupted. "I want to be in *film*. I don't have the chops for stage. And I want my nose to appear less big. If I want a big nose, I can build one. Nicole Kidman. She built a nose for Virginia Woolf. I want to ensure myself that range."

"I don't buy that. It's not like your nose is *that* big."

"I want to do this. I'm *going* to do this. With Claire's money or mine that I save."

"No. Because . . . by the time you save that kind of money, I will have brought you back to your senses. I want to speak to Cybil."

"What?"

"Yes!"

"No! That's— No! I'm twenty years old! I'm not five! She's not my teacher!"

"She's telling you—incorrectly—that your nose will keep you from— She's *shaming* you into changing yourself when you are perfect. As you were *knitted* in—"

"Don't say it!" Lizzie looked at her plate in despair. She wanted the night to be fun and delicious and now her crepes and eggs were cold. "I know you think you're right," she said coolly. "Let's stop. Give it some time."

"But promise me you won't do it—without telling me first. Please."

"Why? So you can lock me up?"

"Well, there's that . . . But if you do it, I have to prepare myself too, Bug. I'll be . . ." Ally turned away. Tears spilled.

Lizzie closed her eyes. "You'll be what?"

"Heartbroken," Ally choked out. Then she raised her voice in anguish. "You're funny and gorgeous! Heads turn when you walk down the street!"

"Weather got one! Weather was twelve!"

"Weather *needed* one. You don't remember. Her nose was

bizarrely, abnormally wide. I'm not opposed to fixing cleft palates. I'm not opposed to—"

"Mom," Lizzie pleaded, "please don't cry." She grabbed a napkin and handed it to her. "Please don't. Maybe I can explain this better . . . another time."

Ally tried to pull herself together. She had been like this for months. Since Claire's diagnosis, the lung cancer, she'd been weepy, didactic, and weepy again. She launched into lectures on anything and everything with no invitation and no restraint. She cried all the time. "What if you *die*?"

"How exactly would I—?"

"Under anesthesia!"

"Worst-case scenario. Point zero one chance of—"

"So? The worst-case scenario happens!"

"Okay, forget it." Lizzie moved her tray aside and climbed off the bed. "I'm finished discussing this tonight." She flew to the bureau and pressed play on the DVD player. "And so are you." She climbed back up and settled herself. Her mother was grieving and crazy and grieving.

Ally glared at her for a moment, then turned and took a bite of her crepes.

They both calmed.

Earlier that night, she'd reduced the flour, gluten-free for Lizzie, to thin the batter and crisp the edges the way Lizzie liked them. "The syrup is hot. Take it," she said and held out the pitcher.

Lizzie took it and poured syrup onto her crepes. She sipped orange juice and ice through a straw and focused on the movie for a moment.

Ally couldn't. Her eyes darted from her crepes to Lizzie, to Lizzie's nose, then back to the TV, where Dustin Hoffman, as Benjamin Braddock, was claiming his baggage at LAX. "Dustin Hoffman has a big nose."

Lizzie said nothing.

Ally gazed around the room.

She'd moved in four years ago, back into the brownstone, into the room, her childhood room, and cleared the remains: the stuffed animals, framed awards, framed photos of Amelia Earhart and Nellie Bly. She left the walls empty except for a map and set the TV up to watch news in bed, but she rarely did. "And don't forget you're Israeli," she mumbled. She couldn't let it go.

"Seriously? I totally forgot I'm half Israeli!"

"If you want to look like some all-American, Christie Brinkley, cookie-cutter, white-bread—"

Lizzie reached out, took Ally's arm, and squeezed it. "Not another word. Not tonight. I'm sorry I brought it up."

Ally looked at her beautiful daughter. "Me too," she said.

JAKE WRAPPED HIS ARMS around the AC unit and lifted it high as if it weighed nothing. No hesitation. No effort.

Ally watched him. "Wow," she said. She could barely budge it with her foot when she'd dusted it off for Harry.

Jake was fit, she thought as she watched, but not in an artificial way, as if he had pumped himself up at a gym. He was fit as if he did real work, construction or something outdoors. As if he fought fires. As if he saved lives.

"Where to?"

"This way," she said. He followed her through the garage and inside.

As Ally stepped in, she was relieved. The kitchen, the house, the whole house, was orderly. Muriel had cleaned early that morning, and well. Everything was ordered, put away, immaculate, from baseboards to ceiling, and Ally was grateful. Muriel had tucked away every marker, puzzle, sticker, paintbrush, doll.

"Can you use the thing?" She strolled across the kitchen and felt light-headed, leading him out to the hall, to the stairs. The house had heated up during the day.

"What thing?"

"That goes underneath. My landlord said to use the thing."

"The universal support bracket?"

"That," she said and started upstairs to the second floor.

"You have one?" he asked, following her.

"I do. Two."

Ally led him to Lizzie's room. "That one," she said, pointing to the window farthest from the bed. "I don't want it blowing on her when she sleeps."

"You got it," Jake said. He squatted to set the unit down. "Can I move these books?"

"No, no. Please. Use the desk."

Lizzie had organized her Nancy Drew collection, fifty-six books, across the floor, starting with *The Secret of the Old Clock*.

"Your daughter likes to read."

"The criminal mind. Spies. Secrets. She's obsessed."

Jake smiled and gazed at the books.

"Let me show you where the second one goes." Ally left and walked down the hall toward her bedroom. Jake followed but kept his own stride, slower and more relaxed than Ally's.

The fact that she was alone with a stranger—a man, no less—hadn't struck her until she entered the room where she slept, where she undressed, and Jake stepped in, close, behind her.

Muriel had left a pile of underwear, freshly washed, on the bed. Ally swooped in, gathered it up, and pointed to the corner. "That window, please. The one over there." She moved to her bureau, opened a drawer, and shoved the underwear deep inside.

"Nice room," Jake said, looking around. He slid his hands into his pockets. "Big bed."

Ally turned and looked at the bed. It was a king. "My daughter sleeps with me most nights. She's in New York. Have you ever been?"

"No." No, he hadn't.

Ally nodded, turned, and strode out and back down the hall. She headed downstairs and Jake followed. "Can I have a beer?" he asked politely. "If you have one."

Ally turned. On one hand, of course, what else would a college kid want to drink on a Friday while he worked? On the other hand, a beer? "Are you twenty-one?"

"Yes, I am, but the law is for purchase. Not for consumption." He tilted his head as if explaining the rule to a child.

"Oh," Ally said. She hadn't known that. "Sure, then," she said, stepping into the kitchen. She moved toward the fridge. "I only have Stella."

"Of course you do," Jake said, walking out past her into the garage.

By nine that night, Jake had installed the two ACs. He embedded a dead bolt in the back door and secured six of the first-floor windows. He washed a basement wall with bleach, raised Lizzie's bike seat, built her bunk bed, and placed the bottom bunk on risers so that a trundle could slide underneath.

He did all this with a transistor radio by his side. The Sox were playing, and, sadly for Jake, the Mariners won.

Ally found pizza dough in the freezer. She should have been

grading and not in the kitchen puttering around, assembling snacks and a pizza for Jake. But she was on edge, unnerved by his presence, all of his sounds: The radio chatter and near distant whir of his heavy black drill. His footsteps across her hardwood floors . . .

When Ally needed to calm down, she cooked. She cooked or baked, or cooked and baked at the same time, a habit that started when she was just six, about to turn seven.

"I want to show you something," he said, stepping in and startling her. She was pulling the pizza out of the oven. She placed it on the counter as Jake walked out, and this time it was Ally who followed.

"I want to show you how to do this."

The second floor was dark. At the top of the stairs, Ally turned on a lamp.

"Do this now, for next time," he said. Reaching down, he took Ally's hand and placed it around a can of oil.

Ally looked at him. What was he doing?

"Lubricating oil. Aerosol. Don't spray it into your pretty eyes."

Ally grimaced. Please. Come on. Her pretty eyes?

But Jake was focused. "Here's how." He stepped around Ally, behind her back, but kept his right hand wrapped around hers, around the can.

"Jake, please," Ally said, spinning to face him. "I know how to spray a . . ." She laughed but then froze as Jake placed his left hand on her waist and turned her around, commanding her to do what he wanted her to do. With his right, he held her hand, and the can, over the hinge.

"You have to spray down," he instructed kindly. "You have to be on top. So the oil moves down and into the grooves. When the metal pieces slide over each other, they vibrate, and the door acts like a soundboard."

Ally stood on her toes as she reached, and Jake closed in from behind to help. Quickly, she realized she was too short. "Okay," she said. "I see—I see what you're doing—but I need a chair or a stool or something."

"No, you don't. I'll do it this time." He turned her around with his left hand again, took the can from her, and did it himself.

Ally stepped aside and gazed down the steps. "Spray down. Got it. Thank you," she said, feeling the print of his hand on her waist.

"You're welcome," he said, moving the door back and forth. It was silent.

"Okay," said Ally, sounding as businesslike as she could. "Wow. I don't know how to thank you. I made you a pizza. Eat it here, take it back to the dorm."

"I'm not going back," he said, turning to her. "Remember? I quit. The semester's over?"

Ally paused and looked at him. "And you prefer cash? So, eight hours . . ."

Jake shook his head. He turned and placed the spray can down. Then he turned back and took her by the elbow as if he had done so a hundred times. "Let's stop," he said, gently pulling her toward him. He released her elbow, then cupped her face and kissed her firmly on the corner of her mouth.

He didn't find her lips. He didn't find her cheek. But firmly and in complete control, he planted his lips on the corner of her mouth as if to ask her permission first.

Ally drew a breath of surprise. She was startled by the motion, the timing, the nerve.

Startled a little, but not entirely, completely surprised.

The afternoon had been charged, for sure. She, of course, was attracted to Jake. But who wasn't? Any living, breathing woman, fifteen years old or five hundred . . . And Ally had put on a game face, she thought. Nothing would happen. Surely he wasn't attracted to her. And if he were, by any chance, Jake would have to be so sure, so assured and confident, to make a move on his professor.

What kind of student would do that?

But there they were, and there he was in Ally's house. She had invited him in, after all, or had he invited himself?

"Oh," she said, staring at him, feeling winded. She couldn't think.

"Is that okay?" Jake asked.

She didn't know. Lizzie was away. That was true. Her daughter was three hours south in New York and safe with Claire.

She was with Claire, Ally's mom.

On Sunday, they'd hop the Amtrak at Penn. Ally would fetch them at one o'clock at PVD on the Gaspee Street side. But she was supposed to be grading papers. Yoko's papers. That night. Not kissing one of her students.

"Let me stay. Please," Jake said. He looked into her eyes and squeezed her elbow. He had her elbow again. Then he stepped back to give her some space, room to think, to see him, to breathe, to catch her breath.

He slipped his hands into his pockets and then slipped them out, and a second later, he kissed her again, this time in the middle of her mouth. "Sorry," he said and let her go completely. "I can't help it. I've been wanting to do that for three years."

What? Ally thought. He did? Years? *Three* years?

They gazed at each other, and neither one spoke.

She wasn't startled the second time, and she didn't resist. She saw it coming. She wanted him to kiss her again. He tasted like Stella, malty and sweet. "Oh my goodness," she said and looked down.

He tasted like college and kissed her the way she'd been kissed back then, on the second floor of Healy Hall or in a dark, sodden corner of Champions bar. Suddenly the past rose inside her, that feeling from ten years before, all that raucous, innocent fun, and something released, nerves maybe, and made her laugh.

"You're laughing," Jake said, seeming embarrassed.

"No, no, I'm not," she said kindly, but she was. "I'm your professor, Jake. Come on. I'm thirty-one."

"I'm twenty-one. So?"

"Please. It's totally yucky and . . . inappropriate, and I'm sure against some rule."

"Why?" he said. "What rule? I'm attracted to you, and I'm pretty sure you're attracted to me."

"I am, Jake. I am. But who isn't? Look at you. Please. Everyone's attracted to you."

Jake smiled.

She looked at him and then downstairs. She imagined Claire standing there, Lizzie with her backpack, both looking up from the first floor. You get only *one* mistake, Claire said when Ally got pregnant in college. One. She'd made hers.

Claire was right, Ally thought: Grown-up professors did not do this. They didn't kiss students. Maybe the men did, but not the women. What was she doing? What was she thinking?

She turned to him. "Think for a second. If I were your professor, and I was a man and you were a woman . . ."

"And?"

"What if—you needed a recommendation? A credit for class— which you *did*? It might seem like—"

"That's not *exactly* what's happening here."

Ally smiled. "I made a pizza." She turned away. "You must be starved."

"I am."

"Good." She stepped away and went downstairs. This was right, she thought as she did. To walk away.

Jake followed.

On the first floor, they cut through the dining room toward the kitchen. "Do you always lead?" Jake asked.

"No. My little girl Lizzie leads. She's the boss. She'll be back Sunday."

"You said that already."

"Oh, I did? Right. She's got a report due. Tuesday. On her birthday. Nathan Hale. Benedict Arnold. It's about spies." She entered the kitchen and moved toward the pizza, pretending to ignore him, to forget what had happened seconds before, rambling on about Loyalists and Patriots, Lizzie's obsession with espionage.

Then she stopped and drew still. Other than the cutting board, the entire kitchen was clean and in order. The entire house. Thank you, Muriel, she said to herself as she stood there. Thank you. Thank you.

She spun and faced him. "It has to be a secret." She whispered as if someone could hear her. Someone on campus. Two miles away. She choked out the words.

Jake stopped, motionless, eyes wide, surprised.

"You can't, you know, write about it. In your—"

"I don't have a—"

"You can't tell—you can't even *think* about it after tonight."

He nodded. "Okay."

Ally felt her heart beating. Was she doing this? They stood there and looked at each other and waited. "This is my daughter. I could get fired. I'm in enough trouble."

He lifted his hands, palms out, as if to say he understood, as if to say it would all be all right. Everything. "Professor Hughes," he said gently. "Just to remind you . . . today I'm done."

This was true. Ally nodded. It helped her a great deal to hear this again.

"Friends," he said. "That's all we are. You're not my teacher. I'm not your student." Jake swallowed.

Ally nodded.

Every inch of her body felt swollen, as if she might implode if the pressure of wanting him wasn't relieved. She had wanted to touch him, to taste him, to know him so badly for so many hours, all afternoon, all evening, all semester, if she'd been honest with herself, not even knowing him, not knowing that he was the Jake of the eighty-page papers, the boy in the back.

Jake was the boy in the back.

The sun had set, the sky darkened, and as Ally watched him, what a specimen he was, sweating in the heat, repairing what needed repair in her home . . . he was already inside in a way.

ON SATURDAY MORNING ALLY called Lizzie three times, and three times she didn't pick up. She felt the phone vibrate in her back pocket but couldn't hear it. She was in Queens, inside a shooting range, trying out a Glock and a Ruger.

"This is what I love!" said Agent Jones. He stood on the other side of the window. "When two things don't match. The image and the girl." He studied Lizzie. "Barely legal. Total knockout. Should be modeling Victoria's Secret . . . but shoots like Jelly Bryce!"

Lizzie was all leg that day, bare and tan, in cutoff shorts and boots with four-inch heels that raised her statuesque five-ten frame to six foot two. Her long blond hair fell over her ribs. She stood slouching, wearing the range's requisite goggles and ear protection.

"See, she's got that model pose. The slouch. Legs spread. Loose hips. It's all in the hips."

Noah just smiled. He wasn't surprised.

"She hasn't missed once. The bull's-eye once. I've never seen anything like it in my life! This is the first time she picked up a gun?"

Noah shrugged. He didn't know.

Lizzie had met him the month before. They'd met on the set of her first film: her thirty-sixth audition and first part.

They gave her the role of Noah's assistant, and Noah had asked her out: three times to lunch and once to dinner. Then he had asked her to join him that day, training for his role as J. Edgar Hoover. FBI agent Alan Jones was teaching the actors both to shoot.

And sure, she had only one line, a single line in the whole film, but one little line in a movie with Noah, directed by Marty, the famous director, was one line she was happy to have.

Cybil, her agent, told her to simply listen and talk. Talk and listen. She shouldn't emote or try to act, Cybil advised. Lizzie was perfect for roles that required "restraint," she said.

"Simple, honey. Keep it simple."

Lizzie had discerned the hidden message: It didn't matter if she was talentless. With her looks, she'd work, as long she knew her limitations, and as long as she fixed that nose.

Inside the range, she raised the Glock, bent her knees, and stretched her right arm perfectly straight. Four years of yoga had prepared her for this, plus endless games of KGB and CIA, of cops and robbers, and archery lessons Saturday mornings at the Ace Archers range in Foxboro.

She steadied her breath, and as she exhaled, she grew still and pulled the trigger.

"Bull's-eye again!" Jones cried. She reminded him of his grand-daughter. "What a follow-through! What an eye!"

Noah smiled and wiped the palms of his hands on his jeans. He was nervous. "I'm meeting her mom for the first time tonight. What should I bring?"

"For the mom?" Jones said.

"Like, a hostess gift."

"You want to impress her? She's cooking? The mom?"

"Dinner."

Jones took a moment and thought about it. "Here's what you bring. All three things: A vintage red. Flowers. Chocolates."

"Dark or milk?"

"Mixed. Imported."

"What kind of flowers? Roses?"

"No. Too cliché. Call a florist. Something in season."

Noah nodded. That's what he'd do.

He turned to see Lizzie click the safety back to its place. She lifted her goggles, turned, and waved to them through the window.

Sammy, a range clerk, sidled up to them and whistled through his teeth. "Which of you ducks is plugging that bitch?"

"Excuse me?" said Jones indignantly and turned to face Sammy.

"You get to tap that bitch or what?"

"Out of my face," Jones said and took a step toward him.

Sammy backed off with his hands in the air. "Got you, chief." Then he did a double take, recognizing Noah. "Hey! You're that guy!"

Noah didn't confirm his suspicions.

"'Hurry up, woman! There's no time to waste!' Right? Am I right? That's your line? 'Hurry up, woman! There's no time to waste!'" He yelled the line in a lousy British accent, imitating Noah. "That was you?"

"That was me . . . playing a part." Noah smiled politely.

"You're Lancelot?"

"No, not really. Just in the movie."

"Yes, you are. You ride a horse. You use a sword. You're a knight. Are you a knight? Like, for real?"

"No. I'm an actor."

"Are you Brad Pitt? No, no, I got it! You're Marky Mark!"

"Nope."

"His brother?"

"No."

"But I'm right. You're famous, right?"

Jones intervened. "Yeah, he's famous. Now, move on out."

Sammy did, happily. "My bitch will freak!"

The week before, at Balthazar, Noah had complained about his schedule and the hardships of his movie-star life: five-star hotels, three-star restaurants. He hadn't been home in months. He longed for his bed, for a homemade meal. He missed his mom.

That's what he said.

"You can have mine!" Right there, between courses, she called Ally and asked her to cook up a dinner for them, at home, in the brownstone, in Brooklyn. Nothing fancy. Ally would cook a meal for Noah, soup to nuts, and he'd have a night of normal for once. Ally was cool, Lizzie explained. So down-to-earth. Too down-to-earth. Ally was real. Noah would like her, and she would like him. Lizzie was sure.

"Lizzie," said Jones as they later took a break, "I know a guy, runs tactical recruiting down in Virginia—"

"Agent *Jones.*" Lizzie smiled and slipped off her goggles. "I am an *actress.*"

"How do you know? At twenty years old? Maybe you are, maybe you're not."

"I'm flattered. Thanks." She headed to the door that led outside.

"Where are you going?" Noah called after her.

"Calling my mom! She called three times!" Lizzie opened the door to sneak out.

"HRT, honey! Hostage rescue! You could save the world!"

"If I could *kill.* A person. Which I can't." She held up a finger and slipped through the door, outside to the lot.

"You invited *Teddy?*" Out in the lot, in the blazing sun, Lizzie was sweating. "Teddy? Mom!"

Ally was home, writing a grocery list for the meal. "I don't want to be your *chaperone* cook. I want to have a date."

"But Ted's *so* uncool," Lizzie whined.

"What's not cool?"

Lizzie rolled her eyes and paced the lot. "The Wharton thing. Choate. The yacht thing. Noah is super *understated.* He doesn't brag. He keeps it real. You know what I mean?"

"I know what 'keeping it real' means, yes."

"Teddy *brags*. He's so into *stuff*: his latest cars, the Maldives house . . ."

"Okay, sorry," Ally said, amending her lists, a grocery list and a list of to-dos. "I should've asked first, but I can't cancel now."

"Yes, you can."

"I'll call him and tell him to keep it real." She added cocoa to her list. "Chocolate cake?"

"And tell him, please, not to kiss ass. Noah *hates* fake."

"You know," Ally said, putting down her pen, "he might not *know* who Noah is."

"Teddy will know."

"I've never heard of this Noah guy."

"That's because you're a Luddite, Mother."

"I am not. Just because I don't *hack* the world like you and your friends—"

"You are, but thank you. And thank you for cooking. He can't wait to meet you. He's actually nervous."

"Great." Ally erased cream from her list. "Chocolate cake? Good?"

Lizzie smiled. "It's bliss. You're the best."

Lizzie *loathed* Teddy McCooey, Ally's friend from Georgetown. Back in the range, she apologized to Noah. "Did you see *The Talented Mr. Ripley*? My best friend owns it. *Worships* it. Like, on an altar."

"I don't think so," Noah said. "Did I?"

Lizzie continued as if he had: "Dickie Greenleaf's best friend.

Freddie Miles. Philip Seymour Hoffman played him. He's fat and rich and *arch*. This guy *is* that guy, like, come to life. I'm so sorry."

An hour later, Jones left for Brooklyn, and Lizzie and Noah waited for a cab in front of the St. Regis Hotel. Noah was scrolling through florists on his phone. "I need to nap. Pick up my dry— What should I wear?"

Lizzie didn't answer. She was lost in thought, musing about the shooting range. "Jones looks like that guy Mike from *Breaking Bad*. He didn't look like FBI."

"What did you expect, James Bond?"

She smiled. "I could be a Bond girl."

"Yes, you could," Noah said, still focused on his phone. Lizzie stepped toward him, wrapped her arms around his neck. Noah looked up as she leaned in to kiss him and turned his head so her lips met his cheek. Lizzie pulled back. He wouldn't kiss her. He hadn't kissed her. She found his ear. "Noah," she whispered, "are you confused?"

"About what?" he said obtusely. Looking at his phone, he continued to scroll.

Lizzie wondered how bright he was, Noah. She wasn't sure, and she hadn't had a chance to vet him yet, investigate him behind his back, the way she did with all new friends. "Me, I feel attracted to you and—"

"All men are attracted to you?"

"Well, not all. But *real* men. Men who like girls."

"Real men don't like girls. Real men like *women*."

"Wait, not *real*. I mean straight. Are you—*straight*?"

Noah looked up. He leaned in close to Lizzie's ear. "I had a six-o'clock call last night. I shot until five and never went to sleep."

Lizzie pulled back. He was mysterious. "You're *tired,* you're saying? You're saying you're straight but *tired*?"

"I'm saying I'll see you tonight." A cab pulled up. "There's your ride."

"Fine," Lizzie said and drifted to the cab. "But remember, don't be offended!" She tried to hide her disappointment. "By my mom!"

Noah looked up. "Why would I be?"

"Because, like I told you!" The bellman opened the cab door. "She doesn't go to movies or watch TV! She has *no idea* who you are!"

Noah smiled. "That's the whole point! That's what's fun!"

LIZZIE WAS RIGHT. ALLY never watched TV. The last time she'd seen a first-run movie in an actual theater was 1994, when she was eight months pregnant with Lizzie.

She knew nothing of Noah Bean.

"He won't even kiss me," Lizzie moaned. She circled the kitchen table, laying placemats, placing silverware. "Honestly, I think he's gay. He's always reading *Cosmo* and *Vogue*."

Ally was frosting the chocolate cake. "When did you meet him?"

"Three weeks ago. My first day on set."

"He asked you out?"

"Couple times to lunch, once to dinner . . . all twenty questions: Where are you from? What do you want out of life, out of love? And then he whips out *Elle* magazine. Weird, right?"

"He wants to get to know you."

"Then he should kiss me. Fork on the left?"

"Fork on the left. He's taking it slow. Sex isn't everything."

"Sex is *something*," Lizzie complained. Ally handed her a chocolate-covered spoon. She tasted it. "Yum! Amazing!"

"Thank you," said Ally, returning to the bowl.

Lizzie sat down. "Can we say I made it? The frosting and the cake? Can we say we made the dinner together, so he thinks I cook? He's old-fashioned."

"Sure, let's lie."

"Can we? Please? What do you care?"

"I don't," Ally said, pouring the batter into a pan. "But you should be *yourself* with him, honey. And not pretend to be someone else."

Lizzie sat forward, thinking, picking through a bowl of olives. "Noah's against my nose job, too. Just so you know . . ." She popped an olive into her mouth.

"He is?" Ally said, turning from the counter toward the oven. "I like him already."

"Which is ironic," Lizzie added wryly in a singsong voice. "Because you're both so perfectly formed, with puny noses and puffy lips and perfect smiles. I guess you can feel superior together and fight that good fight together. I guess."

Ally ignored this. "I can't wait to meet him." Suddenly feeling untethered and excited, she set the timer, took off her apron, and looked around.

The meal was on track. The house was in order. Tidy and clean. Muriel had come down the day before to visit her father up in the Bronx. Ally was thrilled to pay for her ticket to and from Providence. She missed Muriel. Together they'd cleaned the brownstone all day, and Ally was pleased.

At ten after eight, Noah rang the bell.

"Did anyone follow you?" Lizzie asked, leading him inside,

taking the flowers, chocolate, and beer. Noah had brought a six-pack of Stella.

"No," he said and peeled off his cap, glasses, and scarf.

Wherever he went, paparazzi hid and then jumped out of corners with long-lens cameras, snapping and flashing. Lizzie feigned concern and disgust, but truly she loved it: not the attention, but the cat and mouse of the whole game. Dodging the lenses. Noah had learned how to hide, to stay low. He even used a double. But somehow photographers always found him, and Lizzie was impressed. She wanted to know what they knew that she didn't.

"You're a smart kid," Teddy said. He and Lizzie and Noah, too, buzzed around the kitchen, preparing to eat. "How do I get your mom to Augusta?" Teddy had bought, and brought with him, a set of new golf clubs.

"Georgia? In August?" Lizzie said.

Ted pulled out a putter. "Golf is the sport of a patient man. Right, Noah?"

Noah smiled. He stood in front of the open fridge, loading in the Stella, bottle by bottle.

"Lizzie's mother—you haven't met her—she is a woman who *tries* a man's patience."

"No, she doesn't," Lizzie insisted and opened the cupboard for wineglasses.

"I've been fighting for months—*months*—to get that woman *out* of this house. On a trip. Any trip."

"She's been busy." Lizzie turned to Noah. "My grandmother died in March. My mom took care of her."

"See this baby?" Ted held up the club. "This will *inspire* her. These babies cost thirty-two grand. There's gold in here."

"She doesn't play," Lizzie said to Noah. "She's *never* played. She never *will* play."

Noah smiled.

"That's true," said Ted. "But a man can dream. Right, Noah?"

"Sure," said Noah, straightening up and closing the fridge.

Teddy leaned the club in the corner.

"What's on your *feet?*" Lizzie asked as he approached her to open the wine. Teddy was wearing high-top sneakers, odd with his khakis and button-down shirt. They were also gold.

"You like 'em?"

"No."

"Nike only made twenty-five pairs. They're signed by Kobe." He opened a drawer and took out a corkscrew.

"*Bryant?*"

"The one."

"Your sneakers are signed by a rapist?"

"*What?*" Teddy argued, grabbing a bottle and plunging the screw into its cork. "How do you even— You were, like, five."

"I was, *like*, nine," Lizzie said and slid a glass toward him.

Teddy popped the cork and looked at Noah. "2010 Cabernet. Lokoya. Work?"

"Sure," Noah said.

Teddy poured.

"Ladies first," Lizzie instructed.

"*Guests* first." He turned and handed the glass to Noah. "As for

Kobe—you know they *settled*?" He peered at Lizzie as he poured a second glass. "She wouldn't *testify*."

"Oh, then she *must* have been lying," said Lizzie.

Noah just watched.

"The shoes are for *charity*. You against *charity*?"

"I am," Lizzie said. "And faith and hope, and love."

Luckily for Ally, the feud continued and no one saw her enter and blanch and stop in her tracks in total surprise.

"A pleasure," said Noah, a moment later, extending his hand.

Ally shook it and stood there staring.

This was Claire's kitchen, now hers. The kitchen where she took her first steps. Blew out candles on birthday cakes. Where she saw her mother cry and cry the night her father never came home, when she was six . . .

And Jake was here? The boy from the back? But his name was Noah?

Lizzie's date?

Jake from Providence?

Jake, ten years later, smack in the middle of Ally's past and her new life?

He had lost weight. His hair was shorter. His face looked older. But it was the boy from the back, no doubt, and something in his eyes was saying hello.

"I know you," she said.

"I told you, Mom," Lizzie said and turned to Jake. "She said she had no idea who you were."

"No," Ally said. "We've *met* before."

"Mom, please. He's *everywhere*. Everyone thinks they've met him before."

"But I have," Ally begged.

Jake interrupted. "I had you at Brown, Professor Hughes."

"What?" Lizzie said and spun from the fridge with a cheese tray. "No way! Come on! No way! What?" She looked back and forth from Ally to Jake and back again.

"Wow," said Ted, pouring a third glass of wine.

"Gender and Sex," Jake continued. "Women and Work. Fem Economics."

"Yes," Ally said. "Your face is coming back."

"I almost didn't get credit," Jake joked. "But your mom let me slide."

"You almost failed him, Mom? You did?"

Ally unsteadily moved toward the oven to check on the chicken.

"Was she a hard-ass? Tell us!" cried Lizzie.

Teddy turned to Jake. "*You* went to Brown?"

"Just to play ball. I never finished."

Ally grabbed the oven mitt, fumbled, and dropped it. She reached to the floor, picked it up, stood, and steadied herself on the counter edge. "Your name," she said breathlessly, "it wasn't Noah."

"They made him change it," Lizzie offered. "His real name is Jake."

"Jake," said Ally.

"There was a Jake Bean in SAG," he explained. "The Screen Actors Guild. They don't let actors have the same name. Noah's my middle name."

"Oh. I see." Ally turned and handed the oven mitt off to Lizzie.

"Excuse me a sec." If she didn't go, she thought she might faint. She needed a second to catch her breath and slow down her heart. "I need—a Tylenol. I have this little—you know—headache. Lizzie, the chicken. Please take it out. Ted, wine for me."

"You're drinking tonight?" Ted asked, surprised.

"Yup," Ally said, and she flew out the same way she'd come.

On the third floor, she escaped into the bedroom. The phone. The phone.

Where was the phone?

She had left it on the bed.

That same bed. The same bed. Where she and Jake, or she and Noah, or she and whatever his name was now . . .

She had to call Anna.

Anna Baines knew about Jake. She was the one. And she would answer as Lizzie would, always after three calls. It was a thing. It was a promise. A pact they had made when they were ten. A pact Ally made with Lizzie later, and Anna made with her children, too.

Three calls.

After two, Anna picked up.

Ally had moved to the master bath and locked the door. "Guess who's here!" she whisper-yelled, hushed and hysterical.

"Put down that iPad!" Anna yelled at her eight-year-old son across the kitchen. Anna lived in Denver. "Sorry. Go."

"Do you remember Jake?"

"Jake, Jake . . ."

"The boy at Brown?"

"Wait!" Anna said. "No, I don't."

"You do! Come on. He was my student! Claire had Lizzie. I had the weekend. He came to—to—put a lock in our door—and stayed for two days." Ally swallowed. "We did it—we did it—in every corner, on every surface of that sweet little house."

"Wait, wait . . . It's coming back . . ."

"That UTI!"

"That nearly killed you!"

"Yes!"

"Yes!" Anna cried. "That terrible UTI!" She remembered. "The boy with the perfect penis."

"Right. The boy with the perfect penis is downstairs now, with Lizzie, waiting for me to serve them dinner!"

"What?"

"They're seeing each other!"

"No!"

"Yes!"

"Did he know— I'm confused—wait, did he know you're her mother?"

"No! I don't know!"

"Did he *recognize* you?"

"He didn't look surprised. I feel sick."

"He knew, then, that you're Lizzie's mom?"

"Unless he totally forgot about me."

"No. You're unforgettable, Ally."

"Please," Ally said. She fingered the bath towel hanging from the door. She clutched it for ballast. The palms of her hands were sweaty and cold.

"Does Lizzie know?"

"I don't know. No."

"You have to go downstairs. You have guests."

"No kidding! What do I do?"

"You fake it through dinner, and after they leave— Is Teddy there?"

"He's pouring the wine! He brought the wine! Four bottles!"

"Maybe—maybe Lizzie knows. Maybe it's a test," Anna offered.

Ally paused. Would Lizzie test her? What would be the point? "No," she said, considering this. "She was surprised. She couldn't *fake* something like that. She's not that good an actress."

"Ally."

"She's no Meryl Streep!"

"Way to be supportive."

"Can we stay on point?"

"Mom!" Lizzie yelled from the first floor.

"Coming!" said Ally. To Anna, she said, "I have to go." She didn't move. She sat on the edge of the tub and breathed. She looked at the ceiling. Looked at her feet. It had been months since she had painted her toenails. Why did she always wait so long?

"The chicken's getting cold!" Lizzie yelled.

"Coming! Start!" She turned her attention back to Anna. "I have to do this. Please stay awake. I'll call you later."

"Call me—and, Ally?"

"Yes?"

"Was the weekend good? Ten years ago? I seem to remember you loved this guy."

"Loved him? No."

"Yes, you did."

"No, I didn't!" Ally protested a little too much.

"*Something* was good. The sex?"

"The sex." Ally closed her eyes to think. She had to swallow before she spoke. Her mouth was dry. "Honestly, it was marvelous."

JAKE LIFTED ALLY IN one swift motion, as if she weighed nothing. He propped her up on the kitchen counter.

The palms of his hands found her knees, and he spread them apart and moved between them. He cupped her face and found her mouth in a third kiss.

Move, Ally thought. She wanted to lie down, to feel the weight of his body on hers. She wanted him for hours in a bed, between sheets, not for minutes on the counter, even as spotless as Muriel had made it.

"Let's go upstairs," she whispered frantically as Jake brushed her neck with his lips. He returned to her mouth, and she nudged him forward and slid off the counter.

Out from under him, she left the kitchen, moved to the hall, and headed upstairs. Jake followed. On the staircase, he pushed past Ally as if they were racing.

In her bedroom, he flipped on the light, reached the bed first, and climbed up on all fours. He turned and rose to his knees to collect her.

She stopped in the doorway. "Jake, I have to tell you . . . something," Ally said softly, her voice filled with worry.

"What?" he said.

Ally paused. She hated to admit it. "I haven't done this in a . . . long time."

Jake blinked. "Okay."

"I don't mean months. I mean years."

"It's okay, Ally," he said reassuringly. It was the first time he used her first name. It almost took her breath away.

Ally looked down and studied the floor. "I mean, I've done it a few times—actual sex—since I got pregnant."

"A *few* times?"

"I've fooled around. But the actual act? The actual thing?"

"Your daughter is ten?"

Ally nodded.

"So you've had sex a *few* times in the last *ten* years?"

"Eleven," said Ally. "Twice in eleven. Kind of."

Jake thought about it. He looked at the floor. He looked at Ally and smiled. "That is a shame," he finally said. "That is tragic. For all men. Everywhere." Then he studied her. "Ally?"

"Yes?"

"Don't do anything for me tonight."

"What?"

"Let's let tonight be all about you."

Ally smiled and took a deep breath.

He was still there. Despite her admission, he knelt on the bed, ready to take her. "Get over here."

She moved to the bed, unsure. He met her at the edge, leaned in, and kissed her. He twisted her body into a cradle, dipped her, and placed her down on her back.

Long and flush, he lowered his body on top of hers. They kissed and kissed, and kissed and kissed.

She had forgotten how wonderful it was.

A man.

A man with large, calloused hands; long, heavy limbs and rough hair; large muscle groups, so foreign; weight and strength. Jake's smell was musky and sweet. Staggering.

He started to unfasten her blouse from the bottom, button by button. "Tell me to stop."

Ally said nothing. Don't stop, she thought.

Ever. Ever.

He made his way up, button by button, as if he had done so a thousand times, and never moved his lips from hers.

When he finished, he rose to an elbow, parted her blouse, tugged her bra down, and lifted her breasts up and out. He ducked to devour them.

Ally's head fell back onto the pillow.

Goodness.

He's an expert, she thought, running her fingers through his hair, full and brown and thick. Thank goodness he needed a haircut, and how could this kid, at twenty-one, be so adept, so skilled, so smooth? How could he be so lovely? she wondered.

Jake sat back, pulled off his T-shirt, and placed it beside him on the bed.

Ally's lips parted. Her eyes grew wide.

His body was sculpted, smooth, and unreal, as if he'd stepped from a magazine cover. His chest and abs, his broad shoulders and lean, athletic arms, looked as if a sculptor had chiseled them.

"You're so pretty," Jake whispered, breaking her reverie, seeming to be caught in his own.

Ally snapped to. "What? Please! Look at you!" She rolled her eyes.

"Please what?"

Ally didn't feel pretty. Sure, she knew she'd been pretty once. All young women are somewhat attractive.

"You are," Jake said, gazing at her lips. "That smile. That *smile*."

She did have an infectious smile. But she had kept her baby weight, had stopped jogging, and hadn't had a haircut in years. Years.

"Everyone thinks so. Everyone says so."

"What? Who?" Ally wondered how that could be. She never wore makeup, never dressed up. She only shopped for Lizzie. She'd pick up a pair of jeans here, a sweater there, in Newport's nicer Goodwill shops, but mostly she lived in sneakers and sweats and jeans she'd bought in DC to make room for her freshman fifteen.

"What is this? I think you have a . . ." Jake smiled and reached forward, over her head.

"What? What is it?"

"You have a sticky—"

"A what?"

"A sticky note stuck to your—"

"Me?" she said, embarrassed. She turned her head to see what it was as he plucked the pink sticky note out of her hair and showed it to her. A Russian phrase was scrawled across it in red crayon. Lizzie's writing.

"Oh, that's sexy. They're all over. My daughter—she's teaching herself Russian. I think this says, 'I hate you, Mom.'"

"*Russian?*" Jake laughed.

"She's a little on the—gifted—side. Hebrew and French too. It's insane."

He plucked the note from Ally's hand and sailed it off the side of the bed.

"I'm sure there are—more," she said, peering under the top sheet. "Sometimes I find them stuck to my butt as I walk out the door." She lifted to her elbows and looked around for more. There were a few, seven or eight, which was odd, Ally thought. Hadn't Muriel changed the sheets? She must've forgot.

Jake rolled off her and helped to collect them. "You were in college when you had your kid?"

Ally paused. She looked at him. "Yes. I was your age," she said. "Exactly."

"That must be a pretty good story."

Ally sighed.

"Can I hear it?"

"Now?"

"Why not?" Jake said and lay down next to her on his side, propping his head up on his hand.

So Ally explained . . .

"It started in Economics," she said. "Junior year. I was twenty. Just like you."

"I'm twenty-one," Jake corrected her.

Pierre Ben-Shahar had flashed her his beguiling smile. They had started to date that September, and after a party on Magis Row, they had sex.

He'd entered her once without a condom, Ally's first time, on a mid-September night, but only for a second. "Maybe four. Four seconds. Maybe ten. But no more than that," Ally had explained to her mother.

Claire was furious.

Ally discovered she was pregnant on Halloween night when Pierre insisted she dress as a brick and he as a bricklayer.

"He was inside me for two seconds. Twelve, maybe fifteen seconds. Twenty seconds, tops. He didn't even come," she explained to Jake.

Pierre had the Alexander Popov of sperm, she decided after the birth. That was the only explanation.

Two years before, Popov the swimmer won two golds in the Summer Olympics, and Popov the sperm had clearly dived into Pierre's pre-ejaculate, swam, survived, and swam and survived, hiding himself inside of Ally for at least two weeks before he made Lizzie.

He was a survivor, that little sperm.

That was her theory.

And Ally was too.

Despite being twenty and pregnant in college, at Georgetown, no less, a Catholic school, Ally thought motherhood was absolute bliss.

She was born to be Lizzie's mother.

Lizzie was simply meant to be.

So senior year, she powered through, nursing and sleepless, and knocked out a notable senior thesis that brought her to Brown.

"What?" Jake asked. "What was it on?"

"Really?" she said and buried her face in her hands.

"Tell me."

She paused. "It was—it was a—gender analysis of Barbara Kennelly's Pension Reform Act; 1993; pension benefits, cost of living, you know, post separation and divorce; who voted, why, how it died, blah-blah."

Jake smiled.

"I also wrote a *second* on the economic ramifications of paternal abandonment in southeast DC."

"Wow!" Jake said.

Ally smiled. "Talk about *inspired*. I was so mad. Both got published. Big journals. Peer-reviewed."

The papers took Ally to Brown, she explained, with grants and a TA appointment as she worked toward her PhD.

It was not her plan. Feminist economics.

"Sometimes you lead your life," she said, "and sometimes your life leads you."

The work put a roof over her head, and Brown had safe, loving day care.

"And I had a beautiful baby girl."

Jake lay there listening.

She didn't need the courtship, she said, the engagement, the parties. The gifts, the showers, the white dress, the day. She didn't need the marriage or the man.

Especially not Pierre Ben-Shahar, who had threatened to kill himself *tout de suite* unless she aborted *tout de suite*. He escaped that summer across the Atlantic, hopped back and forth from Paris to Haifa and back and back, one month with mom, another with dad, and never returned to the States again.

And never returned Ally's calls.

"His loss," Jake said. He reached out and tucked a strand of her hair behind her ear.

Ally sighed.

She had made peace with her life alone. Alone with Lizzie. But peace or not, she hadn't seen a penis in many years. The lack of sex, of intimacy, the lack of a man, was, at times, excruciating.

And other times, not.

She focused on Lizzie, designing her lectures, joining committees, writing on the side under pseudonyms, and all the sweet and relentless courting of one nasty chair who stole her from the Economics Department.

She had to stay in and stick it out, Claire reminded her. Tenure, tenure! She needed tenure! Providence for life! If she worked hard and played by the rules.

Ally knew she'd never get it. Her mother had no idea what it took or how it worked. She wasn't even sure she wanted it.

That was it. That was the story. She gazed at Jake.

Jake, her student! Jake, like some hero from a daytime soap! Jake in her bedroom! The boy in the back, half naked!

He leaned in and kissed her on the lips, then rolled back on top of her, kissing her harder, even more deeply.

Suddenly Ally was tugging at his belt.

She couldn't resist. She couldn't wait. She wanted him now. She had suffered long enough.

She sat up and pulled his belt apart, then fumbled with the button at the top of his zipper.

Jake grew still, looking pleased and surprised.

Ally wanted him. She wanted to release him. She'd felt him building against her belly, pressing against her inner thighs.

She pulled down his zipper, and Jake rose back to his knees to help. He pulled down his jeans and kicked them off. Then did the same with his gray cotton briefs.

Oh no! she thought when she saw him in the shadows, huge and ready and poised for her. Her jaw dropped and her mouth opened wide. She couldn't help it. "Oh my goodness."

It was— He was absolutely perfect.

Astonishingly perfect.

Wider in girth, straighter, firmer, longer and wider, wider and longer, stronger somehow, than any she'd ever seen before. He was— It was magnificent. "Oh my goodness," she said again. She couldn't help but stare as she slid off her jeans and panties, too.

And then the phone rang.

The phone.

The cordless phone at the foot of the bed.

"Shoot!" she said in anguish. "Sorry!"

Jake smiled and slid to her side.

"Oh my goodness. Hold that thought." She knew it was Lizzie and Claire calling. They were calling, of course, to say good night. It was after ten. "I'm so sorry. I have to get this."

"Your kid?"

"I think." She reached around him to pick up the phone.

"WEATHER SAYS YOUR FEMINISM is *so* 1960s, Mom." Lizzie handed the pasta to Jake. "She says you're a product of the time you were born."

"I wasn't born in the sixties, honey."

"You weren't?"

"No!" Ally laughed.

"You don't know when your mother was born?" Jake leaned across the table. He spooned the pasta onto Ally's plate.

"Teddy, could you wait?" Lizzie scolded, glaring at him.

"Sorry. I'm hungry," Teddy said, looking up from his meal, chewing.

"I thought you were *patient*," Lizzie sniped.

He put down his fork.

"Nineteen seventy-*three*," Ally said as she laid out the chicken. "Thank you, Jake."

Jake sat down and served himself.

"Weather says you're a postfeminist."

"Weather's wrong."

"How is she wrong? What are you, then?"

"Do we want to do this?" Ally said. "Now?"

Lizzie continued. "She said you are. But we're not. We're *neo*feminists. Modern consumers. Not afraid of beauty or sex. Not afraid to define ourselves, market ourselves, sell ourselves. Wait, is this cheese?" She looked at her plate.

"Buffalo mozzarella, honey."

"Oh, thanks." She turned to Jake. "I can't touch dairy. Weather says dairy and gluten are poison."

"True, if you're *lactose intolerant*," Ally said.

"Or you're celiac," Jake added.

"Weather weighs almost two hundred pounds," Ally continued kindly, fairly, taking a seat. "Should she be giving diet advice?"

Really she wanted to kill Weather: Stephanie Rachel Weather Weiner, Lizzie's best friend from theater camp from when they were ten. Weather, with her fourteen piercings and forearms covered in kitten tattoos.

"All that genetically modified gluten. Italy, France. *Saudi Arabia* banned it," said Lizzie.

"Isn't cheese dairy?" Ted asked, digging in again now that Ally was seated.

"Not all cheese," Lizzie explained. "Dairy is *cow*."

"Weather has too many cats," Ally quipped, trying to lighten the tension at the table. "Nine. Is that legal?" She picked up her fork.

"Cats or not, fat or not, she is rocking Lady Bracknell. In our class. Acting class. Oscar Wilde. She dyed her hair *gray*."

"I think when you mess with your face," Jake said, "you're

moving away from something authentic. It's easy to see what's fake up there. It's a big screen."

"That's a good point," Ally agreed, looking at Lizzie hopefully. "Jake should know." She turned to him. "Lizzie said you've had some success?"

"*Some* success?" Ted bellowed, looking at Ally. "He's huge, Ally! Huge! Huge, huge!"

"Okay!" she said. She knew exactly how huge he was.

"What big screen?" Lizzie continued. "Theaters will be obsolete in ten years. Spielberg said that on NPR. Spielberg and that *Star Wars* guy. We'll be watching TV on our phones."

Jake took his napkin and wiped his mouth. "The point is, who do you want to be? Helen Mirren or Jennifer Grey?"

"Neither," said Lizzie. "I want to be me."

"Jennifer Grey?" Ally asked.

"*Dirty Dancing*," Jake explained. "The girl who played Baby. She chopped off her nose and it killed her career."

"No!" Ally cooed. "She was so cute!"

Lizzie rolled her eyes and grabbed the wine. She poured herself another glass. "My mother is obsessed with old movies, and Noah is obsessed with old women: Helen Mirren, Judi Dench—"

"You've had enough wine," Ally said.

"I've had a glass."

"Two, I believe."

"So cheers! So great! So let's get drunk!"

"Good," said Teddy. "This is Lokoya from Napa. Did I say that? Three hundred bucks a bottle, ladies. Drink all you *like*."

Lizzie turned to Jake. "You can be fat and homely and old, and no one cares. For women, it's different." She looked at Ally. "It's okay for some football player to jack himself up for the NFL—twenty-three-inch biceps—*biceps*—for *his* job—the size of my *waist*—but it's not okay for an actress to change her body for hers?" She was upset.

"Lizzie," said Ally as gently as she could. "That's a good point. We're not ganging up—"

"You are! You and Noah! You're like a *team*."

Jake and Ally glanced at each other.

"And Ted, with nothing to add."

Ted looked up. "Nothing to add? I brought twelve hundred bucks' worth of wine."

"I know you agree with me," Lizzie said.

"Well, I *might*," Teddy replied. "In *theory*, yes. But I, for one, would miss your face."

"I would too," Ally said.

"Me three," said Jake.

"Let's forget it," Lizzie muttered. "I'm the youngest . . . at this table. There might be something I know about this world—this age I live in—that you guys don't. So you can think your judgmental thoughts and feel superior with all your *birthdays*—and I will do what I want with my nose." She drained her glass in one fell swoop.

Ally studied her.

No one spoke for a long moment. Lizzie put down her glass. Ally pushed pasta around on her plate. Jake dropped his napkin, then picked it up and broke the silence. "So, Ted, do you travel? A lot? For work?"

Teddy looked up and eyed Jake. "Only to Silicon Valley. Why?"

THE PHONE WAS RINGING. "My daughter, Lizzie, she gets upset. She's sensitive." Ally grabbed the phone and her underwear. "She's supersmart and can only put up with my mom for so long."

Jake laughed. "You want me to go?" he asked sweetly. "You want to be private?"

"No," Ally said. "Unless you want to."

"Whatever you need." He reached to the floor to find his briefs.

"I won't be long." She answered the phone. "Hello?" she said. "Sweetie?"

"Mommy?" said Lizzie.

"Hi, honey." She glanced at Jake. He was pulling on his briefs.

"Grandma won't let me sleep in my slippers."

"What?" Ally said, pulling her underwear back on, distracted.

"She won't let me sleep in my slippers."

"I'm sorry. How are you otherwise?" She couldn't focus. "Are you having fun?"

"No."

"Is she there?"

"Downstairs."

"Where are you?" Underwear on, Ally looked down and pulled her shirt closed. She fastened the button between her breasts.

"Brushing my teeth. Can you come here?"

"I wish, honey. But, sweetie, I told you. My TA went home. Back to Omaha. The capital city of?"

"Yoko?"

"Yoko."

"Nebraska?"

"Yup. She got that disease that made her sleepy. Mono? Remember?"

"Will she come back?"

"In the fall."

"And be better?"

"Yup, but for now, she's home, so Mommy has to finish her work."

"Grandma said you get it from kissing."

Ally paused before she spoke. "No, honey. Grandma's wrong. It's in your liver. It's in an organ inside your body."

"You sure?"

"I am. It's *not* from kissing."

Then suddenly: "Please grade them here!"

"No, sweetie. I'll see you Sunday. You'll have fun."

"I won't!"

"You will. Tomorrow you will. Why are you up? It's after ten."

She looked at Jake. He was still at attention in his briefs. The light from the windows had landed on him, there in the dark, and outlined him, his cuts and curves.

"She won't let me sleep in my slippers."

"Okay."

"And she's smoking. I think. Again."

Ally cringed. "Walk down the phone. I'll take care of it. Where are you now?" She ripped her gaze from Jake.

"Going downstairs."

Ally scuttled to the end of the bed. "Where is Grandma?"

"In the kitchen."

"What was for dinner?"

"Nothing. Burgers."

"Oh. That's— Sorry. That's my fault." She waited a moment, stood, and abandoned the bed, moving toward the hall. She glanced back as Jake sat up. He tucked a pillow under his head and pulled a blanket around his waist. He waved.

On Cranberry Street, Lizzie handed Claire the phone. Ally could hear them in the background. "She wants you."

"What? Hello? Ally?" Claire sounded startled.

"Hi, Mom." Ally stood in the dark hall, gazing downstairs.

"A couple of things." Claire addressed Lizzie. "I need to speak to your mother alone."

Ally rolled her eyes and waited. She waited some more. "Why can't she sleep in her slippers?"

"What?"

"Her slippers. Why can't she wear them?"

"It's hot. The soles are dirty."

"Please let her."

"Did she have a growth spurt?"

Ally paused. "I don't know. Did she?" She turned and went into Lizzie's room.

"Her skirts are too short."

It felt so empty without Lizzie there; all the shadows, the dapple of ambient light from the windows casting across Lizzie's motionless things.

"This is the *city*, Allison. She looks like a little you know what."

"No, I don't. What?" Cradling the phone, Ally bent over and straightened the sheet on the new bottom bunk.

"A *hooker*," said Claire.

Ally paused. She turned, sat down, and took a deep breath. She waited for Claire to keep going. She did:

"I'll take her shopping tomorrow at Saks. She needs new clothes. And flip-flops, Ally? She needs proper shoes."

"That would be lovely." Ally sighed.

"Her hair is too long. The ends are split. I'll take her to Barrett."

"You can braid it."

"This isn't—a *prairie*."

"*French* braid it."

"I'll take her to Bergdorf's after Saks."

"Isn't there—a barber on Montague Street?"

"We'll go to John Barrett, and, Ally?"

"Yes?"

"She won't eat my food."

"That's—my fault. I forgot to tell you . . . She's a vegetarian. Now. As of last week."

"What? Why? How should I know?"

"I'm sorry. You shouldn't. I should have told you, but just let her sleep in her slippers, okay? And *do not* smoke around her, please."

Claire paused. "Getting your work done?"

Ally looked guilty. "Yes," she said and rose from the bed, bumping her head on the top bunk. "Ow." She headed into the dark hall. "Can I have her back? To say good night?"

"Lizzie! Your mother!"

Ally held the phone from her ear. For a moment. Then she entered her bedroom again.

"Oh, and, Ally? She asked me to buy her that gun. For her birthday."

"No," Ally said, gazing at Jake lying there. "No gun. No BBs." He stared at the ceiling, a bed pillow pulled up over his chest. "A toy gun is fine, but nothing with ammo. Foam is all right." Jake smiled. "Mom? You there?"

Claire was gone.

"Hello?" Lizzie said, back on the line.

"You can wear your slippers."

"Please come here."

"No, sweetie."

"Mommy, *please*."

"You can do a night."

"*Two* nights."

"You get to go shopping tomorrow, in town."

"I don't want to," Lizzie said. She sounded as if she was going to cry.

"I miss you too, but the city is fun."

"No, it won't be."

"*Try.* I love you."

"I love you too."

"I'm hanging up."

"Bye," Lizzie said. She spoke to Claire. "She said I could wear them!"

Ally paused and looked at the phone. Then she hung up. She looked at the window and thought, for a second, about heading south. She could gather her papers, drive to the city, and surprise Lizzie in the middle of the night. She'd read them in Brooklyn. Grade them in Brooklyn.

Why not?

"Hi," Jake said, drawing himself up to his elbow.

Ally turned, almost surprised to see him there. "Hi," she said.

"VENTURE CAPITAL," TEDDY EXPLAINED as he chewed a bite of the chocolate cake. "I got in early on all the Web two point oh stuff— This cake, you *made* this from scratch, Al?"

"What is that?" Jake eyed him coolly. "Web two what?"

Teddy licked his lips. "All beyond the static page. Interactive Twitter. Foursquare. Kickstarter. Facebook. I got in early. If not for Facebook, I wouldn't be here. It's how I found Ally."

Ally forced a smile.

"*You're* on Facebook?" Lizzie asked her, picking at raspberries from a bowl. "I'm shocked."

"Last fall. For a month."

"My lucky month," Teddy added. "The week I found her. I hadn't seen her since senior year."

"When he dropped me."

"No," said Ted. "No, no."

"The last time I saw you?"

"The last time I saw—you were—*breastfeeding*. I was twenty-one and dumb. I got—weirded out and left."

Lizzie laughed. "Why?"

"Her boobs got enormous, and one was, like, hanging out, and you"—he pointed to Lizzie—"you were *sucking* it. I was—*traumatized*."

"You *backed* out," Ally said. "Bumped into the door on your way."

Teddy reached for the wine. "It was not a courageous moment. I admit. But I got you a present."

"A baby cup," Ally said, nodding. "I think we still have it. Sterling silver. And a stuffed donkey."

"An ass?" Lizzie said. "You bought me an ass?"

Ally had created the Facebook account with one intention that October: to find Jake. Not to talk, or anything else, but to see what had become of him. To see if he was alive and well.

She hoped he was.

Four weeks later, ninety-one people had friended her, including Anna, eighty-nine students, Meer, and Ted. Teddy asked if she was single, how was the kid, and would Ally like to go get a drink. With him. On him.

When she couldn't find Jake, she agreed to coffee and canceled her account. Or tried to. She wasn't sure if she actually had or not.

She didn't care.

She was a stalker, she told herself, disappointed. She had no right to look him up. But then she considered asking Lizzie to work her magic, all that trolling and sleuthing she did through high school, sometimes till morning, bleary-eyed and thrilled by her latest hack.

But Lizzie would've asked for the *whole* story, the entire story, and Ally was too conflicted to tell it.

"Everyone wanted your mom at Gtown. She was the *get*. Did you know that, Lizzie?"

"Well, she got *got*," Lizzie said dryly.

"That, she did."

"Hey, you know, Noah?" Teddy said, changing the subject. "Speaking of getting: I'm raising money. Series A. For this new site." He turned to Ally. "Is this okay? The toys thing? With you?"

"Sure," Ally said and picked up her fork. "Why wouldn't it be?"

"The *sex* toys thing?" Lizzie popped a raspberry into her mouth. "At the *table*?"

"That's right." He turned to Jake. "Sex toy site. Silicon Valley won't touch it."

Ally gazed at her waiting dessert. Her stomach felt tight and twisted in knots.

"Tough to find funding," Teddy continued. "Banks passed. PayPal passed. But worldwide sex toys—upscale, hygienic—shipped discreetly through UPS? It's a gold mine. We should sit down."

Jake shook his head. "Thank you, but I don't do that."

"You don't what? Use sex toys?"

"I don't decide where I put my money."

Ted ignored this. "Well, tell your *guys* we're going to brand it for sexual wellness. Nothing violent. Nothing dirty. Sexual *wellness*. Sexual *health*. Of course we'll have whips and dildos and lube, and handcuffs and feathers—"

"Coffee anyone?" Ally rose and made a getaway to the cabinets.

"Call each other," Lizzie said. "Swap numbers."

"Decaf? Regular?" She pulled down mugs from a shelf.

"Regular, please," Lizzie called. "Noah? Or Jake? I want to call you Jake." She laughed and studied him. "I still can't believe you had my mom."

"How was Ally? At Brown?" Teddy asked, cutting himself another piece of cake. "Was she good? Did she suck?"

Ally paused as she poured the coffee. "You don't have to answer that."

"I don't mind," Jake said and put down his fork. He picked up his napkin and wiped his mouth. "But what do you want? The dinner-party answer or the truth answer? You want the truth?"

At the counter, Ally froze. The truth answer? What was that?

Lizzie lit up. "The truth! The truth!"

"Well," Jake started, smiling slyly. "Sometimes—sometimes you have a teacher—who leaves a kind of indelible mark. Sometimes—not often—you have a professor you never forget, and that professor, for me, was your mom."

Lizzie smiled and looked at Ally. "Go, Mom! To Dr. Hughes!" She raised her glass, and Jake did too, and Teddy too. "Hear, hear."

Ally turned around, relieved. "Thank you," she said, putting down the mugs. "That's because I gave him a credit he didn't deserve."

"That's not why," Jake said.

"Okay, well. You guys drink up. I'll clean up." She turned around, back to the sink.

"I'll help." Jake rose and gathered the wineglasses. Lizzie's first.

"Jake, please," Ally protested. "You're the guest."

"I want to help."

Lizzie and Teddy stayed seated. "Just want another . . . if no one cares." He cut a third piece of cake, then licked the cutting knife up and down and put it back on the tray.

Across the table, Lizzie studied him. "Now that has your saliva on it."

Teddy paused and looked at her. "At least I eat." He reached into his pocket, pulled out a hanky, and blew his nose. "You're getting skinny. Don't get too skinny."

"It's for work."

He smiled. "Work? Del Frisco's, right? Great steak there, by the way. What do you do? Hostess? Waitress? That's what you mean by work, right?" He blew and blew as Lizzie watched. "Excuse me. I'm sorry. I know it's— I should excuse myself . . . frigging cold. In August. It's weird." Then he folded the handkerchief in half, crumpled it up, and placed it down next to his plate.

Ally and Jake made small talk behind them. They moved, back and forth, from the sink to the fridge and back to the trash, and back again to the dishwasher.

Hushed and quiet, shy and reserved, they did the dishes and discussed Jake's success: What it was like to be an actor. How it happened. If he was happy.

He fell into acting, he said, in LA.

"Sometimes you lead your life," he said. "And sometimes your life leads you." He had followed his brother west to work: Beverly Hills. The Palisades. Rich people. Handyman stuff. A flat-screen

TV, a dollhouse, a bunk bed, as it turned out. "For this director," Jake explained. The director was looking for a guy for this part. "Lancelot. You know, the knight?"

Ally nodded. Of course she knew Lancelot. King Arthur. The Round Table.

"They called me in. I read the lines. They gave me a test and that was it. Took off from there."

She smiled. "Exciting. Must be fun." Like clockwork, she handed him dish after dish, and Jake placed them carefully into the washer.

"A lot of it's waiting," Jake said. "Goofing around . . . going to parties. Too many parties." Then he asked about her work. Why she left Brown for Brooklyn College.

"No tenure," Ally explained. "Applied to about fifty schools and got an offer right here at home." Suddenly she was overcome. Her eyes welled with tears, but she held them in. "Four years. Since we've been back. This is it." She motioned to the room. "The house I grew up in. I spit up *peas* at that table."

"I'm sorry," Jake said tenderly. "About your mom. Lizzie told me."

Ally nodded. "It was . . . We were . . . here with her. When she got sick. And at the end. That was good. And now I'm taking the year off. Not teaching. This September. First sabbatical, starting now." She needed it badly: the rest and refocus.

Jake nodded. "I'm sure you deserve it."

Ally smiled. "I feel like I do. First vacation in twenty years."

"More paid vacation, less sick leave. Especially for women. Isn't that right?" Jake then said.

Ally turned and stared at him. In May she'd had a story in *Elle* saying just that. Almost verbatim. "I agree," she said and nodded.

At the table, Lizzie leaned in and lowered her voice. "Who will deal with your hanky there?" She was thinking about Ted's appetite. His hygiene.

Ted looked up and licked his lips. "What?"

"Who will pick up your wet little hanky? Maybe you should clear your own place."

Lizzie had tried for six long months to dig up dirt or worse on Ted. She'd tried her best to hack his accounts, his phone, his iCloud account. She'd tried to crack his Wi-Fi at home. Nothing worked. He was walled in. Too well. Too protected.

"Sure," he said. "But your mom likes to—"

"No," Lizzie said. She was tipsy. "Not my mom. You're a big boy. You can clean up. My mom's so—*fragile*—these days. You don't—want to get her sick."

Ted said nothing.

Lizzie had checked his real estate records, probate court records, registrations, and 13Ds. She'd found nothing. "She doesn't want your cold," she said. "No one—no one wants your cold."

Ted paused and put down his fork. He picked up his handkerchief, leaned back, and slid it into his khakis pocket. "You're right when you're right."

Lizzie nodded. "We shouldn't pass our diseases around." They stared at each other meaningfully.

"Too true," he said. "Too true."

"**IS SHE THERE EVERY** weekend? Your daughter?" Jake asked, lying on the bed in the dark.

Ally stood there, phone in hand. "No. Hardly ever."

"She can handle it. Can she?"

"Maybe. Maybe she can. Maybe she can't. My mother is . . . What's the word? *Exacting*, I guess." She shrugged. "I think I should head to New York tonight."

Jake looked surprised.

"Not that I don't want to do this. I do. I'm just . . . a little . . ."

"What?"

"Conflicted."

"Sure."

"I'm a mom." She tried to explain. "My daughter comes first. Before work, before me, and, of course, before any man I meet."

"She sounds like she needs a good night's sleep."

"Maybe, but—"

"Twice in ten years? Ally. Twice?"

"Yes to all that. I know, I know. But single mothers . . . It's hard to explain." She took a deep breath. She was embarrassed. "And you know what? The real thing is . . . I don't know you. You don't know me. Even if you *weren't* in my class, which you are, which you were—even if you weren't twenty-one, which you *are* . . . I'm not into . . . flings."

Jake shook his head. "This isn't a fling."

"It's not?"

"No." He lifted up to sitting, slid off his watch, and handed it to her. "Take it," he said.

"Why?" She did. She took his watch.

He turned and arranged the pillows behind him. He leaned back and said, "Two minutes each. Life-defining moments. Top ten. You got the clock. I'll go first."

Ally smiled and hesitated. She looked at his watch, then at Jake.

"Let's get to know each other, Ally Hughes."

In the dark, she could barely see the hands. Jake leaned toward her. "The face lights up. Button on the . . ." He showed her the button and his fingertips grazed hers. Ally looked up. This brief contact made her heart race.

She pressed the button and the face lit up. Reluctantly she watched the second hand move to the twelve. "Okay, go." She was still standing up at the edge of the bed.

Jake took a breath and looked at the ceiling. "Born in Boston. Last of four boys. Dad took off when I was two. Mom taught first grade, so we had no money. At three, got a baseball. That was big. That was major. Moved in with Grandma, above a bar, all of us, at five. Little League at six. Oldest brother shot when I was nine.

Shot, but survived. I started pitching. Arrested for possession my junior year, high school."

"Arrested?"

"*Convicted*. Served two months at Elk Island. House of Corrections."

"Possession of what?" She sat on the bed and turned to face him. She was intrigued.

"Cocaine."

"Wow." She pulled her blouse down over her underwear, over her thighs.

"My older brother dealt. I delivered. It's a long story, but it got me into Brown."

Ally smiled. "Jail time. Of course."

Jake smiled. "They wanted my pitching. I had straight As and the baseball thing so . . . Four partial scholarship offers. Chose Brown, to pitch for the Bears . . . Three weddings later, five nephews, I quit school and decide to hit on my smokin' professor."

"Is that me?"

"Yup."

Ally smiled. "Time," she said and stretched her legs toward him. He picked up her foot and bit her big toe and put it down again. Ally smiled. She gave him the watch.

Jake lit up the face and waited. "Okay, okay, wait, wait . . . Go."

Ally thought about it. Defining moments? Defining moments. "Born in New York," she started and smiled. "Only child. Dad died when I was six. Pretend to remember him, but I don't. We have that in common." Jake nodded.

"Lizzie too. No dad." She paused. "My mom was depressed. For a long time. Still is. Still is, I think. Never got over him. Then I got out. Accepted to Georgetown. Knocked myself up—I told you that. Had my baby, Elizabeth Claire. Moved to Providence to TA, for my PhD, and lived for nine whole years in this house. Turned thirty-one two months ago, and . . . and this student hit on me . . . The one I always thought was . . . so cute."

They stared at each other, both silent.

"Now do you know me?" Jake asked and smiled.

"No," she said, staring at him, basking in how handsome he was.

"So she's safe there, and you're safe here? Dead bolt, windows, me, done. Everyone's safe, and you can be Ally for a few hours? Ally, not Mommy?"

"I'm always Mommy."

He nodded and placed his hand on her ankle. "Good mom. Good daughter. All these roles we play."

"It's not a role," Ally said, shaking her head. "It's who I am."

He walked his fingers, his middle and pointer, to the center of her shin and up to her knee. "Good professor." He leaned forward onto his stomach. By Ally's side, he propped himself up and inspected her leg. "Killer gams, by the way . . ."

Ally smiled.

He took her leg, rotated it, and kissed the nook in the back of her knee. Then he continued to walk his fingers past her knee and up her thigh.

Ally watched. The side of her mouth curled into a smile. What was he doing?

At the top of her thigh, he splayed his hand. His fingers spread out around her leg, and he gripped it as if to measure its girth.

Then he leaned in and kissed a freckle. "Since we're playing 'get to know you'. . . how many freckles do you have? Do you know?"

"No."

Jake nodded. "Maybe you don't know someone . . . until you know how many freckles they have . . ." He circled the freckle with his finger. "One," he said and gazed down the bed, back to her foot. "Do you mind?"

"What?"

"If I count."

Ally smiled. "Is this, like, a thing?"

"A thing?"

"To seduce me?"

"Is it?"

"Is it what?"

"Seducing you?"

Ally exhaled and closed her eyes. She opened them again and watched as Jake found the freckles on her leg, one by one, and drew invisible circles around them. "Two, three . . . I just want to know . . . four, five, six . . . something about you that no one else knows . . . seven, eight . . . that maybe even . . . you don't know." He leaned in and kissed the seventh and eighth.

THUNDER RUMBLED OVER BROOKLYN. The warm, thick air grew windy and cool.

At the front door, Jake thanked Ally and pulled her into a tight embrace. Ally froze. "I meant what I said, Professor Hughes," he said and released her. "I never forgot you."

Ally nodded, forcing a smile. "Nice to see you."

He turned and Ted walked him out, on his heels. They went down the stoop, discussing Ted's site: the live demonstrations, the customer reviews . . .

"One moment, boys," Ally said, pulling Lizzie back inside. She closed the front door. "It's going to rain." She stepped into the closet, found an umbrella, stepped back out, and lowered her voice: "You were a *little* rude to Ted—"

"I'm *sorry*," said Lizzie and took the umbrella from Ally's hand. "I am. I am." She opened it up to see if it worked. "There's something—*off*—about him. I just can't put my finger on—"

"Nothing's *off*. He's a little spoiled. That's all. A little—"

"No. That's *not* all," Lizzie insisted. The umbrella wouldn't lock.

"This is broken." She gave the umbrella back to Ally, and Ally disappeared back into the closet. Lizzie continued, whispering too. "It's weird. You feel it. I know you do."

Ally returned with a second umbrella. "Teddy is smart, funny, cute—and *generous*."

"If he's so cute, then *do* him, Mother," Lizzie said, not unkindly.

"Elizabeth, please."

"Have *sex* if he's so cute. Do it already." She opened the umbrella and stood underneath. "But, no, you won't, because he's strange—and we can't say why. He seems like a catch, and yet—"

"He was our *guest*. He is my friend."

"I'm sorry, but he has a secret, and I have the right to be worried. I do. I'm the kid." She closed the umbrella and mocked her mother, pretending to sob: "You're beautiful, honey. Even your nose. You're sacred, sweetie. If you want to marry some preppy freak, I have to prepare myself too—"

"Stop," Ally said.

Lizzie smiled. "And Noah? What?"

"Noah's lovely."

"*Lovely?*"

"Great and cool and great."

Lizzie nodded. "And that's what you need. A *great* man. I cannot *believe* he had you at Brown!"

"Small world," Ally said as she reached for the knob. She opened the door and drew Lizzie close. "Call me tonight. We need to talk." She kissed her on the ear.

"I love you, Mama." Lizzie kissed her back and walked out.

———

"Did you remember him?" Teddy asked an hour later. He sat at the table and finished the cake while Ally scrubbed the pans in the sink.

"I remember his writing," Ally said. "These papers—went on forever. The last one was on this erotica writer, Anaïs Nin."

Teddy looked up. "Erotica? Porn? Porn, you mean? *You* taught porn?"

Ally stopped scrubbing. "He was . . . Catholic, I think, and so freaked out by the threesomes, orgies, hermaphrodites . . ."

Teddy was suddenly standing behind her. "Sounds fun to me." She could feel him at her back. He whispered in her ear: "Teach me, too?" He placed his hands on top of her shoulders and started to massage them.

Ally turned and said kindly, "Not a great night . . . and you have a cold."

Teddy's face fell. He stepped back and leaned against the table, perching his buttocks half on, half off. "You need to get out of Brooklyn, Al. Out of this house."

Ally turned to the sink, embarrassed. She picked up a Brillo and started to scrub a casserole dish. "I'm sorry. You're right."

"We got together. Your mother was sick. You said you were stressed. She passed away and you were sad. When I'm upset, *all* I want is to hop in the sack. We have fun. Don't we?"

"Yes."

"Have you ever been—*frigid* before?"

Ally paused and looked at the dish. "*Frigid?*" she said quietly, wondering if in fact she was. She turned. "But we fool around."

"Yes, we do, but we're *adults*. Grown-ups, Ally, and I can't get past second base."

Ally nodded. He was right. That was true.

Teddy looked around the kitchen. "I think you're stuck. In her house. You can't have *fun* in your *mother's* house. You can't get out from *under* her—spell." Ted reached into his pants pocket and pulled out the soggy handkerchief. He blew his nose. "You need a vacation—or a shrink."

"Maybe," said Ally. "My best friend's a shrink. I'll ask her."

"Or maybe you're not attracted to me."

"Please," she insisted, turning around. "You're attractive. You are."

"I know!" He laughed. "I know I am! I've got appeal."

"You do."

"But that doesn't mean . . . Some women need—some need a meal. Some need commitment." He was musing.

Ally nodded. "Some do," she said, "but tonight, I'm tired. Five-course dinner, cooked from scratch. Lizzie and her nose . . ."

"All right," he said. "I'm an ass. I got you a new set of golf clubs. There." He pointed to the corner.

"Ted."

He straightened and lifted his buttocks from the table and tucked in his shirt. "I want to take you down to this course. I like you, Al, I always have, and I'd like to take this to the next level."

Ally studied him for a moment. "Aren't you—*seeing* other people?"

Teddy paused. "Not *really*."

She rubbed her eyes. "I thought you were. I had this sense—"

"You want to go steady? We can go steady."

Ally turned to the counter and picked up a piece of tinfoil. She wrapped it around a chicken breast.

"You want me to pin you? Give you my ring and my varsity jacket?"

She turned and handed the chicken to Ted. "Did you play sports?"

"No," he admitted. "Only the golf."

Ally smiled.

At the front door, he kissed her. "You know what I thought? All night tonight?" He lowered his voice.

"No. What."

"Ally has a fantastic ass. It's perfect."

"Thank you."

"I'd pay for that ass. To *own* that ass."

She gently pushed him out the door.

"That turns you on," he sang as he left. "You're pushing me out *because* you're turned on." He trudged down the stoop. "Am I right?"

"Nope. Good night, Ted. Thanks for the wine."

"Night, Al. Love you."

Ally waved and watched him walk off toward Hicks Street. Then she looked up at the low-hanging clouds and held out her hand. It had started to rain.

In the kitchen, she washed down the table.

Maybe he was right, she thought, Ted.

Claire was still so alive in these rooms.

She drew still and pictured her mother there, sitting at the table, ever so erect, ever so tall, but shrinking in girth as the chemo ate her away.

"He's *eager*," Claire had said with a smirk, of Ted. "About you." She raised her brows, thinned but still arched, and sat still in the way she sat still toward the end, as if moving even an inch might cause pain. She wore that pale pink, thinning robe, with the white scalloped edge. "He never married?"

"No," Ally said, holding the kettle under the faucet.

"What's his *problem*?"

Ally smiled. "What's mine? I'm over forty and I'm not married."

"You were *abandoned*," Claire said mercilessly, as a matter of fact. "On purpose." She reached for her Parliaments. "I was abandoned *by accident*. It wasn't *me*. Accidents happen. Old people drive. Daddy died. But Pierre left you *on purpose*. That's yours. Your problem. What's Ted's?"

Ally thought better than to respond. Not right away. She placed the kettle on top of the burner and turned on the gas that lit the flame. "Just because he's not married, that doesn't mean he has a problem."

Claire's eyes shifted. "Yes, it does."

Ally was choosing her arguments carefully, trying to avoid them if she could.

"Anyway, he's *courting* you."

"Maybe he is."

"He is. He asked me"—Claire turned her head toward the stove—"if I thought you would."

"What? Would what?"

"Get married."

"He did?" Ally said and opened a cabinet. She took out a tea tin. "Ted did? When?"

"Last week. While you were out getting the Popsicles. Lime. When we ran out of lime."

In Ally's bedroom, Jake's old T-shirt hung on the hamper.

Mortified, she picked it up, dashed to the closet, and threw it inside, deep in the back. She had called Anna. "Do you think it's weird that I won't sleep with Ted?"

"How was dinner?"

"Wait. First. Do you think it's weird?"

"No," Anna said in a soft voice, trying not to wake her husband.

Ally walked into the bathroom. "Because—because I had a colleague. This adjunct at Brown. She had sex with the pizza guy. Every time she called Domino's."

"And?"

"*And* she had sex with her oil-change guy. *And* her dentist. In his office. He closed the door and they did it on the chair. It reclined."

"Ally?"

"Yes?"

"It's not *weird* to want to be *in love* before you have sex. Everyone's different. You need love and intimacy. Some women don't. It's not a *crime*. Now, how was *dinner?*"

Ally started to take off her clothes. "Have you ever heard of Noah Bean?"

"You're killing me here."

"Have you?" she said and peeled off her shorts.

"The actor?" said Anna.

"You *have*?" Ally said and gazed at her legs. She looked at them in the mirror too.

"Why?"

She took off her underwear. "Well," she said. "That's him. That's the boy with the perfect penis."

Anna paused. "What are you saying? I'm confused."

"Are you awake?" She piled her clothes on top of the toilet. "Did I wake you up?"

"We went to bed early."

"Oh, I'm sorry."

"Ally? What about Noah Bean?"

"That's the guy. He changed his name."

"Wait, I don't get it," Anna whispered, sounding panicked, growing more alert by the second.

"You're asleep. I'll call you tomorrow."

"No! Stay! Are you—saying . . . Are you saying that . . . *you* slept with Noah Bean?"

"He wasn't Noah Bean back then. But yes, I did."

Anna then screamed.

Ally held the phone from her ear. Anna's husband, startled, woke up: "What! What! What the hell happened?"

"Ally had sex with Noah Bean!"

"Who?" he bellowed. "Who the hell is that?"

"Are you telling John?" Ally was mortified.

Anna returned. "How come you never *told* me this?"

"I didn't know!"

"'Hurry up, woman! There's no time to waste!'" Anna yelled in a convincing English accent. She was imitating Jake in his role as the knight.

"What are you saying? Hurry up what?"

"His famous line: 'Hurry up, woman! There's no time to waste!' He's Lancelot, Ally, and *People*'s Sexiest Man Alive, from three years ago or maybe four . . ."

Ally sighed. She looked in the mirror and studied her belly fat. "But whatever." How did it get there? She took the roll of it in her hand. "He's a person. A regular person."

"No, he's not. Google *People*."

"I will *not* . . . Google *People*."

"You're such a snob."

"I'm not a snob." Ally turned to the side and did a plié. "I'm in a—dilemma. Call me back when the shock wears off."

Anna laughed. "Did you tell Ted?"

"No. Not yet."

"Lizzie?"

"I will. What's weird, what's also weird: He quoted me."

"Huh?"

"He quoted this story I wrote for *Elle*."

"Wow."

"I think. Unless—"

"He *remembered*," Anna said coyly. "Ally?"

"Yes?"

"Get me an autograph? Please?"

Ally growled. "This is—that is—not helpful. I'm hanging up."

Anna hung up, and Ally hung up and looked in the mirror.

People's Sexiest Man Alive?

She studied the stretch marks across her hips. The pockets of bulge in her inner thighs. She'd never had a problem with her thighs before!

Until this year.

Damn, she thought. She should join a gym.

Forty-one.

Forty-one was the worst.

She turned back around and stood up straight, as straight as she could, and sucked in her belly.

She straightened her neck and lifted her head, but the slight double chin remained.

She peered in close to examine her face: the little red spots and three fine lines. It was as if they had *appeared* on her face. Across her forehead. *Overnight.*

She ran her fingers through her hair, sure it had started to thin.

Maybe it was stress, she thought, and stepped out to find a T-shirt to wear. One that did not belong to Jake.

She left the bathroom, went down the hall and into the bedroom.

All that stress. All that grief. The changes in her body. Maybe she didn't feel confident enough, and that was why she wouldn't sleep with Ted.

When had it been? When had she agreed to coffee, after he found her on Facebook?

While she'd been trolling for Jake.

Jake.

January, she'd agreed to coffee. She remembered snow on the ground. Two or three months before Claire had died?

Claire had been sick, and Teddy had been so bighearted. Called all the time. Sent food. Ran errands. Came the moment Claire died. Attended the wake. Sent a bouquet, an enormous bouquet. And he had been so very patient . . .

About the sex.

Ally had claimed to be too stressed. Then too busy. Then too sad. That's what she thought and that's what she said.

She had too much to do before and after: the hospice, the funeral, Claire's estate . . .

Teddy was cute. Teddy was bright. Teddy was happy to travel to Brooklyn to eat, to walk, to read the paper . . .

What was wrong with her?

She'd had flings. Well, one. With Jake. She wasn't in love with him back then. Was she?

In a tank and sweatpants, she climbed into bed.

Maybe Ted was right about her. Maybe she *was.* Frigid. Repressed. Maybe she needed to embrace pleasure for pleasure's sake. What was wrong with pleasure? Nothing. What was wrong with fun? Nothing. She rolled over and grabbed the phone.

"Ally?" said Ted as he picked up.

"Let's go away. Next weekend. Let's go and . . . you know. I'm ready."

"You are?" he asked, sounding surprised.

"Something is wrong with me. Let's do this."

She would have sex.

Sex with Ted.

Yes, she would. "Bring protection. I'm not on the pill."

"I didn't think so," he said with a laugh.

Ally looked at the ceiling and waited. He joked, of course, but when had it become *mandatory* for all single women to be on the pill?

"Don't worry, Al. I'm done with all the baby making."

"What?"

"Vasectomy. Four years ago. Snip, snip."

"Really?" said Ally. She was surprised.

"How about the Hamptons? Nantucket? Name it. We'll fly."

"Good," Ally said. She didn't care where. "What about diseases?"

"Yes?"

"Tests? Have you had—recent tests?" She wanted to disappear under her covers. She hated this conversation. Hated it.

"Not twenty-one, honeybun."

"What does that mean?"

"It means don't worry."

Ally paused. "Okay," she said. "Good night."

"Sleep tight. And, Ally?"

"Yes?"

"I can't wait."

Ally lay awake until two o'clock.

Then she wondered about the dishes.

Had she run them in the washer?

They'd chatted about it, she and Jake, but once he had loaded the dishwasher full, did he actually run it? Did she?

She wanted to wake up to clean dishes, dishes that meant the dinner was done, dishes she could put clean, clear away.

She got up to check.

Halfway downstairs to the first floor she paused. Something below caught her eye.

On the table by the door, a navy blue cap sat on a scarf with gold-rimmed sunglasses tucked inside.

Ally stared at it for a moment and then approached.

She recognized the hat. Through sweat and rain and drying again, the Boston Red Sox baseball cap had formed itself to Jake's head.

She took out the glasses and slipped them on.

She gazed at herself in the hall mirror and tried to look like an actor or model: at first with annoyance, a look of disgust. Then contempt. Then she tried bored. None of it worked. The glasses didn't suit her. She set them back down.

She picked up the cap and held it to her nose.

Crazy, she thought. Totally bonkers. Standing there, smelling her daughter's date's hat. That was the moment. She had crossed over from partially sane to officially nuts. The nutty professor. She inhaled as the doorbell rang.

Startled, she threw the cap as if she'd been caught. She sailed it like a Frisbee, and it bounced off the wall and landed again on top of the scarf.

Quickly, heart racing, she tucked in the Ray-Bans, turned, and steadied herself on the rail.

The bell rang once, so it wasn't Ted. Ted would ring twice, three times, four, and Lizzie had a key.

The bell rang again.

"Coming!" she called.

Two in the morning or not, she knew.

She knew who it was.

She knew it was Jake.

CHARLIE'S PENIS LOOKED LIKE celery, Ally thought, but cut in half. A thin stalk of celery. It was her first. The first real penis she'd seen up close. Really close.

She was seventeen when Charlie Bergen had begged her to give him a hand job that night. They were parked in the limo during St. Ann's prom. Somehow, somehow she talked him out of it.

Three years later, down in DC, Pierre's had curved to the left like a banana. Exactly like a banana, she thought, when she first saw it. A medium-size deli banana. The kind you can still buy in Brooklyn delis for twenty-five cents.

Six years later, when Lizzie was five, Meer insisted that Ally attend the Raunch Culture Conference in Boston for her. Since she couldn't go.

Ally forgot his first name, but he taught Gender Studies at Cambridge in England. Edwin, Edward, Edmond, Edgar. Something with an E . . .

She did remember the name of his penis.

He'd introduced it. "Allison, please meet Mr. Major Johnson. The

Slut Slayer. He's saying hello. Can you say hello?" Ally nodded. "Hello, Major Johnson. Pleased to meet you." The Englishman smiled. "Mr. Major Johnson, the Slut Slayer, please. That's his full title." Ally smiled. "Pleased to meet you, Mr. Major Johnson, the Slut Slayer." Edwin or Edmond enjoyed this. "Would you care to shake hands?"

She didn't have sex with Mr. Major, but she did make out with the man himself in his hotel room, after which he *insisted*, in a charming British accent, on taking *the slayer* to absolute climax while Ally watched.

The Major looked like a four-inch carrot, an organic carrot, a natural carrot, the kind, Ally thought, that tapers toward the tip.

Jake Bean's was number four. And what a beautiful fourth he was.

All good things to those who wait, Ally thought, staring at him in the shadows. Jake then turned her onto her belly.

She heard the rip of the condom wrapper, and when he entered her from behind, Ally came like a twelve-year-old boy. Within seconds, the pleasure intensified, exploded, and spread through her entire body, down her limbs and into her fingertips and toes. "Oh no," she whispered, after it subsided, her head bowed. "I'm so sorry. How did you do that? So, so sorry . . ." She fell to her stomach.

Jake pulled out and lay down next to her. "Why?" he said. "Why are you sorry?"

"I just went from zero to sixty in four seconds . . . like a BMW . . . I'm so . . ." Embarrassed, she hid her face in a pillow.

Jake's penis had filled Ally in a way she'd never been filled before, not by Pierre, not by food, not by any other forms of fulfillment. The utter satisfaction, the feeling of completion, was both physical and existential. She would have gladly died there with Jake deep inside her, if not for Lizzie, and some other stuff . . .

"I'm incredible," Jake joked.

"You are," she said, still hiding her face. Then she looked up. "Come back and finish. Let's let you finish." She pressed her body into his and kissed him.

"No," Jake said, kissing her back. "I don't want to."

"What? Why not?"

"I don't want to come."

"What?"

"Tonight's about you."

"Why? Please. That's not—"

"I like to wait. It's the journey that counts. The means, not the end." He smiled.

Ally studied him. "Oh, wait. You wrote about this in your paper." She lifted up onto her elbows. "Tantric sex?"

"Yes, but this is more Zen Satori."

"What?" Ally laughed and looked down. Nothing had changed. He was still at attention, full in the condom.

"I have this brother into all things Asian: beliefs, women. Moved out to Cali for 'Buddha on the beach, dude, twelve out of twelve.'"

Ally smiled. "But doesn't it hurt? Don't you get, whatever, blue balls or something?"

He shook his head. "No, because, you know . . . You don't suppress it."

"Suppress it?"

"Strain. You just—relax. You slow down your breath and relax your muscles and focus on the girl instead of yourself. Especially, like, your abs, you know? You relax your abs so nothing builds. There's no tension."

Ally studied him.

"It's hard to describe."

"But what's the point?"

"I don't know," Jake said and then thought it through. "Control, I guess . . . All these guys, spreading their seed every-which-where, with no control . . ." Ally listened. "Like we learned in your class . . . Guys who make women wear those tents, the Islam thing, and because why? They can't trust themselves—or other men—to not go nuts? Control yourself. Try."

Ally took a breath. "Are you sure?"

"Yeah. So we can go and go and go, and then, if I want to come, I do. But I'm not a slave to it. And—and—it's better if I wait."

"It's better when you wait?"

"Everything's better . . . when you wait."

Ally smiled.

So Jake, the student, made his professor come that night: Once on the bed and then on its edge. A third time against the bathroom sink. Then a fourth and a fifth in the kitchen, up against the fridge and across the floor. And lastly, a sixth time, up against the tile in Ally's bathroom, with a toothbrush in her mouth.

At four they finally fell asleep, tangled in each other's limbs.

TEDDY WAS SURPRISED WHEN Lizzie buzzed up that night after dinner at one o'clock. One in the morning. He couldn't say no. It was pouring outside. He buzzed her in, looked around the loft, and scrambled to pick up the fast-food wrappers, change, receipts, printed research, socks, and clothes.

He was too busy to actually shop for something to sit in, a bed to sleep on, a desk to work from . . . and so before he moved into SoHo, into his loft, he hired the beautiful Bunny Dunn.

Bunny decided to warm up the space, the poured-concrete floor, ductwork, beams, with a deluge of clubby, costly antiques.

But for all its design and all its worth, Teddy neglected his home. The floors were covered with a thin film of grit, the windows with soot, and the furniture with a layer of dust.

Lizzie thought this was fascinating. Telling of something. She didn't know what.

His closets and cabinets lay oddly empty, his stuff, instead, he had piled in corners, scattered on surfaces, underfoot. All the low- and high-tech toys of the moneyed American boy, Lizzie thought.

She gazed around, taking account of all the items: Four World Cup Brazuca balls. Five MacBook Pros. Two iPads. Three iPods. Two iPhones. A Xerox WorkCentre copy machine. *Esquire, Maxim, Men's Health,* in six-foot stacks. *The Wall Street Journal, Financial Times,* and *The Economist* in four-foot stacks. Two sets of golf clubs. A grand Bose home audio system and seventy-inch 3-D HDTV . . . She counted by threes, by fives, by fours: Thirty-one baseball caps. Thirty-two pairs of Vineyard Vines shorts. Thirteen Patagonia vests . . .

He did not own a mop or a broom, a spatula or a box of salt.

Ally had ventured to visit him *once.*

"You can't tell your mom." Teddy swept coins off the coffee table.

"You're right," Lizzie said, sitting at one of his many desks. "She would freak. She hates porn."

"But if you want your nose, these models, these girls, are making a fortune." He stuffed the change into his pocket. "But think it through."

"A fortune?" she asked, intrigued. "How much?"

"A grand a day from what Fishman says." He knelt on the floor, reaching under the table.

"A thousand a day? Wow," she said, studying his workspace. "Or *you* could give me the money."

"No," he said. "I've earned what I have, and you should too."

On the surface of his desks sat keyboard after keyboard and more hard drives than she cared to count. Above the desks, along a shelf, five monitors ran together, daisy-chained with FireWire cables.

"How does it work?"

"He has a studio. They set you up in a private room. You strip.

Play around. There's a computer—with a camera. I guess. I haven't been there myself."

"I'm alone? In the room?"

"Of course. It's safe. The guys are online. They sign in and out." Ted got up and walked to the trash can next to his desk. He threw all the coins from his hands inside. "The golf clubs *failed*, by the way."

"Can I wear a disguise?"

"Like what?"

"A wig? Glasses?"

"Yeah, you should. And use a fake name."

Lizzie thought maybe if she wore a wig, covered her freckles and her birthmarks, maybe no one would recognize her. "Who's this guy? Who is Fishman?"

Teddy explained.

He and Fishman had met at Wharton in '98. Fishman was thin, with an oversize head, and fancied himself a movie producer. When his comedies failed, he decided to produce porn with story. "Narrative porn for the thinking man," Teddy said. He set up a studio out near LA but failed there too. The thinking man, as it turned out, tuned in to porn to stop thinking.

Back east again, he partnered with investors and managed to build a sex-cam network, twenty-nine sites, that catered to the US and Western Europe.

"What about— How do you come in?" Lizzie asked.

"I don't come in." Teddy was back down on his knees, fishing under the couch. "He's my buddy."

"Oh," Lizzie said, turning back to the desk. "So if I'm a cam girl for, what, a month? You think I could walk with twenty grand?"

He rose on his knees and stretched his back. "Your grandmother's money was meant for grad school. Don't bug your mom. She's still in mourning."

Lizzie nodded. "I'm still in mourning. We're all still in mourning."

Teddy turned and studied Lizzie as she rose and walked to the window. "Actually," he said, watching her as she lifted the blinds and stared out into the pouring rain, "maybe not. It's a bad idea."

"Why?" she said.

"Forget I even— If your mom found out . . . That would be the end."

"I won't forget it," Lizzie said, looking out onto Canal Street: the wet puddles, dilapidated buildings, red blinking lights. "Give me the number." She looked at her fingertips, covered in soot. "Do you ever clean? This place is a sty."

"That's nice. Polite. You ring me up in the middle of the night— What are you even doing down here?"

"I met Weather. The club was lame . . ." Lizzie smiled, crossed the room, and sat, again, at Ted's desk. "Give me his number. Seriously. I'll check it out."

Under the sofa, Teddy found a pudding cup, a chocolate-covered spoon, and french-fry envelopes filled with salt. "Only—if you tell me—if you help me. How the heck do I get your mom? To go on a little vacation with me? What do I do?"

"Well, first, you hire a maid."

"Fuck you, Lizzie."

Lizzie smiled and rested her elbow on a keyboard. A monitor sprang to life. She spun in the chair, surprised and excited. "Oh, look at this . . ." She slipped a pair of headphones on.

On the monitor, a woman in pigtails sat on a desk, sipping a Jamba Juice, talking on her iPhone. Her panties read, "The Party Starts Here." Other than that, she was totally naked, and her tiny pert breasts stood at attention as if she was cold. Lizzie listened. "She's talking about her PSATs."

"That's—the site. One of the sites." Teddy had grabbed a paper and pen.

"Teddy?"

"What?"

"Why are you watching this?"

"I might invest." He drew near and handed her Fishman's number. "This is his cell."

"My mom would *kill* you," Lizzie said, smiling. She took the number and slipped off the headphones.

"No kidding."

"I won't tell."

"Look, Ally wants Juilliard. Now you can go and get your nose, too."

"I'll never get in," Lizzie said. "And she won't even notice, by the way. They shave the sides by a *millimeter*." She tucked the number into her jeans, rose, and meandered toward Teddy's front hall. "This is nice of you. Really. To help me. That's what my mother loves about you. You're so kind. So *generous*."

Teddy looked up. "I'm happy to help. Now help me."

"Sure. How?"

"Get her to— How do I get her away? Out of that house, out of town?"

"Why? What are your intentions?"

He paused. "To continue to—get to know your mother."

"Why don't you marry her first?"

He perked up. "You think she'd marry me? If I asked?"

Lizzie smiled and slipped back into her sodden ballet flats. "May I please pee?"

"Sure," he said and pointed toward a hall around a corner. "You didn't answer me."

In the bathroom, she opened the cabinets looking for condoms, lube, toys. Something. Anything. But she found nothing but Kiehl's, Kiehl's, Kiehl's, and more Kiehl's.

She peeked behind the curtain: nothing there either, but Kiehl's shampoo, Irish Spring soap, and Kiehl's conditioner.

Then she peed, and as she did, she borrowed Ted's toothbrush. She used it to poke through his overflowing trash. She needed to think, to see, to dig . . . through all the Kleenex, the cough-drop wrappers . . .

Then, at the bottom of the pail, she saw it: a tube of lipstick.

With the toothbrush, she flipped it upright and lifted it out between her fingers. She split it apart to see the color: a deep purple-pink. She read the label on the bottom: *Fuchsia*.

Fuchsia Flash.

Not a lipstick Ally would buy. If she wore lipstick. Which she didn't.

So maybe Ted had a sister, thought Lizzie. Maybe an assistant.

Maybe a friend. Ally thought he was dating around. Now they knew. One thing for sure: It wasn't the maid's.

She stood and flushed and wrapped the lipstick in toilet paper. She tucked it into her back jeans pocket next to the paper with Fishman's number.

"Hopping a train?" Teddy asked, holding the front door open for her. He was glad to see her go.

"Maybe," said Lizzie.

"You need money? You want a car? I'll call you a—"

"No, thanks. I'll walk." She slipped out past him into the hall. "You won't tell her? Right? Ever?"

"*Never*," he said. "She'd murder us both."

"She would."

"All right. We agree. Get home safe."

"Oh, I will."

His cell phone rang. He slipped it from his pocket, glanced at the number. "Look. It's your mom."

"Say hi for me," Lizzie called over her shoulder.

"I don't think so."

MAYBE HE WAS DREAMING, Ally thought. Maybe all men woke like this. She didn't know. But the smell of him, his sweat and some kind of musky scent, aroused her so much that she reached down and drew him softly between her legs.

Jake's eyelids fluttered open. "Morning," he whispered and smiled at her.

She gently rolled to straddle him, but Jake stopped her and laid her back down. Pinning her, he moved on top, pressing with his hips. He rose to his elbows and buried his head in Ally's neck. His right hand raised her breast to meet his mouth. His left hand slipped down the side of her body and behind to her buttock, gripping it for ballast.

Ally met him by raising her knees and bit into his shoulder. She ran her fingers through his hair and pulled it taut. This slight infliction drove him wild.

Then she pulled back and studied his jaw, the stubble that matured overnight as they slept, the lines of his waist, cut and drawn, as if he'd been carved.

Morning sex with a beautiful guy, is what she decided, looking at him. A guy. Not a boy, but not quite a man.

A map of Europe hung over her bed. Pearl pushpins marked the cities she wanted to visit: London, Rome, Barcelona, Paris, Vienna, Budapest, Berlin, Florence . . .

Jake stood naked at the head of the bed, standing on the pillows. He studied her route. "What's all this?" he asked, intrigued.

Ally entered from the bathroom. "I'm saving for a trip. It's only gonna take about forty years."

"Take me on it."

She clambered up next to him and pointed to the pin with the number one on it. "First Barcelona. That's first. For the Majestic."

"What's that?"

"It's a hotel. A five-star hotel." She moved her finger north to France. "Next, Paris, for the Hôtel Ritz."

"No hostels?" Jake said, smiling.

"No backpacks. No hostels. Five-star hotels all the way."

"Why?"

Ally explained:

She was six when she and her mother stayed for two nights at the five-star Fairmont in Nob Hill. Claire had buried Ally's dad in Colma, California, near San Francisco. His childhood home.

At midnight, the second night of their stay, Ally awoke in the king bed alone, alone in the room. She had climbed from the sheets, checked the bathroom for Claire, all the while calling, "Mommy? Mommy?"

Claire was missing.

Tiny Ally, forty-six pounds, in a white nightgown with puffed sleeves, arrived at the lobby but stayed put and stepped back as the elevator doors opened and a horde of hotel guests piled in, careening.

By accident, she couldn't get out. She rode back up in a cloud of perfume and cologne and sweat, staring at ankles and hems and shoes, black men's and shiny high heels with bare ankles.

By the third floor, the crowd dispersed, calling back, "Night!" and "See you at brunch!" and "Be good!" Except for the couple pressed in the corner.

They hadn't seen her, nor she them, until the mob cleared. And as they ascended, Ally watched, for the first time, a man and a woman in the throes of passion: grabbing, groaning, mouthing each other. As if they were racing, Ally thought, to see who could eat up the other one first, like hungry, writhing, zombie monsters.

When the elevator paused and the doors opened on the sixth floor, the couple broke apart and staggered out. "Oh," said the girl, when she saw Ally over her shoulder. "Oh," said the man as the doors closed. "Wait!" called the woman as she tried to keep them open while Ally pushed the lobby button down, over and over, for the second time that night.

"They found me," said Ally, "after midnight. Wandering the lobby, looking for her."

Jake was still. "Where did she go?"

"No one knew," Ally said, shrugging.

The man in charge, in a black tux that night, took her on a tour of the palace. A search.

They checked the library. Checked the dining rooms. He took her to the kitchen, where the chef made her toast and chocolate chip cookies, hot from the oven, with glasses of milk. They walked, hand in hand, through the ballrooms.

"There must have been a wedding."

But at six, she thought they'd entered a ball. An orchestra played. She and the man, whoever he was, danced a few songs out on the floor amid the guests. Ally looked dazed, eyes wide, spotting the bride in a full-skirted white satin dress with semi-cathedral train and tiara. The groom, in his black tux with tails, held her close.

They found Claire at quarter to four, slumped in a chair in the Tonga Room. In her grief, she had drank and drank and drank, and fallen asleep.

"He might have been the manager," Ally mused. "The concierge, maybe. I wasn't scared."

Everyone there took care of her. At the hotel. She felt like a princess.

Except for the fact that they'd buried her dad that afternoon, it was a fairy tale come true. She turned to Jake. "Have you ever stayed at a fancy hotel?"

Jake shook his head.

"I knew it wasn't real. But after that week, and such a sad day— it felt like a dream."

Later, in the kitchen, Ally placed poached eggs on toasted English muffins and slathered them with hollandaise sauce. "I've been twenty-one and broke," she said, concerned about Jake. "I had a baby. I know how it feels." She set the eggs in front of him.

He dug in with a knife and fork. "No cash from you. Sorry, lady."

Ally gave him a mug filled with coffee. "You did the work."

"Professor Hughes, let's be clear—"

"Don't call me that."

"I don't want a dime." He picked up her check and tore it in half, then placed it back down.

"We agreed to eight bucks an hour."

"Seven."

"Seven."

"Which would be what? Forty-two bucks? This check says five hundred."

"But—you might need a bed or a bike. Or *food*."

"I didn't come here to work yesterday."

"No, but then, Jake. This makes me feel like I paid you with sex. Let's keep it separate."

"I wanted to *do* something for you. I wanted to be near you. The dead bolt, the bed—was all an excuse." Jake swallowed and leaned forward over his plate. "Damn, these eggs!" He looked at Ally. "What about you is *not* amazing?"

"Everything." She leaned against the counter, watching him eat. "What about quitting? What's the deal?"

Jake kept eating. "I don't like the people."

"Friends?"

"Not really."

"Girlfriend?"

"No. Would I be sitting here? No college girls."

"What's wrong with college girls?"

He looked up from his plate and swallowed, a bite of egg on the end of his fork. "The best thing about college girls: In ten years they won't be in college anymore, and maybe they'll have something interesting to say." A bit of yolk dripped down his chin. He grabbed a napkin and wiped it off.

"That's not fair," Ally argued. "The women in my class have plenty to say."

"About their *bangs*, and if I refuse to watch *Party of Five*."

Ally smiled.

"If I want to watch a baseball game, I doubt you'll take that personally. And sex is better with older women."

"Is that right?"

"Beyond superior," Jake said. "Older women are better mannered. They're not all princess. They don't perform. As my brother always says, the Zen one, 'Older women are wiser women, and wisdom makes a better man. A better man makes a happy woman. Happy woman, better man.'"

"That's a theory."

"That's win-win." Jake smiled.

"I don't believe that. I don't think age brings intelligence with it."

"Okay, Ally, you're the doctor. You're the genius," Jake said dryly.

Ally ignored this. "Anyway, if you did stay, if it is about the money, I'm sure Brown has some kind of fund."

"I don't want to stay and I don't want your check." He swallowed the last of his eggs, rose, and cleared his plate. "Where's the trash?"

"I'll do it." She reached for the plate. "We have a disposal."

"I'll do it," Jake said, nudging her aside. He went to the sink, grabbed a sponge, and wiped his crumbs into the drain. He rinsed his plate and dried it, too. "You're not my mother. Hand me the pan."

Ally turned and grabbed the egg pan from the stove.

"Do *not* clean up after me. Ever. Please."

"Oh?" she replied and dumped the water from the pan. "I thought after sex, I had to do your dishes and pick up your socks . . ." She swept the orange rinds from the counter and into the sink, and sailed to the fridge.

Jake stopped drying. "That wasn't sex. That was—I was making love."

She opened the fridge, then closed it again, forgetting what she had wanted to get.

"Couldn't you feel it?"

She turned, stood still, and didn't respond. Jake grabbed the pan and rinsed it clean. She looked at him. "I wanted to give some-thing to you. A little good-bye-and-good-luck thing. That's all."

"I don't want your cash. And I'm not leaving yet."

Ally leaned against the counter and ran her fingers through her hair. She was tired. They'd slept for only a couple of hours.

Jake turned the water off, put down the pan, and crossed to her. He placed his hands around her waist, dug his fingertips into her skin, and held her there. Then he kissed her once on each cheek and once in the center of her forehead, politely, as if she was a girl.

"Please," she said, rolling her eyes.

Then he cocked his head to the right, leaned in, and kissed her square on the mouth. His right hand found the back of her head, his left, her ass, and he pressed her into a deep, wet kiss that tasted like toast and coffee. Delicious.

Ally opened her eyes. "Oh no. What am I going to do with you?"

"Whatever you want."

"I have *nine* papers to read. By Monday at ten."

"Go," Jake said, stepping back toward the sink. He grabbed the sponge. "I'll finish up. Strip down the bed. Get out of your hair."

"Don't strip the bed."

"You go to work. I'll come find you before I leave."

Ally studied him but didn't move.

She wanted him to stay. She loved that he felt so comfortable there, in her house. She didn't have to host him. He fit right in, without her direction, without her permission. It was as if he'd lived there for years. "I'll be in that—third bedroom. The one with the boxes. That's where I work."

Jake nodded.

"DID I WAKE YOU?" He was soaked through, reeking of whiskey and warm, wet clothes. He stood in the doorway.

"Jake, it's two in the—"

"I know. I'm sorry." He had stopped at the Henry Street Ale House and laid back shots of Johnnie Walker Gold, shot after shot, after shot after shot.

By the time he paid and found his way back to Cranberry Street, the August sky had split open wide. It was pouring rain. "I'm sorry. I saw the lights on. I . . . left—I'm sorry—I left something here."

"You did," Ally said, turning. She scooped up the scarf, hat, and glasses and handed him the bundle. "Where's Lizzie?"

"Clubbing. With Weather."

She regarded him a moment. "Okay, does she *know*? Does she know about us?"

"No. No, I swear."

"Let's get you a towel. Come in, come in." She stepped back and opened the closet. "I have to tell her. You know that, right?" She pulled a beach towel down from a shelf.

Jake stared at his glasses and cap. "Yeah, I know. I know you do."

"Did you know before? That it would be me?" She gave him the towel.

"Yes," he admitted, taking the towel. He threw it over his shoulder.

"But she'll *think* we were both surprised. It's not as if we could tell her right then. At dinner? With Ted?"

"Right," he said and punched his cap. He slid it on from back to front and then closed his eyes for a long moment.

"Have you been drinking?"

"I have this thing and I need your help." He leaned to the other side of the doorway.

"Could you dry off? You're getting my entire—"

"Sorry," he said, staring at his feet. He didn't touch the towel. He didn't dry off. He glanced upstairs. They had been here before, at the bottom of a staircase. "So we're clear? I—left these—and stayed in Brooklyn—so I could come see you about my thing." His knees buckled, but he caught himself and straightened. "I—you see—I wrote a script. Actors do that. Sometimes."

"A script?"

"A screenplay. I'm trying to get this director to do it—this Marty—and I need your help."

Ally paused. "How much did you drink?"

Jake shook his head. "We stopped by—I don't know, somewhere— and talked, and then she left, and anyway, I'm back, and I hope you can help. That's why I'm back."

"Because of your *script*?"

"That's why I'm back." He looked at his Ray-Bans. He looked at his scarf. "I wear scarves in summer." He contemplated this. "That's who I am, Ally, now. It's who I've *become*."

"Jake."

"I taught myself to write," he said. "You remember this?" He reached into his pocket and pulled out the book, the paperback book, that Ally had given him ten years ago. *The Elements of Style.*

"Oh," she said as he handed it to her. The spine was splintered, the cover torn, pages battered, folded. She flipped the cover. Her name was scribbled across the page. She couldn't believe it.

"My script is about—the fire you taught us, in Women and Work. The Triangle fire."

Ally nodded and gave him the book. Yes, she remembered the Triangle fire. She'd taught it.

In 1911, in New York City, teenage girls had asphyxiated, burned, or jumped to their deaths in a factory fire. The ones who survived changed the course of labor rights.

"No one will buy it. You know why?"

"Why?" Ally asked. The writing, perhaps? "Is it too long?"

"Well, it is supposed to be ninety-eight pages."

"And?"

"It's three hundred. But that's not why. It's because it stars girls—not bending over. No bare butts. No tits or tongues— hanging out. And no one in Hollywood gives a shit. Because the girls wear *clothes.* Long skirts. High necks."

"That's too bad."

"I didn't get it in class back then. But now I'm in SAG, this union, you know, and these girls—Ally, they started it all—workers' rights, so I thought maybe if you talked to Marty—"

"Me?"

"He'll be at a party on Wednesday night. I have to go. They

make you go. My PR people. I get money from the booze guys, but—Marty will be there. And who knows more about women than you? Convince him to make it, Ally, please? For us?"

She studied him. "Me?" she said. What was he saying? "You want me to convince some guy to make . . ." He looked so intense, so heartfelt, so drunk.

"Shit," he said then. He bowed his head and drew still. "Oh, man." He looked left and right.

"What's wrong? What is it?"

He turned around and opened the door. He flew out into the pouring rain, down the stoop, and vomited on the sidewalk below.

Stepping out behind him, Ally cringed.

Down on the sidewalk, he vomited again. "Shit," he cried softly, then vomited again for a third time.

Ally went down the stoop to help. She stood for some seconds in the pouring rain and placed her fingertips on his back. Jake crouched over, waiting, waiting.

"What did you drink?"

He didn't answer. "That's it. I'm done," he finally said. "There's nothing left." He spit and straightened up. "That was your awesome chocolate cake. Chicken, pasta. Sorry."

She tried not to smile. He was even charming when he threw up. "You want some water?"

Jake nodded and gazed at her breasts. He could see them in the streetlight. He lifted his head and smiled. "Good to see you."

Ally looked down and realized her tank top was rain soaked and see-through. She covered her chest. "Come back inside."

They walked up the stoop and into the house.

———

After he had rinsed and spit, after Ally pulled a sweatshirt on, he followed her up to the second-floor bedroom they used as a den.

"I'm sorry," he said. "I feel like . . . I might . . . pass out."

"It's fine. Sleep it off."

"Ally?"

"What?"

"I'm sorry I let you make me go. I was, I was . . . weaker then."

Ally said nothing. She wasn't sure she heard him correctly. She pointed to the couch. "Sleep there," she said.

Jake said nothing and sat on the couch, his head bowed low.

"Not in wet clothes. You're getting the—"

"Sorry," he said and straightened up, his head still bowed. He peeled off his T-shirt and dropped it to the floor. He stood up and pulled his jeans zipper down.

"I'll dry your stuff." She picked up his shirt and tried, tried, her best to focus on his clothes, on the floor, on anything but his bare wet skin.

He pulled down his jeans and took his briefs with them. "Oops, sorry."

Ally turned and tried not to laugh. There was that penis! "Stay in your underwear. Dry. It's dry."

He pulled up his briefs, collapsed on the couch, and closed his eyes. She turned and picked up his jeans from the floor.

"They all want Noah . . . and no one wants Jake . . . ," Jake murmured, closing his eyes.

Ally grabbed a blanket from the back of the couch and gently placed it over his body. Jake drew still and passed out, asleep.

She stood there and studied him for a moment: The cut of his cheeks. The curve of his lips. The line of his jaw. His thick lashes.

He still made her breathless. She could stare at that face forever, she thought.

Mrs. Robinson. That's who she was. What a drag.

She sighed like a schoolgirl, left to make coffee, and stayed awake for the rest of the night.

Down in the kitchen, she opened her laptop and Googled Jake as Noah Bean.

There he was. Everywhere. As Lizzie said. Hundreds of articles, hundreds of photos: On the red carpet. Walking down the street. In three-piece suits, boxers, tuxedos, T-shirts. *Details, GQ,* movie posters. Smiling, smirking, laughing, posing.

How had she missed him? Lizzie was right. She was a Luddite.

Ten minutes later, feeling naughty, a little bit shady, she stopped her search. What if he woke up and walked in on her? This type of thing was Lizzie's realm.

Or it had been. It was Lizzie who, by sixth grade, had traded in her Nancy Drew for Lee Child and Vince Flynn and spent her evenings somewhere on the web, chatting in a language unknown to Ally: arguing over the ethics of spam blocks, certain black hats, trolls, doxing, heisenbugs . . .

Ally had discovered an odd-looking mask, a Guy Fawkes mask,

hanging in Lizzie's room, on her bedpost. In lipstick on the mirror, she'd scrawled the words "ANONS RULE."

"What's an anon?" Ally asked at dinner one night.

Lizzie looked up from her salad and beans. "An anon," she said, "is a member of an anarchist group. A part of a global activist brain."

Ally paused. "I don't—know what that means. Is it a club? An online club?"

"Think of it that way, sure," Lizzie said, forking her lettuce leaves one by one.

"How else *should* I think of it?" Ally squinted the way she did when she knew that Lizzie was lying by omission.

"It's nerdy kids who play pranks. But only on people who deserve it, okay?"

Ally studied her thirteen-year-old and her zit-dappled chin. She didn't like pranks.

In January, five years later, Lizzie had called her mother in tears. She needed to get out of Durham for a spell. She needed to be home. A friend of hers had hung himself . . . there in Brooklyn, and Lizzie was crushed.

Ally discovered the brilliant young man was a hacker, too. He had accessed some online files from MIT and faced time in jail, thirty-five years, and a million-dollar fine . . .

Lizzie had loved him. He was her hero.

She then abandoned her online life and turned her attention to drama instead, auditioning for plays at Duke that spring.

She didn't get parts in *Bat Boy: The Musical* or *Othello*, but she sewed costumes and painted sets, and that summer, she came home transformed: no more nights staying up late, staring into the glow of the Dell. Instead, she went to bed by eleven and woke up at six to run ten miles. She put the Guy Fawkes mask away.

Ally didn't know how to feel. About the change. If she was truly relieved or not.

Hollywood? Acting? After she'd majored in foreign relations? After she'd wanted to secure the free world?

When Jake awoke, he found his T-shirt and jeans dry and warm, folded on the table next to the couch. He found Ally down in the kitchen, apologized, and thanked her. They strolled from the kitchen toward the front door.

"No nose job," Ally said. "She cannot get this nose job." Now that she had him alone and sober. "She needs a man—an older man—not you—and not Ted—to tell her she's beautiful as she is. This—Marty—you want me to meet. He could do it. She talks about him. Is he a big deal? Could he influence her?"

"Yeah, he could," Jake said, nodding.

"It's the dad thing. She's insecure. On some level."

"So come to the party and I'll get Marty to talk to Lizzie. About her nose. Deal?"

"Deal." She unlocked the door. "Can I bring Ted?"

"No."

"Why not?"

"Because."

"Wait," Ally complained. "He's an investor. Maybe—"

"No Ted."

"Why not?"

"Because. I'm taking you out."

Ally took a breath and lifted her head around in a circle. "Jake! You're dating my daughter!"

"What? I am not!"

"She thinks you are!"

"She doesn't even like me!"

"Yes! She does!"

"She thinks I'm a bore. Lizzie is *funny*. She needs someone funny, someone like, I don't know, James Franco."

"Who?"

"No one. Never mind. Look. When I figured out who she was, that was it. I set up this dinner. I never touched her. She thinks I'm gay. She asked me yesterday if I'm gay. We are *not* dating."

"Either way, I have to tell her."

"I don't care! Tell her! I'll tell her! You know what she'll do? She'll laugh. She's an amazing—amazing—girl. I don't date girls."

Ally considered this. "I don't know."

"Let's make a bet. If she thinks it's funny—which she will—you come to the party. I leave New York on Friday night."

"Fine," Ally said. "We both tell her, and if she's okay, if she's not crushed, I'll come."

"Good. And Marty will say he loves her nose. Marty loves it. I love it. We all love her nose."

"But you can't take me out. I'm—involved."

"Where's your ring?"

Her ring? "Ted comes."

"Ted stays home. This time we're doing things *my* way."

Ally grimaced. "You know I'm forty now, Jake? Forty-one?"

"Thanks for the sleep, the coffee, dinner. You ready?"

"For what?" Ally said begrudgingly. Jake slid on his cap, pulled the rim low, and slipped on his shades. He swung the door open. Ally gasped.

Out on the sidewalk, a crowd of paparazzi erupted. Flashes flashed. They all yelled at once. "Noah! Noah! Noah, over here!"

Ally stepped back and Jake closed the door. "I'll send a car Wednesday. Eleven o'clock."

She was confused. "Eleven in the morning?"

He smiled. "No. Eleven at night. That's when the party starts, *Professor.*"

NINE FINAL PAPERS SAT on the ottoman. Tucked in a chair, red pen in hand, Ally started to try to read them. Which one first? She wasn't sure: "Nin, the Major Minor Writer?" "Anaïs and the Younger Man?" "Nin and the Narcissist?" "Lies and Liasions?"

She couldn't decide. Boxes surrounded her. She worked in the room and used it for storage. She'd discovered some childhood clothes recently, Christmas dresses and patent leather shoes. A red velvet coat lay across a box, waiting for Lizzie to try it on. It might fit, Ally thought, staring at the coat. Lizzie, at ten, was taller than Ally had been at twelve.

She should have been reading.

Why wasn't she reading? That coat reminded Ally of her first kiss. Her first *real* kiss.

Chase Fenton had left the foyer to help his mother with something upstairs. Ally was standing in first position, practicing pliés, waiting for Claire.

Gazing down at her patent leather shoes, she decided she was too old for Mary Janes. Thirteen! she scoffed, and still in buckles? Claire *had* to buy her a new pair soon. Without straps. She had to.

Chase's father, Mr. Fenton, stumbled from the powder room singing and happy. Some carol. He saw Ally, straightened his tie, tucked in his shirttails, and teetered to her. He looked dazed. "Leaving, Ally?"

"Yes, Mr. Fenton." The red velvet coat hung over her arm.

"Where's your mother?"

"I don't know." She looked toward the kitchen. "Saying good night?"

"Well," he said and staggered close. "It's nice to see you. Honey. It is. We should see—more of you." He reached his arms wide, threw them around her, and pulled her in close. Then he pulled back and kissed her, parting her lips with his tongue.

Ally was stunned.

She'd been waiting for a kiss. She had been sure Chase would kiss her that night, if they could steal a moment alone. They'd talked about it in math class. He'd sent her a note: "We're kissing. Tonight."

But *Mr. Fenton* kissed Ally at the Christmas party. Not Chase. He kissed her, stumbled off, and forgot a minute later.

Ally remembered. Her first kiss. Her first French kiss. Her first French kiss with a senior partner at Goldman Sachs.

When she got home, she took off her shoes and handed them to Claire. "Goodwill," she said. "I'm too old for these." She ran upstairs and called Anna. "Yuck!" she said, laughing. "His actual tongue!" She could still taste the gin.

Ally looked up from the red velvet coat. She heard the sound of a lawn mower. Or she thought she did. The smell of freshly cut grass wafted in. Someone—someone was mowing her lawn. Jake? She got up to check.

In the backyard, Jake slowed down and cut the engine as Ally walked up through the soft green grass. "What are you doing?" she asked, laughing.

"What does it look like?"

"Jake!"

"What?" He wiped his brow, covered with sweat. The day was unusually hot for late May, already in the seventies. Jake was barefoot, in jeans, and bare chested. He'd taken off his shirt. "I want to do this."

"But why?"

"You need it. This house, this yard . . . needs help. I want to cut back that stuff near the door. It's safer that way. And maybe some sensor lights? Ever thought of that?" He looked unhappy with the state of the yard.

"Thank you," said Ally. "Really?"

"Why not? This is how the Bean boys roll."

She could only smile. How could she fight him?

"Foreplay begins by mowing the lawn."

"Foreplay?" she said. "I thought you were leaving!"

"Taking out the garbage. Opening the door. Putting down the lid without being asked. Treat your lady like the queen she is."

"*Your* lady? I'm your lady?"

"Mine for the moment. Total ownership. All my brothers are happily married. Works for them. You don't agree?"

Ally shrugged. "I don't know, Jake. What do I know? Look at my life."

Jake smiled. "Listen, you fold your towels in thirds. That's class. We fold our towels in half at our house. You're doing great."

Ally laughed and studied him.

Why did she feel as if she'd known him for years?

"That fence, the links, sticking out there?" Jake pointed to the chain-link fence that bordered the yard. "I want to fix it. I'll do my work. You do yours. I'll meet you in the shower in ninety minutes."

Ally stood there, hands on her hips. "So I'm supposed to—go back upstairs—read all about Gore Vidal and Henry Miller—while you're here naked and sweating? Please!"

"You can do it," Jake said facetiously. "I believe in you. Go."

She looked at the mower. "You shouldn't push that around in bare feet. You could lose a toe."

"*You* could," Jake said. Yanking the pull cord, he fired up the blades.

"YOU *SLEPT* WITH MY mother?" Lizzie asked, shocked. She stared into space, eyes wide, trying to parse and file this confession. "You and my mother had actual *sex*?"

It was Tuesday morning. They sat at the bar at Bubby's in TriBeCa.

Jake was nursing a mug of coffee and eating his way through a basket of biscuits. Deeply hungover, he nodded at Lizzie. The Grey Goose people had paid him to attend a party that morning, starting at midnight, ending at five. Now it was ten and he cupped his hands around his coffee as if it might keep him from floating away.

"That's why she called!" Lizzie said. "She called me a hundred times yesterday!"

"Could you keep it down?" Jake asked kindly. His head was pounding.

"I'm sorry, but this is too incredible." Lizzie was delighted.

"Call her back. She wants to talk."

"I cannot believe I *missed* this."

"What?"

"There had to be clues . . ." Her thoughts raced back over Saturday night: Jake's arrival, Ally's reaction. Then she remembered. "She ran! When you met! When you shook hands!"

"What?" Jake bit into a greasy biscuit.

"She bolted upstairs! She totally freaked! I cannot believe— How stupid am I?"

"That's your—that's your *takeaway*?" he asked as he chewed a buttery bite. He put down the biscuit and picked up his mug. "That's your concern? That you didn't somehow . . ."

Lizzie only half listened. Excited, she pulled her purse from the bar and took out her phone. "Wait, so she knows?" she asked, distracted.

"She knows what?"

"That you're telling me now?"

"Yes."

"You talked?"

"We did."

She shook her head. It was all too great. She texted Weather, fingertips flying over the touch pad. "Weather is going to love this . . ." She put the phone down on the copper-topped bar and turned her attention back to Jake. "I cannot believe she *screwed* a student."

"Screwed?" Jake cringed and placed his mug back down on the bar. "It wasn't *screwing*."

"But you were her student! She's so naughty!"

"No, she's not." He looked away and motioned to the barkeep to refill his coffee. "But you're okay? You're not upset?"

Lizzie checked her phone. She couldn't stop smiling. "Upset? No. I mean, it's vile."

"Why is it *vile?*"

"Because she's my *mom.* Do I have to explain?" She slid off the barstool.

"She is your mom, but she is a woman."

"No kidding. Can you buy my juice? I have a thing. I have to bounce."

"Sure, but . . . there's a part two."

"Oh, Weather!" Lizzie cried and picked up her phone to show him the text. "Weather wrote back: 'Badass Mom!'" Lizzie's fingertips flew in response. "Weather worships my mom so much . . . She is so in love with my mom . . ."

Jake took his chance. "Me too," he said.

Lizzie glanced up and smiled but kept texting. She didn't hear him.

Jake said it louder. "I am in love with your mother too."

She heard him that time and looked up to see him, sheepish and blushing. All the laughter left her eyes.

Jake, again, cupped his mug in prayer.

Lizzie stopped texting and put the phone down, back on the bar. Then she thought better, picked it up again, and put it away, back into her bag. She slipped back onto the barstool and sat there, eyebrows furrowed. She moved a bracelet up and down her wrist. Finally she turned and said, "You didn't know? That we were related? Until you saw her?" She sounded hurt.

"Yeah," said Jake. "We were both surprised."

Lizzie nodded. "That's your story?"

"My story?" Raising his eyebrows, he shook his head. "I didn't . . . put it together."

Lizzie squinted. She didn't believe him. "But you knew Hughes. You knew Providence."

"It was *ten* years . . . ago." Jake shrugged and looked at her, eyes wide, over his mug. "You called her *Mom*."

Lizzie studied him. "You know," she started, "just because you act—*sort of* well—in front of a camera—doesn't mean—"

"What? What? What do I have to—have to—*say*—to make you believe me?"

"First, stop *stammering*," Lizzie snapped with condescension. "And second, there's nothing you *can* say. I know you're lying. You weren't *surprised* when you shook her hand."

"Come on. I was—"

"Stop," she said forcibly, cutting him off. "Stop. It's insulting. Do you think I'm dumb? I skipped grades twice and finished school at *sixteen.* I did Duke in *three* years. My IQ is higher than ninety-nine percent of the population's. Point six."

Jake said nothing.

Lizzie continued. "I threw myself at you—for a month. I offered to spend the night with you—at your hotel—for three weeks. Please. You *used* me to get to my mom. Admit it, *Jake.* Stop lying and act like a man. Just admit it. I know the truth. There's no need to—"

"Fine!" he blurted out. "I was in love with her ten years ago! I thought I still was, but I wasn't sure, and I am! You're right! I did it! I lied! I'm sorry!" he said.

Lizzie leaned on the bar and smiled. That was all. She wanted to break him. She wanted to win and she did. That was it. "*Good,*" she said, forgiving him instantly. "Actually, it all makes sense."

"What makes sense?" Jake said bitterly.

"You and my mom. You're both good-looking. You're both criers."

"What? I'm not a—"

"You both have that sincerity thing, which is so Nick Drake and annoying. You're sweet. You're both shitty liars."

"That's true," Jake agreed.

"In fact, you may be perfect for each other!" Lizzie laughed. "How weird is that?"

Jake studied her for a moment, remembering the weekend in Providence. "You know, we *met* when you were ten."

"*We* did?" she said. This was a morning filled with surprises. "You just keep rocking my world."

"Your mom hired me to build a bunk bed. For your birthday."

"You *built* that?"

Jake smiled. "I put it together." He sipped his coffee. "Man, you two are nothing alike."

"Yes, we are." Lizzie slipped from the stool again. "No one thinks so 'cause I'm tall and gorgeous and she's short and, you know—"

"What? Pretty? Smart? Sexy?"

"Yup. See? I told you we are." She reached into her bag and took out her phone. "I have an audition. I have to bounce." She texted Weather again. They were meeting.

"For what?"

"A cam-girl thing, but don't tell my mom." She leaned in and took a last sip of juice. "Wait. You talked. Does she love you? My mom?"

"No. I didn't admit it—to her." Jake straightened up. "Cam girl, like—?"

"Does she love you? Do you think she does?"

"I don't know."

She reached for her wallet inside her purse. "I'm doing the reach. You buying breakfast?"

"Yeah, I got it, but, Lizzie, wait. What kind of cam girl?"

"The only kind." She slipped her bag over her shoulder. "You should tell her. See what she says."

"Like—*sex*-cam girl?"

"It's only an audition, and Weather is coming."

"Why would you—*do* that?"

"To buy my nose."

"Wait. Can we—*talk*? Before you go? About this?"

"No. I'm late." She leaned in and kissed him on the cheek. She flew down the ramp. "All those clues!" she called across Bubby's. "I love this life!" She pushed through the door.

Jake, alarmed, hailed the barkeep to bring his bill. He reached into his bag, pulled out his phone, and dialed Ally.

ALLY AND JAKE STARED at the ceiling. Steam rose and pinked their cheeks.

They were both naked in a hot bath, Ally lying on top of Jake, her back against his chest, the back of her head resting on his shoulder.

He ran a tiny bar of soap over her body as if he was playing a Ouija board. "You think you'll get married?" he asked as he circled her belly with the tiny pink bar.

"Oh my goodness," Ally said, closing her eyes, luxuriating in his soft caress. "I can't date, much less get married . . ."

"Why not?" he asked, switching hands and moving the soap to her left breast. He circled it around, then moved it back down and across her waist, taking it again with his right fingers.

"Logistics," she said. "I make seventy thousand a year . . . fifty after taxes . . . I'm on my own . . . College will be, I don't know, thirty-five, by the time Lizzie goes . . . per year . . . I can't afford a babysitter."

Jake considered this. "How will you ever meet anyone?"

"I won't," Ally said without self-pity. "But that's okay. I have a plan . . ."

"Tell me," he said. He ran the soap along the short diagonal path that divided her leg from the start of her torso. Ally's bikini line, if she had one. And then he moved it between her legs. "Tell me the plan."

She winced with pleasure and closed her eyes. "Oh my goodness, that feels so . . ."

"What's the plan? I want to know the plan."

Ally smiled. "Are you sure?"

"Yeah. What's the plan?" He brought the soap back to her belly.

Ally relented. "When Lizzie's out of school . . . living responsibly on her own . . . I'm going to take a French-style lover."

"French?" Jake asked, annoyed because he wasn't French. He was Irish and Italian and Polish. American. "Why does he have to be French?"

"No. French-*style*," Ally corrected. "Meaning we love each other, and he pays for my life, but we're not married."

Jake paused. He looked at the wall, at the tile. "Your plan is to find a *sugar daddy*?"

"*No*," she insisted. "A lover. We're *in* love. It's all civilized and grown-up and loving. We're just too old to—"

"You're his *hooker*?"

"No!" Ally laughed. "He's madly in love. With me. He is. He's just too busy for some conventional hetero-normative—"

"Hetero-normative? You mean, like, marriage? He's too busy to marry you? What?" Jake was mocking her. "This is the plan—from Brown's foremost Fem Ec professor?"

Ally laughed again. She leaned forward and placed her bottom between his legs. She reached and turned the faucet back on. The water was cooling and she wanted it hot.

"So how does it work? With your pimp?"

Ally grimaced, bent her knees, and swiveled around, facing Jake. She pulled her knees up to cover her chest and Jake placed the soap on the edge of the tub. "Well," she said, "every week he sends a car and his driver takes me to a five-star hotel. Wherever he's staying. Sometimes New York. Sometimes the driver takes me to the airport and hands me a ticket."

"And?"

"I check in and go to the room. But he's not there. He's never there."

"Why not? Where is he?"

"He's busy."

"Too busy? When you came all that way?"

"Yes. But the bed is *covered* in gifts."

"Gifts?"

"Shopping bags filled with lingerie, chocolate, shoes . . ."

Jake shook his head. "I'm calling Meer. First thing Monday. Ally Hughes is no feminist."

Ally rose. "That's right. And Meer will agree: Ally's no Marxist. Ally's no feminist: a term that only means two hundred things to two hundred people. And Meer is the proud *post*feminist because she's 'sex-positive'—she says. Another term that drives me nuts— because it implies that if I hate porn, I'm sex-negative. Which I'm not."

"Obviously."

"Then she says—*accuses* me—of being more third than second wave. Says I've proclaimed some critical stance from second wavers, and so I say, well, if she must *define* me, peg me, whatever—she's welcome to call me a retro-essential-feminist-*mother*-with-first-wave-leanings." She took a breath. "You can too."

Jake smiled. "Did I push a button?"

Ally relaxed back into the water. "Sorry. But Meer's constructions—so ivory tower—they drive me— I don't know. So many people—they feed and clothe girls, protect women—with no allegiance to Meer or anyone's *movement*."

Jake leaned forward and placed his hands on Ally's thighs, smoothing them in the sudsy water. "Back to the hotel?"

"Sure." But then she sat up. She couldn't help it. "Meer stole me from Economics. She thought I was *exactly* like her. Point by point. But I'm not, so now I'm her giant mistake—a huge disappointment—because I believe in the *evil* free markets. Capitalism. So now she wants to kick my butt to the curb."

"Who would kick that pretty butt?"

"Meer," she said and relaxed back again.

"Breathe," said Jake. "She's not in the room."

"I know."

"Breathe."

"Okay, so I get all dolled up. Garters and stuff."

"Good. Better."

"Lace." She smiled and rested her head on the wall to the side of the tap. "He finally comes." She stretched out her legs on top of Jake's. "We eat, catch up, and then he bends me over the bed and we screw for hours."

Jake looked jealous for a moment.

"Then I wake up and he's gone. I'm alone."

"Without a good-bye?"

"It's morning. He's off! And that's the end."

Jake rolled his eyes.

"So I stay in bed, watch the *Today* show, drink a little coffee—"

"He needs to *marry* you."

"I take a dive in the hotel pool—"

"One of those things—that stuff on the bed—all those gifts—there should be a ring."

Ally smiled.

"A diamond ring. Call me old-fashioned."

"The bellman comes up, takes down my bags—"

"The ring, Ally."

"Why, Jake? Why the ring?"

"To make it *real*."

"The ring makes it real?"

"It makes it a *start* to something real."

Ally smirked. "Then I go home and it happens again, every few weeks in all different cities around the world. Paris, London, Rome, London . . ." She sat forward, up on her knees, then stretched out her body on top of his. The tops of her thighs on top of his thighs. Her belly to his belly. Her lips to his lips.

"*Shitty* plan," he said, and she kissed him. "Fancy shit and a guy you only see twice a month?"

"I know," she said. "I'm so ashamed." She wasn't at all.

Jake's leer moved past her and landed on a pail perched by his foot. Vinyl sea creatures sat inside it, frogs, fish, snails, next to goggles and a gold bottle of No More Tears. He kicked it all off the edge of the tub.

"Whoops!" Ally turned toward the crash. "You did that on purpose!"

"Yup." He smiled. They locked eyes as he gripped her ass. Ally felt him grow. Quickly again, it happened so fast, in a matter of seconds, he was large, inflamed, and pressed against her inner thigh.

They had made love already twice in the bath and he wanted her again? Ally was flattered, embarrassed, pleased.

He peeled a tendril of hair from her cheek and tucked it away behind her ear.

She studied him too: His dark blue eyes. The valentine curve of his fleshy lips, bright red and broken from all her sucking. His thick, wet lashes.

She'd never made love in daylight before. She could see him so clearly. Every pore. Every scar. Every freckle.

But it had to be noon. She had so much to do, besides grading papers. "Jake," she said gently, "I've loved this so much . . ." She studied his pink, dewy face.

"But we should get out and get on with our day?"

Ally nodded and smiled regretfully.

"CAM GIRL? CAMMING? WHAT is that?" Ally stood at the kitchen counter, chopping onions to cook a brisket.

She needed something to savor that morning, a fleshy food, warm and dripping, to bite and chew and swallow. She'd tripled the wine and the brown sugar and simmered the beef for six long hours on low, low, low, until it would practically melt in her mouth.

"They set up a camera and people sign in and it's live," Jake explained, his cap pulled low and sunglasses on. He was walking north on Fifth Avenue, weaving through tourists, back to the St. Regis.

"It's *live*?" Ally asked, chopping and holding the phone with her shoulder.

"Yes," he said.

"What do they do?"

"People pay money to, you know, watch."

"Watch what?"

"To tell the girls—what to do."

Ally stopped chopping and put down the knife. "Are you kidding?"

"That's why I'm calling."

"Like sexual things? Naked things?"

"The girls get off or dance around. Some have sex."

"Is it recorded?"

"It can be," said Jake.

Ally said nothing. She turned and looked around the kitchen. What was going on with this child? What was Lizzie thinking? "Has she—has she started this yet?"

"She said she has an audition today. She's going this morning with Weather."

Ally turned and walked out of the kitchen, furious. "That *Weather.* That girl—always has the most bizarre— You should see her." She didn't speak as she walked down the hall and up the stairs to the third floor.

After some moments, Jake wasn't sure if she'd hung up or not. "Are you still there?"

"I'm here."

"You okay?"

"No."

"Can I help? Can I come over?"

"I won't be here. I'm going into town. I'm going to find her and lock her up." Ally stepped into her closet, looked around. She found a pair of jeans and pulled them on over her underwear.

"Tell her I told you. She asked me not to, but I don't care."

"Thank you," she said, zipping up her jeans.

"I thought you might—"

"Yes. Thanks. It's right that you called. How did you leave it? Was she mad?"

"We left it fine."

"We have a rule. I call three times and she calls back. She's breaking the rule. It's unbreakable. She's ignoring me."

"She just laughed. I told you she would."

"Good," Ally said, unrelieved. "Will you see her on set?"

"No, that's done. She did her line. But I can call her."

"Please, and tell her to call me. Please."

"Sure," he said. "Sorry."

"Jake?" she asked plaintively. "Why would she *do* this? Did she say?"

"She wants her nose."

Ally closed her eyes in anguish.

Minutes later on Cranberry Street, Ally, dressed, flew down the stairs. She grabbed her purse and keys from the table. She grabbed an umbrella from inside the closet. The bell rang as she opened the door.

The UPS man stood on the stoop. "Morning, Ally."

"Morning, Frank." Surprised, she signed for the unexpected box. She thanked Frank, took it inside, and set it on the floor at the foot of the stairs.

Quickly she glanced at the little white sticker in the top left corner, to see who'd sent it. "La Perla?"

Then she stood up, as straight as an arrow. It must be a gift, but from Ted? Ally drew a quick breath in.

Ted?

Or Jake? Or Jake.

AFTER HER FIRST THREE sexless years, Ally decided that not having sex brought about its own brand of thrill. Maybe not widely known or exalted. In America. Or anywhere else in the world, for that matter. But celibacy, chosen or not, was underrated, she decided. It was. She was sure. She was sure that monks knew some kind of joy, a spiritual pleasure, sensual even, that sex-having people did not understand.

"It's the kind of pleasure that brings you back to when you were ten," she explained to Anna one day on the phone. Before puberty reared its head. "Remember? When life was about morning cartoons? Snuggling with your doll? When you were eight?"

"Actually," Anna explained, "the whole idea of a *latent* period in middle childhood? All that Freud shit? That's been debunked. Middle childhood is sexual. Sort of." Anna was studying psychiatry.

"I'm not talking *Freud*," Ally argued. "I'm talking about the *pleasure* of being barefoot in spring. Riding bikes. Apple slices. All those bubble baths. Baking cookies, cocoa in winter, lemonade in summer . . ."

"I don't think we had the same childhood," Anna said.

Ally ignored this. "My point is: Pleasure was *about* something else. It was different, sure, but comparable, right? To sex? Just different. Right?"

"I think you need to get laid, Ally."

She knew it was silly to be modest now, now that they had had sex in the bathtub twice in the bright light of morning. But she couldn't help it.

She wasn't the type to walk around naked in front of anyone, even a man who had seen every inch of her body in daylight.

Quickly she dressed and brushed her hair, thinking of all she had to do: the papers, the grades due Monday. Monday by noon. She had to buy bananas. The hampers were full and she had to buy bleach to wash the whites. She had also promised to drive to Connecticut, to an antique toy store, to buy figurines for Lizzie's report. The diorama was due on Tuesday. Tuesday, which was Lizzie's birthday. She needed vanilla to bake Lizzie's cake. She needed to sign her up for camp.

"Can I come with you?" Jake asked, stepping from the bathroom, pink and clean, zipping up his jeans.

"Where?"

"To Mystic, right?"

Ally paused. She looked concerned.

As much as she had enjoyed herself, enjoyed Jake, Lizzie was due home in a day. Sunday morning. Yes, that meant they had twenty-four hours, but the whole thing had to end sometime. He couldn't spend the night again. Could he?

Or could he?

Did he want to?

That would be cutting it way too close.

But another part of Ally, an aching part, wanted him to stay and stay and stay. She looked down at his sock on the floor. She wanted that sock to stay there forever. On her floor. Next to her bed. She would never complain about that sock. "Jake," she said kindly, pleading in a way, turning to him.

"What? Say it. We've had our fun?"

"That's not what I was—"

"You don't want company on your drive?"

Yes, she did, but—

"Let's grab lunch."

"What if—what if—someone sees us?"

Jake picked up his button-down shirt. He couldn't find his T-shirt. "At some little store in a whole other *state*?" He pulled his arm through it.

Ally put her brush down and looked at the bed, its rumpled sheets and fraying blanket. She then looked at Jake as he buttoned his shirt. If she sent him home now, would she see him again? Ever? No.

"Come on," he said, rolling up his sleeves. "We'll eat oysters and churn butter." He ran his fingers through his thick wet hair. "It's a beautiful day." He turned and started to straighten the bed.

"You don't have to—" She crossed to him.

"Yes, I do." She joined him and they pulled up the top sheet together, then the blanket. Jake began to tuck them in.

Ally then stopped. She was struck by how easy it was to make a bed with someone else. It's a two-person job, a bed. It's a two-person job, this life.

And then she said, "I don't tuck."

Jake looked up. "Why not?"

"Why tuck when you'll kick it out tonight?"

Jake grabbed the pillows. He threw them to her and she arranged them.

"You know," he said, picking up his sneakers, "it's fun to escape from your life for an hour, but it's more fun to do it with a friend."

LIZZIE HAD FASHIONED HER costume at Weather's. They stood in front of the bathroom mirror.

She was pleased. Brown ringlets hung to her waist. Fake red nails extended her fingers. Colored contacts turned her eyes blue. She drew, with precision, two fake birthmarks, one on her back and one on her belly, with waterproof mascara, and they both wore stilettos, shorts, and white tank tops.

"Wife beaters," Lizzie said as they gazed at themselves. "That's what these are called."

"We don't look like battered wives," Weather replied. "We look like hookers."

Lizzie turned to her and smiled. "Perfect."

Ally took the train to Fourteenth. She walked eight blocks through the sweltering heat to Lizzie's building.

She buzzed and buzzed with no real hope, then took out her phone and looked for a place to sit and wait.

Across the street, she found a stoop in a patch of shade under some blue wood scaffolding. From there she could see east and west across the whole block. She'd see Lizzie first when Lizzie came home.

"I already texted you. You ignored those," she started, leaving her a message. "And we have a deal. Three calls—you call me back. Three calls. And this is, like, my twentieth. Two days. I'm upset."

She left it at that.

She looked across the street at Lizzie's building and wondered why they both lived alone.

Wasn't it the millennial thing? Kids fresh from school living with their parents? Lizzie could have an entire floor on Cranberry Street.

Ally felt badly. She should have offered. Now she would. She called Lizzie back. "By the way, I'm sitting outside here, at your building, and I'm wondering why you're paying rent when you don't have to. I know you need your freedom—but it seems so silly. It's really a very American thing. To insist on living on your own. Okay? Call me."

Lizzie ignored her mother's call. They rode the train to Brooklyn, hopped off on Carroll, and walked to Red Hook.

Across Third Avenue and under the Gowanus, they found the building. Only the ground floor looked alive, with a limousine depot and a small shop selling radiator parts. Fishman had rented the top two floors, the ninth and tenth, with fourteen offices inside each. The rest lay fallow, collecting soot.

They looked for the entrance for fifteen minutes and finally found it around the block, where Fishman was waiting.

Khakis, polo, no socks, tan, he looked as if he'd stepped off the Jitney, and maybe he had. "Pleased to meet you!" he called. "Thrilled!" He shook their hands. "Which one's Jenny?"

"Me," said Lizzie. "This is Weather."

"Great," said Fishman. "Ted's like a brother. Teddy is great."

"Yes," said Lizzie. "Yes, yes, he is."

On the ninth floor, they walked through the polished, winding halls.

"The building was built in 1901. It was a factory. Sugar, they say. A sugar mill." Fishman led them past door after door, all of them shut. Music floated out into the hall. "You work the same studio. Room is yours, twenty-four-seven, except for one to three at night, when the cleaning crew comes. No charge." He turned around and smiled.

They both smiled back.

Lizzie then heard the song "Putin Zassal" from inside a room. She recognized it. "Pussy Riot! The Russian group! Love!"

Fishman frowned. "But Russian isn't our brand. I'll remind her."

"You have a *brand*?" Lizzie asked, curious. Ted hadn't mentioned a brand.

He explained:

Six years before, he had personally funded a marketing study of "Global Internet Porn Habits." The study broke web searches down by region, then by country, around the world.

With the results, he and his partner decided to focus on Western Europe, specifically Belgium.

Belgians, he said, the research said, trolled the web for American girls. So did the French. So they decided to sell them a type. "The models who work here have to look *stateside*."

"What does that mean?" Lizzie asked.

"American college. Innocent but slutty. Fresh but willing."

The girls nodded. They understood.

The sites, he explained, charged five bucks a minute, American dollars, for the live meetings. "Four hundred thousand clients a day," Fishman bragged. "Our models are cut into the flat minute rate at fifty percent, plus tips. Fifty percent!" he said with a smile. "Some make four hundred bucks an hour."

He didn't say more. He didn't say he'd installed hidden cameras in every studio.

Or that they'd recorded the sessions from start to finish, from four different angles, close-up and wide.

The hundreds of hours of digital footage, naked footage, sliced and diced into ten-minute shorts, compiled, and sold worldwide as a series, this was his secret.

He didn't say that *American Girls,* volumes one, two, and three, had earned investors, including Ted, millions of dollars.

Finally, Fishman had found success.

Instead, he walked them into the pantry. "This is free to anyone working." He opened the cabinets to show off boxes of candy, health bars, chips. A small table sat by the window with three midcentury chairs around it. "Soda in the fridge. We keep it pretty stocked. Microwave there." He pointed to it and then turned. "Questions?"

The girls shook their heads.

———

Down the hall, in the payroll office, Josh was typing as they entered. He was twenty-two and wore a black baseball cap backward. "That hag, before, pushed thirty, yo." He didn't see Lizzie and Weather in the doorway. "Rolls of fat ain't curves, you old hag."

"That's enough, Josh. We've got guests." Fishman opened his leather briefcase and took out his phone. "I apologize for Josh. This way, ladies."

Surprised, Josh turned and looked at the girls as Fishman led them back into the hall.

"I just need photos. Back, side, front," Fishman said as they walked. "Again, please keep your underthings on." He opened the door to an empty room and led them inside. "I'll be out here. Knock when you're ready."

In the room, the girls looked around. It was empty except for a folding chair.

"What a jerk. That IT guy?" Lizzie said.

"I thought he was cute." Weather pulled off her tank top.

"Wannabe Eminem bullshit. Please."

"This is fun." Weather giggled and pulled down her shorts.

"This is *creepy*," Lizzie replied, lifting her tank top up and off. They piled their clothes onto the chair. Lizzie looked at the door. "Are we sure we want to do this?"

"Why? What's wrong?"

"I don't know. We're naked here."

"What did you think? I have bathing suits that show more than this."

"I know. Okay, why am I freaking?"

"Free snacks!"

"Exactly. Everything's covered. For now."

They laughed. Weather moved to the door and cracked it. "Ready," she said.

In the hall, Fishman was texting. He looked up at Weather, entered the room, and closed the door.

For the next few minutes, the girls posed with pursed lips and sleepy eyes, and Fishman shot them with his iPhone—click, click, click. "Give me some sugar." Front, side, and back. And that was that.

That was the tryout.

"Thank you," he said. "My partner's at home with a sick kid today. No camp. Let me text these and we'll have an answer in five minutes. Thank you, girls."

"Thank you," they said at the same time.

"Jinx," said Lizzie.

Fishman smiled.

Back across the river and up north a bit, Ally bought a large iced coffee at La Follia on Third. Manhattan's Third. It was three by then, but the sun was south and blocked by the building whose stoop she had borrowed.

"Here's the thing," she began again, flooding Lizzie's voice mail. "Say it's not wrong. What you're doing. For argument's sake." Her gaze floated across the street to Lizzie's window, four stories above. Hydrangeas sat on the windowsill. "Get naked. No problem. Feel your power. Except that *other* people think it's a problem. *Other* people think it's wrong. Twenty years pass and you're my age, and maybe you're feeling less empowered. Work dries up. Acting, let's say. Or you want to quit. Good-bye, acting! Hello, philanthropy! Hello, teaching! You apply for jobs, and *somehow* . . . This boss, that boss, they all know that you, Lizzie Hughes, Duke graduate, Juilliard graduate, hopefully, that you, in fact, were a sex worker once . . . That's what they call them, by the way. Like table server or camp counselor or ice-cream scooper. Elizabeth Hughes: sex worker." Ally took a breath and stopped. "Anyway," she said and then continued. "They all reject you because of this job from when you were twenty. This phase. Photos, video, it doesn't matter. It's out there, on record. Forever."

A recorded voice then cut Ally off. "You have reached the maximum time."

"I have?" She looked at her phone, confused.

"To send your message, press one," the voice said.

"Wait, one?" She pressed one.

"To listen to your message, press two."

Ally pressed one four more times. "Send, send. I want to send."

"To rerecord, press three," said the voice.

"No, please, wait! I'm pressing one! I'm pressing one! This is important!"

"For more options, press four. To cancel, press star."

Ally looked at her phone and pressed four. "More options, more options . . ."

It didn't work. "Sorry," said the voice. "Please try again."

"But wait!"

"Good-bye."

Somehow the message got through anyway.

THEY TOOK HIS CHEVY and Jake drove. He headed south along I-95 in the afternoon sun.

Ally rolled down the window and laid her head back. She slipped off her shoes and placed her bare feet on the glove box. "This is amazing!"

"What?"

"Not driving!"

"What do you mean?"

"Riding in the passenger seat! It's such a treat!"

Jake smiled and looked at her. "Tell that to women in Saudi Arabia!"

Ally smiled. "I always drive! I'm sick of it! I'm never *not* driving. This is like a dream . . ." She closed her eyes.

The passenger seat felt like bliss after a decade of driving, driving, always driving.

She relaxed into the leather seat, into the speed, feeling the motion of the car, feeling the sun and wind on her face as they sped along.

What a fantastic feeling. How strange and wonderful, to ride in a car without the burden of actually driving it, without the stress of protecting Lizzie and Claire as she drove.

Jake was taking her for a ride.

She surrendered to it.

He turned on the radio. The Sox were playing the Mariners again. But Wakefield had given up five whole runs before the fourth inning. Jake was upset. "Shit!" he said and pounded the steering wheel.

Ally opened her eyes. "You okay?"

He shook his head.

She listened to the radio for a few minutes. "Men and baseball. Talk to me. What's the obsession?"

"This isn't baseball."

"It's not?"

"This is the Sox."

"Uh . . . but the Sox are a baseball team, right?"

"Yes, but . . . it's not about baseball. It's not about winning or salary caps. It's not about 'roid rage or designated hitters or any of that . . ."

"Then what's it about?"

"Hope."

"Hope?" Ally said, finding him more charming than ever.

Jake glanced at her and explained. "This is a team . . . This is a *town* that loses and loses. Every year. Every year, we come close and lose. Like, it's who we are." He looked ahead at the highway again. "Boston can't win. It's what people think. We lose 'cause we're cursed. The curse of the Bambino. But we're not." He glanced at Ally. "We know we're not. We know that someday the Sox will win the Series again. And when they do, after waiting so long, it'll be amazing because we waited. Because we were patient. Because we hoped and believed we could." He turned up the volume.

Ally considered his words.

What was he saying?

If the Red Sox could do it, shake off their curse, if the Sox could do it, then anyone could.

She thought of Claire, and how Claire had said, "No good man will marry you now." She looked up at the Baltic blue sky and hovering clouds. "No good man will want you now. Not with a child."

Claire was wrong, Ally decided then and there. She thought about the Sox and studied the weeds that pushed through the divider that split the highway north and south. The flat white faces of Queen Anne's lace claiming the right to bloom, to reach, despite the interstate's treachery.

No good man? What was Jake?

The Sox could win. The Sox would win.

At the Tin Soldier on the south side of Mystic, she talked the shopkeeper down. "Thirty-four ninety-nine?" she complained.

"I can't let him go for less than that," Francis, the owner, said to Ally. He was eighty. "Look at the detail." He held up the tiny tin soldier. "Gaitered trousers. Button shoes. A land pattern musket."

Ally turned and looked at Jake. She turned back to Francis. "I don't know if Hale saw combat. Did he?"

"They all kept muskets," Francis griped, irritated. "It was a ground war. Don't you know about a ground war?"

"No," Ally said. She thought he was sweet. "Okay. He can be

Hale. I'll take Hale and George Washington, and the Sixth Regiment British sets. All four."

"And the furniture," Jake added.

"And the tavern furniture, please," Ally said, nodding. "Please."

"Fine." Francis turned to the glass cabinet. He unlocked it, plucked George Washington from the shelf, and reached for the boxed sets of British soldiers. "The Washington's thirty-four ninety-nine too."

"Fine," Ally said, even though it wasn't. She knew she'd regret spending so much.

Francis then left and headed to the front to ring them up. Ally followed, but Jake caught her arm, pulled her back, and kissed her. "Well done," he said.

She smiled.

"Old men like that—they make me—make me—want to be bad. I can't explain it. He makes me want to commit a crime." Ally smiled. The store was empty. No one would see them kissing in the back, in the dark, surrounded by creepy antique toys.

It had been years since Ally'd kissed in public. Even in any kind of private public.

Suddenly they were pressed against each other, kissing and groping. Jake backed Ally against the glass case and lifted her dress around his waist. Under her sundress, fully covered, he pulled down his zipper and took himself out, erect and ready. He found Ally's panties, yanked them aside, and entered her, lifting her up off the floor.

"Here? Here?" Ally whispered, thrilled and surprised. "What are you doing?"

"You," he said.

And he did.

———

An hour later at a picnic table restaurant, they lapped up bowls of New England clam chowder. As Ally ate, she studied Jake. She thought of him, selling cocaine. Behind bars. What was it about taking risks, about being bad, that made a woman feel so good? Fear? Adrenaline? She felt so alive. That simple soup, the silky clams, the bacon and potatoes, the massive amounts of slimy cooked onion—it all tasted better, she thought, in that moment, than any soup in the whole world. The sea air smelled fresh. The birds sang. People laughed. It was the prettiest day of the year and Mystic was the most charming town.

Oh, and Jake was the sexiest man alive.

After they ate, they strolled by a park, hand in hand, and decided to fit in some batting practice.

Jake swung his duffel bag out of the trunk, gave Ally a bat, took a glove for himself.

They threw and caught and kissed for an hour. Jake taught Ally his curve-slider grip and Ally hit a double that nearly took his head off.

"I know what we should do," he said, driving back. "Tonight. I have a great idea."

"Tonight?" Ally said. "What about my— I have papers."

He looked at her and smiled. "Have you ever role-played?"

"Role-played? No. Wait, what do you mean?"

"Pretended you were someone else during sex?"

Ally rolled her eyes. "My sex life has been pretty—tame."

He glanced at her. "I took this theater class. Last semester. Acting. It was cool. Want to try it? Role-play?"

"I don't think so," Ally said, but she was intrigued.

"Great," he said, pretending to ignore her. "Here's my idea: We drive somewhere. Somewhere far. Farther out. New Hampshire. The Cape. We find a bar. Get some beers—"

"No, wait. We can't both drink. One of us has to drive."

"Okay, you, then. I'll drive. You get the beers. And I pretend to be someone else and you pretend to be someone else, and we meet again for the first time."

"That sounds weird."

"We pretend to be strangers. I pick you up."

"But what's the point?"

"There is no point. It's fun. Remember fun? It's this thing you can have that makes you feel good?"

"No, I don't think I remember," she said, pretending to try to remember.

"I can be the jail guard. You can be the bait. I can be the doctor. You can be the nurse. You can be the doctor. I can be the patient. I can be the pimp, you can be the—"

Ally interrupted. "Yuck. That's not fun."

"Whatever. You choose."

Ally looked at him. "I don't know. I hate to keep saying this, but I have so—*so* much to do."

"You get to step out of your life for a minute. You get to be someone else."

"Okay, but I like my life. I like who I am."

"Okay," he said. "It was just an idea." Jake was silent, eyes fixed ahead. "I can't give you a plane ticket, Ally, or send you a car."

Ally turned. "Jake, please. I was kidding."

"I can't give you Europe or five-star hotels."

"Please—"

"But I *can* . . . give you a break. A little vacation from your life."

Ally considered this. He was so kind, and he was right. She needed a break. "You have," she said. "This has been wonderful." Then, at the bottom of her bag at her feet, her phone rang. She scrambled for it, pulling it out, thinking of Lizzie. "Meer," she said, seeing the number.

"Don't pick it up."

"I won't," she said. "Why is she calling me on the weekend?"

The trees along I-95 bloomed with pale green, late-spring leaves. Millions of them filled in the nothingness, the emptiness of winter between the branches, creating shade for the summer to come.

Ally, too, felt as if she was waking up after a chill, a hibernation. Or was it hiding? Had she been hiding?

Jake placed his hand on top of her leg, palming her thigh again, stretching his fingers out and around it. He looked upset. The end of school maybe, Ally thought. All that uncertainty. All the change.

She laced her fingers through his fingers and couldn't resist his calloused hands; his strong hands and heavy limbs, coarse hair; his broad back and chiseled waist; the path behind his ear, along the side of his neck. His clavicle. The way his eyes lit up when he smiled. The way he blushed. His massive muscle groups, so unfamiliar and irresistible . . .

And so she agreed and they remained on I-95 and drove right past the Providence exits.

They circled the city and headed east toward Route 25, toward Cape Cod, as the sun set.

"HONEY, IT'S JUST, CHOICES matter," Ally said, still on the stoop. "What can I say? That's my point. It seems like nothing, I'm sure, to you now—but our choices, they're like dominoes. All set up against each other. One goes down, the next goes down . . ."

Ally studied the tenement building, its doorway arched with a mural of giraffes and a bonsai tree. Why giraffes in Stuyvesant Square? she asked herself. The world was so weird. New York was so weird. Everyone who passed was wearing scrubs. Navy-blue scrubs, bright-green scrubs, bright-blue scrubs. Everyone was talking or texting on the phone.

"It's hard to see it—when you're young. You've only had so much time on the planet. But when you're older, you can look back—and see how one thing led to another and that thing led to something else." She paused. "I don't mean to lecture you, Bug. You've probably erased this message by now. All of them. Anyway, I'm at your building. Still. Call me back."

Ally hung up and thought about it, then dialed 411 to find a number she didn't have.

"CTA," the operator answered. Lizzie's talent agency.

"Cybil Stern, please," Ally said. The operator connected her.

"Cybil Stern's office." It was Cybil's assistant.

"Hi there. This is Allison Hughes, Lizzie's mother. Is Cybil there?"

"Yes, she is, Mrs. Hughes. One moment, please." The assistant then put Ally on hold. Ten seconds later, she picked up again. "Actually, Cybil is in a meeting right now. Can she return?"

"Return?"

"Your call?"

"Oh, yes, of course. Can you tell her it's an emergency, please? That I need to speak to her *immediately*, please?" The assistant agreed and Ally hung up and dialed Weather.

Somewhere in Red Hook, out on the sidewalk, Weather sobbed. She couldn't help it.

Lizzie consoled her as best she could as she pulled off her wig and then stuffed it into the bottom of her bag. "The American girl? The *stateside* girl? Fresh but willing? Hannah Montana, pre–'Wrecking Ball,' dancing around to Taylor Swift in front of a bunch of perverts? Please. That's the job you're *crying* about?"

"So?" sobbed Weather.

"Belgian bankers rubbing it out? Horny husbands in southern Connecticut, slumming in the pool house, fleeing with their laptops from Lululemon wives and whiny kids?" She was trying to make Weather laugh.

"He said they don't serve the tristate area."

"Yes, and I have a bridge to sell! Bridge! Bridge! Only a nickel!"

Weather giggled, but then her laughter turned into tears. More tears.

"You're just like my mom," Lizzie complained.

"I'm sorry! It hurts!"

Lizzie stopped walking. She made Weather stop. "Hold on, wait. Clean yourself up." She dug into her bag and pulled out Kleenex. Ally had slipped them in there at some point with Band-Aids, safety pins, mints, and Mace . . .

Weather's cheeks were flushed and her nose was running. She took a few tissues and wiped her face. "I'm feeling *rejected*," she whined again.

"By *porn* producers?"

"You can't talk! You got the job!"

"We're not talking Marty or David O. Russell. We're not talking *Spielberg*."

"I know, but still! How will I get an *acting* job if I can't get a *porn* job?"

"You don't want a porn job! No one wants a porn job!"

"You do!"

"No! I want a *nose* job. I am doing this for *six* weeks. Eight weeks max, and that is it. Now, cheer up! Come on!"

Weather balled up the wet Kleenex and threw it like a brat onto the sidewalk. Lizzie bent over and picked it up, walked to a trash can, and threw it inside. She turned and scolded her friend. "Don't litter."

They started walking, and seconds later, Weather started sniveling again. "You think I'm too fat? They didn't like the fat?"

"You're *gorgeous*. Stop."

"Maybe the tattoos? Some people hate cats."

"You *dyed* your hair for your art, okay? I don't think the *gray* hair helped."

"Oh, I forgot. You're right," Weather said. She suddenly remembered and fingered a strand of her dyed gray hair.

"It ages you a *little*, but please. Please. They lost a future *Oscar* winner."

"Where are we going?" Weather felt better and looked around. She had no idea where they were.

"I think toward my mom's." Lizzie looked skyward to gauge where they were. She looked for a bridge. She needed a bridge to know where they were, to find her way home.

"Can we stop by? Maybe she's cooking."

"No, we shouldn't," Lizzie said. "Listen to these." She stopped and dug for her phone in her bag. It was under her wig. "Noah betrayed me. Listen and weep." She pulled up her voice mail, scrolled through the messages, and gave the phone to Weather.

Weather listened.

"I just want to add," Ally started, around four o'clock, "when something is sacred, it shouldn't be exploited. Bought and sold. Children are sacred. Nature is sacred. Animals. Flowers. Flowers are sacred."

"Flowers?" said Weather. She smiled. Lizzie smiled.

"Sex is *sacred*. It's not *sinful*. That's not the point. It's not bad. The point is it's *sacred*. Your *body* is sacred, Lizzie Bug. You might not know that yet. You're twenty. You can ace a test on four hours' sleep. Run ten miles. But wait until you wind down. Or watch me as I fall apart, like I did with Grandma. Then you'll know."

"Oh, sad," Weather remarked and looked at Lizzie.

Lizzie nodded.

"Or get sick yourself someday or make a baby—with your body—it's a miracle. Reproduction. The respiratory system. The brain, honey. I know I sound nuts, but we, as a species, we invent nothing—nothing nearing the beauty of the body. So to prance yourself around and shake your boobs for a bunch of jerks—it's an affront to any grateful, deep-feeling person and— Oh shoot! Are you kidding? Oh, man! Did I just step in—goddammit!"

Weather looked at Lizzie. "Did she step in dog poo?"

"I think," Lizzie said and took the phone back. They both laughed.

"You know you can't erase that *ever*. I mean *ever*."

Lizzie smiled and nodded. She knew. "Can I sleep over?"

Weather nodded. "I *cannot* believe she's camping out! In front of your house!"

When the sun began to set four hours later, Ally got up and walked a few blocks the other way. She bought another coffee, this time hot, at Irving Farm. Then she returned to the stoop and called Ted. He didn't pick up. She left a message:

"About the weekend, Ted, it's Ally. I'm in a bit of a—you cannot *believe*— Have you ever heard of *sex*-camming? Maybe you have. It's an Internet thing." Ally cringed. "Suffice to say, my whole life is *unraveling*. No Nantucket. Sorry. Call me."

She sat on the stoop across from Lizzie's and sipped that coffee for two more hours.

At one point, a woman and a girl walked by. A mother and daughter, Ally thought. She tried not to stare. She tried not to judge.

The mother, of course, was busy texting, and the girl, around ten, showed no pudgy limbs or budding, or hips. And yet she wore a mini skirt, heels, a see-through T-shirt that fell from her shoulder, and lipstick and blush.

What happened to clothes? What happened to lining? Ally wondered. When did material turn so sheer?

Then she thought: Wait, what's wrong with sheer? Women should wear what they want. Of course. Then she saw the girl had a book. Oh, she reads. Good, Ally thought. Well, of course she reads! Shit!

At what point had Ally turned into Claire?

After all, Lizzie had worn short skirts, and Ally had never worried back then.

That's because Lizzie was into balls and computers and guns. She refused to wear dresses, collected weapons; dozens of lightsabers, caches of Nerf. She played with the Dreamhouse but mostly she'd rendered it under siege.

She never cared about looking pretty.

Ally remembered when Lizzie was ten, or around ten. She left camp sulking, stomping her feet. "Avery said—"

"What did Avery say?"

"I can only have a baby if a man puts his penis—*in* my vagina." Ally opened the car door for her and she climbed inside. "Is that true?" She sounded betrayed.

"That's one way. There are others." She swung the door shut and rounded the car.

Well, there it was. It was time for the talk. She opened the driver's side door and climbed in.

"Is that what *you* did?" Lizzie demanded.

"Yes," Ally said. "Seat belt, please." She started the car and pulled on her own.

"Disgusting!"

"Seat belt."

"I'm *never* doing that! Ever! Ever!" Lizzie pulled on her belt.

"You don't have to. Science is changing. There are lots of ways—to skin a cat."

"What? Skin a *cat*? What does that mean?"

"It's an *expression*." Ally glanced into the mirror to check for cars. "It means there are ways—different ways—to do the same thing. Sorry. That's all." She pulled out.

Lizzie sat back and slapped her bare thighs. "You said the fishes come out the mouth! You said the dad squirts them out when you kiss!"

"No, I didn't."

"You did!"

She did. Ally remembered. Lizzie was in the bath. She was four. Maybe even three. The fish, as she called them, instead of sperm, "swam down the throat into the tummy and landed on an egg, and a baby hatched."

"Exactly," said Ally, assuming Lizzie would soon forget.

She was wrong.

"Okay, I said that," Ally admitted. "But you were *three*. It was cute."

"I am adopting." Lizzie reached for the radio dial. "I am adopting."

"Fine. Do. But you have some time. You might change your mind."

"I will *never* change my mind."

At ten, in the dark, Ally got up and went home.

At ten the next day, she woke to the sound of the doorbell ringing.

Frank, from UPS, again. "Whole load today."

"Morning, Frank."

He turned and revealed eleven boxes descending in size like a tower on his trolley.

"Oh my goodness," she said, surprised. "What is this?"

"Two more in the truck."

"Two? More?"

"Where would you like them?"

"Wait— Can I?— Wait. Can I *not* sign? Can you take them back to sender or something? I wasn't expecting—"

"You don't want them?"

"Um," Ally said. She wasn't sure.

"Everything okay?"

"Yes, no, forget it. I'll sign. Sorry." She took a deep breath, took the stylus and signed.

She and Frank brought the boxes inside. They piled them at the base of the stairs, next to the unopened box from La Perla.

Frank walked out, back to his truck, to fetch the two others, and Ally skimmed the return addresses. "Oh, man," she said, reading the labels: Cartier, Godiva, Chanel, Blahnik. Gaultier, Gucci, Barneys, Saks.

After Frank left, she found the phone and called the St. Regis. She asked for Jake Bean.

"Certainly, ma'am. One moment, please," the operator said and then disappeared. When she came back, she said, "I'm sorry, ma'am. No one is registered under that name."

"Oh, I'm sorry," Ally said. "I meant Noah. *Noah* Bean, please."

"Certainly, ma'am," the operator said. "Hold one moment." She went away again and came back. "I'm sorry, ma'am. No reservation under that name."

She sat on the stairs and dialed Anna. She had to call her three times.

"He sent me presents."

"Who?"

"Jake Bean. The UPS man showed up with boxes. A dozen boxes. Saks, Cartier. I haven't opened them."

"How do you know it wasn't Ted?"

"Ted buys for Ted. Golf clubs. Scuba gear. Squash rackets."

"And the problem?"

"What does he want? What is he doing? I haven't seen him in ten years."

"Is this about age? Because there was a woman last week in the news. She married her truck."

"And?"

"Ally. Mary-Kate Olsen, the toddler from *Full House*. The toddler *twin*. Remember that show? She's with Sarkozy."

"The French president?"

"No. His brother. But still, the guy's a *thousand* years old. And then there's Woody—"

"Please don't go there—and you know it's different for women. "There's still a double standard out there. We think it's changed, but it hasn't, Anna—"

"Yes, it has. Jennifer Lopez, Casper Smart. Joan Collins is seventy-seven. Her boyfriend is—"

"Please. How do you *know* this? How do you even—?"

"I looked it up! And you know what I think? You've been comparing *every* man—for the last ten years—to Noah Bean. Or Jake. Or whatever."

"No."

"Like I did with John, you fell in love at first fuck."

"Don't be so crass! We didn't fuck. The whole thing was tender—and loving. He said so!"

"See? You loved him! I knew it! Ha!"

"I didn't say that. I said the *sex*—was loving."

"Fine."

"By the way, Lizzie is doing porn."

"*What?*"

THEY DROVE AND DROVE as night fell, until they spotted the perfect bar with neon signs and a pebble-strewn lot set back from the road.

Friar Tuck's.

This was the place, they both agreed, as Jake pulled in. They could practically smell the draft beer, the frozen potato fries soused in tallow, the greasy cod, twenty-cent wings, fried oysters, and cheap cologne. They could hear Megadeth on the jukebox.

Jake parked his Chevy in a dark, empty corner at the edge of an even darker wood.

"This is so strange," Ally said. "I'm never out at night."

"What do you mean?"

"I'm never outside, outdoors, at night. It's so easy on the eyes. I forgot." She turned to him. "Remember the first time you went out at night? With your friends? How exciting that was? That's how this feels."

Jake smiled and turned off the radio. "I'm going in. You head inside in, like, twenty minutes?"

"Great."

"You okay out here by yourself?"

Ally looked around the lot. "Of course." She peered into the woods.

"Okay," Jake said. "See you inside."

Ten minutes later, alone in the car, Ally rolled down the window and looked up into the clear night.

Off the coast that far out, the sky was awash with thousands of stars. She opened her phone to check Meer's message but dialed New York instead and waited.

After some seconds, Lizzie picked up, loud and clear. "Mommy?" she answered. She knew it was Ally.

"Hi, sweetie! How's it going?"

"I'm going to bed. I'm tired," Lizzie said. She sounded weary.

"How was the shopping?"

"Good."

"Only good?"

"Where are you now?" Lizzie said, yawning.

"Home," Ally said.

"No, you're not."

"What?" How could she know?

"We tried you at home."

"Oh. No, I'm home. I didn't hear it. The phone ring. Sorry." She changed the subject. "See you at the station tomorrow? Yay!"

"Do you want Grandma? She's downstairs."

"No, I'm here," Claire said. At some point, she'd picked up the line.

"Oh!" Ally laughed. "Hi, Mom."

"Night, Mommy," Lizzie said and yawned again.

"Night, honey. Did you get your hair cut?"

Lizzie hung up.

"Lizzie? Mom? You still there?"

"Yes, I'm here. We'll see you at one?"

"One with bells on," Ally said. "Did she get a haircut?"

"No. She didn't. Did you get your work done?"

"Almost there," Ally lied. "Just a few more."

Claire paused. "See you tomorrow."

"Great," Ally said. "How did the shopping go?"

Without replying, Claire hung up.

Ally stared at the phone for a moment. That was odd. She sat there wondering what was wrong. Maybe the reception? Or something else?

She turned on the radio, and after some minutes, she looked toward the bar and wondered suddenly if she was safe, sitting in a parking lot alone.

She gazed around the lot again. No one was out among the cars, and the music was playing so loud inside that no one would hear her if she screamed. If she screamed. If she had to scream for some reason.

She decided she'd waited long enough. Surely Jake had a soda by now and had picked up a game of darts or whatever.

She grabbed her purse, took the keys from the ignition, and climbed from the Chevy. She locked it twice and walked off quickly toward the bar.

THE STUDIO AT THE end of the hall was designed to look like a teenager's room: cheerleading pendants, One Direction posters, Hello Kitty sheets.

The MacBook Pro sat on a desk across from a mirror so clients could enjoy two different angles at the same time.

"Will it work?" Fishman asked and held the door.

Lizzie stepped in. "Perfect," she said, looking around. "You thought of everything." She was impressed. She slipped a CD out of her pocket and turned to him. "Rihanna? Usher?"

"Perfect," he said, imitating her and turning to leave.

"Any advice?" Lizzie asked as she placed her bag on the bed.

"Well," Fishman said, turning back around, "some guys like action. Movement, dancing . . . Others like something more subdued."

"Subdued?"

Fishman shrugged. "Stripping slowly. Pleasing yourself."

"Pleasing myself," Lizzie said and smiled. "I love your euphemisms."

Fishman studied her. "You're pretty smart, aren't you, Jenny?"

Lizzie paused. "No, not really."

"Anyway, some guys just want to talk."

"Okay," she said. "I can talk."

Then he paused. "But not too much. Don't talk too much."

Lizzie nodded, feigning interest. She was starting to wish she'd never asked.

"It's not intimate. Even if it feels like it is. Men love mystery."

"Who doesn't?" Lizzie laughed.

"Familiarity breeds contempt. Don't you think?"

"I guess. I don't know. I'm twenty years old. What do I know?" She laughed again nervously.

Fishman studied her. "Just don't think you're making friends. He doesn't care about your dreams."

"No, of course."

"He doesn't want to know your favorite food or the name of your pet. He wants to come. That's what he wants. Nothing more."

Lizzie wondered if Fishman was stoned. She thought she could smell the faintest whiff of weed.

He gazed past her and thought about it for the first time ever. No one had ever asked his advice. "Keep in mind," he continued, riffing, "he's having sex with *himself*. He's somewhere out there, all alone . . . *pretending*, like, make-believe, to have sex with you . . . When you think about it, it's pretty sad . . . when he could be— when he's *meant* to be screwing an actual woman. It's not like we *pretend* to eat. It's not like we *pretend* to sleep. But we pretend to fuck 'cause we can?" He looked at Lizzie, his eyes glazed over. Then he snapped out of it. "Well, good luck," he added brightly.

"Thanks," Lizzie said. She was amused but tried to hide it.

Fishman then opened the door and slipped out. "And I'd lose the wig. I think you're prettier as a blonde."

Lizzie looked surprised as he pulled the door shut, and a cold, clammy feeling settled in her stomach.

Minutes later, the screaming came. "No, no! Help!" the young woman screamed, loud and clear.

Lizzie looked up from the CD player. She looked toward the wall to her right, toward the voice.

"Help! Someone! Help!" The voice sounded anguished.

Lizzie's breath quickened and her eyes grew wide. Instinctively, she stepped toward the wall and pressed her ear against it.

The woman cried out, "Call the police!"

Lizzie beelined to the door and stepped out into the empty hall, where she could hear a man's voice too, lower, berating the Screamer next door.

She looked around. The hall was empty. No one was there? Or maybe, she thought, no one else heard or no one else cared?

She crossed to the door as the pleas grew more and more intense. Tentative, she took the knob, turned it, and threw the door open wide.

"What are you doing!" the Screamer screamed. At Lizzie. "Close the fucking door!" The naked Screamer, a tiny young thing, was perched on all fours, and the young man behind her, naked too, was gripping her ponytail, pretending to ride her hard from behind. He laughed.

"I'm sorry!" Lizzie said and pulled the door shut. "Shit! Shit!"

She stood alone in the middle of the hall, her heart racing. "Way to make friends. Way to make friends," she said aloud to no one. She was mortified.

The screaming wasn't real. It was an act.

Across the East River, in Manhattan, on Thirty-Sixth and Ninth, Weather was standing on a makeshift stage at the Joel Fox Acting for Actors Studio.

"I'm sorry, Mr. Worthing. You're not on my list of eligible men." In her best British accent, she pretended to consult a clothbound book. "I am quite ready to enter your name, should your answer be what a truly affectionate mother requires."

"Lizzie?" called Ally, interrupting. She had opened the door and cast the light from out in the hall over the stage.

"Excuse me!" cried Joel from somewhere in the dark.

"Lizzie, are you there?" Ally yelled, interrupting again.

"Excuse me, lady, this is a class!" Joel bellowed.

"Is Lizzie Hughes here? Lizzie? It's Mom!"

"Mrs. Hughes?" Onstage, Weather turned, squinting in the stage lights. She was wearing a floor-length pink satin gown, matching pink bonnet, and wire-rimmed glasses.

"Weather?"

"Hi."

"Hi, honey. We need to talk."

"Um, can it wait? I'm in the middle of—"

"No," Ally said, stepping inside. She looked into the dark. She couldn't see Joel, but she knew he was there. "Mr. Fox? Sorry. It's

Allison Hughes. Lizzie's mom. I'm sorry, but it's an emergency. I need Weather for a minute or—"

"Hurry!"

"Thanks," said Ally, leaving the room.

Weather lifted her enormous hoop skirt, stepped off the stage, and followed Ally into the hall.

"Mrs. Hughes—"

"We have a deal," Ally interrupted. "If I call three times, she calls back. She hasn't called. I'm worried sick."

"Mrs. Hughes," Weather said again. "That guy in there, Joel Fox, calls on me, like, once a month. Not once a week like the girls with boobs and toothpick legs, the ballerinas, but once a month. If I'm lucky."

"I know about the porn," Ally said.

Weather's face fell.

"I need a number or an address. Lizzie is missing."

"I can't. I'm sorry. Lizzie would kill me."

"I will kill you!" Ally drew close. "Do you understand how dangerous this is? How stupid this is? To get mixed up with these kinds of people?"

Weather swallowed and drew on her courage. "Do you understand she's *manifesting* her future? Do you understand that Lizzie is a *warrior*?"

Ally squinted. "What are you saying?"

"She's Lara Croft."

"Who is that?"

"You should be impressed. She has a plan."

"And what is the plan when someone holds a gun to her head or drugs her or abducts her?"

"That's not—part of it," Weather said.

"Camming is a *gateway* crime. Do you know what that is?"

"Mrs. Hughes. I have to go back to—"

"Where is she now? She should be here. Acting class, Wednesdays, four o'clock."

"You should know—she's wearing a wig."

"That's the plan? A *wig* is the plan?"

The door opened and Joel popped out. "Are we done?"

"No!" Ally snapped.

He slipped back inside.

Seething, she turned and faced the wall. She tipped her forehead against it and breathed. "*Why* was that actor naked in there?"

In the studio, the six-foot-four actor playing Jack Worthing had, indeed, been standing next to Weather naked, his lanky pale penis resting on his thigh.

"It's the Fox method. It helps inhibition."

"Does it really?" Ally asked. She turned and studied the enormous holes in Weather's ears, stretched by rings three inches wide.

Odd, she thought. Why did this girl from *Scarsdale*, this girl with the face and smile of an angel, why did she look like a Kenyan Maasai? "Weather?" she said. "Was it your idea? This sex-cam thing?"

"No, Mrs. Hughes."

"Was it Lizzie's?"

"No."

"Then whose was it?"

"I can't tell you."

Ally nodded, turned around, and started downstairs. "I'm sorry he calls on you once a month! You're beautiful, honey. Except for the way you torture your ears. Your acting is terrific. You've always had talent. Real talent. Pay no attention to Mr. Fox."

Weather stood there staring at Ally. She didn't say a word.

"Ask her to call her mother, please!" Ally sang with irony. "You know, the woman who fed her and changed her and paid for Duke."

"Mrs. Hughes!"

Ally stopped and turned. "Yes?"

"If you want to know, ask your boyfriend."

"My boyfriend? Who? I don't have a—"

"Ted?"

"Okay," said Ally, mystified.

"It was his idea."

Ally's gaze, fixed on Weather, shifted to the wall, to a poster for *Hair*. Weather blurred as laughter erupted from inside the room. She leaned in to listen, opened the door, and slipped back to class with a small wave.

Ally, however, stood unmoving for more than a minute. Then she turned and went downstairs.

Out on the sidewalk, she speed-dialed Ted.

In Red Hook, in the pantry, Sasha stood over six feet tall, with white-blond hair, side-swept bangs, and naturally, beautifully bloated lips. She was trying to read the directions for the Keurig when Lizzie walked in. "Hello. Hi. How are you doing there in today?" She spoke with a Russian accent.

Lizzie brightened. Hurray, she thought, the Pussy Riot fan! Finally! She said hi in Russian.

Sasha turned around, delighted. "No! Tell me! Do you speak Russian?"

"A little," said Lizzie, again in Russian.

"Oh! You must see this!" Sasha pointed to the Keurig. "Mr. Fishman, he buy this for us. Do you know to how use?"

"No," Lizzie said. "But I can help you . . . figure it out." She strode to the counter to help.

"Very wonderful," Sasha said, peering closer at Lizzie's hair. "Is fake?"

Lizzie smiled. "I'm undercover, *spying.*"

"No!" Sasha gaped. "Police?"

"No!" Lizzie cried. "I have to model in secret, you know, because of my mom." She plugged in the Keurig. "She'd kill me."

Sasha nodded. "Yes," she said.

The Screamer then entered. She now wore a pink robe and slippers. "Hey, stupid," she said to Lizzie and flew to the fridge.

Lizzie spun. "Stupid?" she said. "You called for help." The Screamer laughed and opened the fridge. Lizzie seethed. "You *screamed,* 'Help! Call the police!'"

"It was *fake,*" said the Screamer, cracking open a Dr Pepper. "Fake rape. Everyone loves it." She took a swig.

"Well, it *sounded* real," Lizzie said. "Sorry for trying to save your life."

"He doesn't even penetrate," the Screamer bragged. "He's not even in. He's not even *hard*." She scowled at Lizzie and chucked the soda can into the trash. "Are you coming, Sasha? Tonight? Party?"

"No," Sasha said and turned to Lizzie. "I cannot pay for New York vodka."

The Screamer shrugged, grabbed some SunChips, and walked out the door.

Sasha smiled. "We don't have party for sixteen in Ukraine. We only have pie and clothesline."

"Oh." Lizzie smiled. "Those two dummies should lock the door."

"No," Sasha said, examining a K-Cup. "No one cannot lock nothing here."

An hour later, after coffee and a nice long chat in broken English and broken Russian, Lizzie returned to her fake teen bedroom to call and report her news to Weather. "You're kidding," she said to herself aloud, fretfully searching through her bag.

Had she left it on the bed? The desk? Where? Had she taken out her phone?

Where was her phone?

Then she stopped and gazed at the door, remembering what Sasha had said. She couldn't have locked it if she wanted.

Panicked, she turned her purse upside down and sorted through the items: Kleenex, Band-Aids, pen, shades; novel, headphones, flip-flops, Mace; sunscreen, lip gloss, tampon, Altoids . . .

Her fingers flew as she tried to determine what was gone: her cell phone, house keys, clutch with cash, she decided in seconds; and, oddly, a new pack of Doublemint gum.

She looked up, furious.

Across the East River and uptown, near Gramercy Park, Ally sat on the sidewalk and waited. She waited for calls: a call back from Lizzie, from Ted, from Cybil. She waited to hear from Del Frisco's on Sixth, where Lizzie waitressed. She waited to hear from Lizzie's friends Zoe, Miles, and E.

Nobody called Ally back.

"DO YOU HAVE TEQUILA?" Ally asked, sitting at the bar at Friar Tuck's somewhere out on the Cape. She didn't know where they were.

"Yep, we do." The bartender smiled. "Straight up?"

"No, thanks, no. I never drink." She ordered a frozen margarita instead, no salt, and cheese fries. She leaned on the bar, looked around, and chewed the nail of her pinky finger.

She couldn't see Jake anywhere.

The main room and the two rooms off it were dimly lit and clouded with smoke. Three different jukeboxes blared different songs from three different rooms.

Jefferson Airplane blasted from the closest, and when Ally turned toward the sound of the song, she found Jake sitting one stool away. "Don't you want somebody to love? Don't you need somebody to love?" He was singing along.

Ally looked away and smiled.

He finished the song, the entire song, and the bartender brought out Ally's food. Then Jake slipped to the stool next to hers. "Something about cheese fries and booze," he said. "Once you get going, it's hard to stop." He was speaking in a thick New York accent. He reached out his hand. "Carl. Yastrzemski. Nice to meet you. Folks call me Yaz. I'm a Major League player. Baseball."

Ally focused on the TV. "Hi," she said, ignoring his hand, playing hard to get.

"I didn't catch your name."

"Didn't throw it."

"What's your name, pretty?"

Ally tried to think of one. "Um," she said. "Margaret Thatcher?"

"You don't know your name?"

"This is so weird," she said as herself.

Jake looked around. "What's weird, doll?"

"This," she said. "I can be anyone? Anyone at all? Sappho? Or Esther? Or Joan of Arc?"

"Ally."

"What?" She leaned in and whispered. "I thought we were doing a doctor and nurse, or something like that. But if you get to be a baseball player, then I want to be—I don't know—a queen. Elizabeth the First." She sat up straight. "Elizabeth. Hello."

He reached out his hand. "Nice to meet you, Elizabeth."

"The First." She held out her hand, permitting him to kiss it. Jake took her hand and kissed it gently. "Otherwise known as the Virgin Queen. Although that's ironic."

"What do you do, Elizabeth the First?"

"I rule England *and* Ireland."

"That fun?"

"Yes. I live in a palace, fight wars, and take lovers half my age."
She sipped her margarita.

"Wow. Cool. You here alone?"

"I'm waiting for someone. A duke." She pretended to look for her
duke. "You alone, Yaz?"

"I'm with my team." Jake pointed to a group of guys hovering around
the pool table. "I'm number eight. Seven Gold Gloves. Triple Crown."

"I'm sure that's impressive, but I don't know baseball. Only
hammer throwing."

"Can I steal a fry?" Jake asked, smelling her cheese fries.

"No. I don't share food. Germs and diseases. You know, the
plague. Smallpox. Not good."

Jake nodded. "Right," he said. "We shouldn't swap spit. At least
not yet. You married?"

"No. Only lovers."

"Kids?"

"No," Ally said. She then changed her mind. "Wait, no. I do
have a child. I have a daughter." She didn't want to leave Lizzie out,
even out of her fantasy life. She took a fry and leaned in. Softly she
said, "This isn't working. I'm not turned on."

"Why don't you choose someone sexy?" he whispered.

"Can we start again?"

"Let's start again."

She slid the fries in front of him. "Eat." Jake grabbed a couple
of fries and smiled. "Are you still Yaz?"

"I'm sticking with Yaz."

She picked up her glass and guzzled the drink. Jake watched as she set the glass down and raised her hand to alert the barkeep for another. "I want to be a groupie," she said. "The kind of girl who preys on stars. Give you myself—in every way—in exchange for—I don't know—your attention and bragging rights. I can brag I slept with Yaz. Cool? The truly consensual trade. Sex to impress. The 'I had sex with a supermodel' thing. But in reverse. The 'I can bring this guy down to his knees—Monica Lewinsky and Bill' thing."

Jake nodded. "Good. That's hot."

LIZZIE BARRELED INTO FISHMAN'S office. "Someone stole my stuff!" she announced.

Josh and Fishman sat focused, working. They both looked up and turned around.

"You're kidding," said Fishman. He seemed alarmed but not alarmed enough.

"I went to the pantry, and when I came back my stuff was gone."

"You haven't signed in and you needed a *break*?" Josh asked.

"I was hungry," said Lizzie. She looked at Fishman. "Someone went into my purse in my room." She then looked at Josh, who was staring right at her, pointedly chewing a green piece of gum.

"What's missing?" Fishman asked and stood from his desk.

"My wallet, my keys, and my phone," Lizzie said.

"I'm sorry. It's a problem. I should have warned you." He opened a drawer. "We haven't caught her, but we have a Russian short on cash."

"Sasha? No. She was with me. In the pantry. She was with me."

Fishman handed a MetroCard to Lizzie. "Take this. It doesn't expire until next month." He crossed to his briefcase.

Lizzie watched as he slipped out some bills and pulled out a phone. "Take these." He handed them to her. "Emergency phone, until you get a new one, and here's money to pay for new keys or a lock for your place."

Lizzie took the phone and the fifty-dollar bills, the newest-looking money she'd ever seen, clean and smooth. "Thank you," she said.

"Take your purse," Fishman said. "Even to the bathroom."

Lizzie nodded.

"Anything else we can do to help?"

"No," she said quietly, feeling as if she was being played.

Fishman nodded and sat back down. "Someone's rolling our rooms for sure."

Josh nodded and cracked his gum.

An hour later, Lizzie felt faint in the humid heat. On a Henry Street corner, next to a mailbox, she slipped off her heels, changed into flip-flops, took off her wig, and stuffed it, hard, down into her bag. She then took off through Carroll Gardens, through Cobble Hill, toward Brooklyn Heights.

She knew they'd try to track her with the phone. Powering off would achieve nothing. She put it in flight mode and took out the battery. Then she remembered the second battery, the weaker one, there to maintain contacts and time.

What she needed, she decided, was a booster bag. A Faraday cage. The kind Weather had made with foil when they were twelve, to shoplift; an electromagnetic shield.

She stopped at a market, bought five rolls of foil, and wrapped the phone like a birthday gift until it was the size of a brick.

Ninety minutes later, she reached Pineapple, then Orange, then, finally, Cranberry Street. She climbed the stoop, knocked, but found the brownstone empty and dark. Her spare key was home in Stuyvesant Square.

So she headed east and hoofed it over the Brooklyn Bridge, watching the golden sun dip west.

When she got home, she discovered her superintendent was gone, in the DR, and wouldn't be back for another day. No one but Julio had a spare key.

Ally had spent the afternoon there, across the street. At nine thirty, she got up and left. She missed Lizzie, and Lizzie missed her mother, by less than five minutes.

That night at eleven, Ally, at home, climbed into an Escalade. Jake's car. The driver dropped her at Tenth and Sixteenth at a hotel in the Meatpacking District.

She checked the address and wandered in and waited in the lobby behind two women who looked like models.

One was over six feet tall, in a Sid Vicious T-shirt, four-inch shorts, and stiletto heels. She also wore a mink-fur vest and striped ski hat with a pom-pom on top. Odd for August, thought Ally, but cute.

The other one wore a T-shirt too, except hers was ripped. She didn't wear shorts or a skirt or pants. She did wear a thong, so the bottom of her butt cheeks peeked from her shirt when she laughed or bent over, and Ally thought she looked ready for bed. Then, she thought, maybe that was the point.

When she stepped up, the concierge winked. "Love the look. So uncommitted."

Ally looked down. What was she wearing that was so uncommitted?

Tretorns. Jeans. A button-down shirt in a yellow and pink floral print. The blouse, she thought, might pass for Liberty, except that she bought it for three ninety-nine on sale at Old Navy. The cotton was sheer, the buttons were plastic, the hems were fraying.

"Hunt Club, love. That's downstairs." The concierge pointed to a door across the lobby with a tiny brass sign. It read, "The Hunt Starts Here."

Ally didn't know about the separate entrance that led to a hall to a secret door that led to a second secret door that led to a bouncer and a red velvet rope, and a guest list, then down a stone stairway that spiraled around and stopped in front of a gold beaded curtain in the corner of the basement.

She finally found Jake and Marty tucked behind a table, shouting to talk over bottles of Patrón. The music was loud and thumping and grating. Apparently it was Hip-Hop Wednesday.

"The unsung American teenage girl!" Jake called to Marty, handing him the extra-long script. "It's totally new! Never been done! These girls, they started a revolution! And they wore clothes!"

"Talk to me!" Marty called and popped dried wasabi peas into his mouth. Marty was known for his films about men: men and gangs, men and sex, men and money.

"It starts with the fire!" Ally yelled over the table. "We see the girls jump from the ninth floor and die! The city wakes up! One girl survives and fights the good fight: Safer conditions! Eight-hour workdays! Overtime pay! Show the whole trial!" Ally looked down and drained her shot, then turned to Jake. "Do you show the trial?" She shuddered and her insides grew warm. Jake shook his head.

"What's the trial?" Marty yelled because he had to. "Is that the third act?"

The music grew louder.

"What's a third act?" Ally yelled. The DJ in the corner was blasting his favorite Kanye West, a song about hoes and shoving his fist into Asian pussy. Jake refilled Ally's glass. "No more!" she yelled. "I never drink!" Then she grew still.

"The third act is the last part," Jake explained, turning to Ally. She didn't hear him. She saw someone . . . or thought she did. She froze and focused across the bar as if she were a lioness spotting prey.

"Is that the third act? The trial?" Marty asked.

"Is that Lizzie's agent?" Ally said.

"Cybil Stern?" Jake turned, scanning the crowd. "Which?"

"The one in black? We met last Christmas." Ally straightened. "I'm sorry. Hold on a sec." She slid from her seat. "Maybe she knows . . . where Lizzie is."

Marty looked concerned. "Everything okay?"

Ally paused. "She told my daughter to fix her nose and dye her hair." She couldn't take her eyes off Cybil.

"Ally, wait," Jake pleaded as Ally straightened her Old Navy blouse, looking ready for a fight.

"And lose thirty pounds and skip grad school."

"Ally, come on." Jake reached out as she walked off. He tried to follow but found himself wedged behind the table. "Ally!"

Cybil was sipping a Virgin Slut. She and the models from up in the lobby chatted in a circle out on the dance floor, crushed by the sweaty, rowdy crowd.

"Now she's doing this cam-girl thing! To make money—to get this procedure—that *you* recommended!"

"Me? No!" Cybil yelled over the hip-hop. "*I* recommended? No, Mrs. Hughes!"

"You didn't?" said Ally.

"Lizzie with a nose job? That's nuts!"

"Really?" said Ally, realizing Lizzie had lied to her. "Can you call her then? And knock some sense into— Whoa! Whoa!" A man squeezing by—an enormous man, over six feet tall and three hundred pounds—bumped into Ally. "Sorry!" he said as Ally caromed, hard, into Cybil, who then knocked into a woman behind her. The woman fell forward onto her friends, then righted, turned, and yelled, "Scumbag, bitch! Motherfucker!"

"Sorry!" yelled Cybil, meaning it, as the dancers circled her irritably.

"Sorry? Sorry? I'll fuck you up!"

Swiftly, and instinctively, Ally and the models stepped in and formed a line of defense.

"I got pushed," Ally said. "I bumped into her. She bumped into you. It was my fault. Sorry."

"Who the fuck are you?"

"No one," said Ally. "I'm no one at all."

"I'll fuck you up."

Holy smokes, Ally thought, as she considered the gauntlet thrown down. I'll fuck you up. Did that mean fight?

Suddenly she was in one of those shows: the catfight shows with the housewives or sisters or someone's ex-wives; women with blowouts, in heels and makeup, in shift dresses, bickering. Except no one here, tonight at the club, was fully dressed. Bras and pajama shorts, Ally thought as she studied the girls; and truck driver hats. At least they were keeping the sun off their skin. She didn't want to fight. She wanted to dress them and put them to bed.

"Motherfucking bitch," the woman said.

Ally raised her hands, palms out, in surrender. "We're not fighting! This is— She didn't *mean* to bump you! Really! I swear! Come on! We're friends! We're all women! We're on the same side! Right? Right?"

Ally had never been smacked before.

She'd never been slapped or shoved or punched.

The seconds flew as a blur of screams and limbs and pain, scratching and clawing and lights, as swearwords were screeched and clothes were ripped and stretched and pulled. Ally was yelling "Stop! Stop!" above the music and cheers and jeers from all sides. Partyers stopped and whipped out their camera phones, laughing, pointing.

"What the—? Please!" She tried her best to budge from Jake's grip as he lifted her out of the scuffle. "I'm in the middle of a—"

Jake threw his arms around her waist and carried her off through the throng. "Ow! Hey!" she said, protesting. "Stop!"

"They're on coke! Stop squirming!"

"What?" Ally said.

He led her into a short dark hall, where they stopped for a moment and caught their breath. "How should I know?" Ally complained.

"Oh, I don't know. The dilated eyes? The fine white powder above their lips?" Jake tried the restrooms, but both were locked. "What happened? Are you okay? Were you and Cybil on the same side?"

"Nothing!" she said and looked away. "We all got bumped and they got mad! I got smacked . . . I think . . . my jaw." Ally felt the side of her face.

"Are you hurt?" He leaned in to see her chin.

"Coke? Really?" No one Ally knew used cocaine at Brooklyn College or at Brown. Wine was popular, vodka, for sure, lattes and chocolate and Skittles abounded, Colace and Advil, but no one she knew used hard drugs. "That was— What are we *doing* here, Jake?" She smoothed her blouse and touched a tiny scratch on her hand. She wrung out her wrist.

"It looks okay," Jake said.

She looked at the ceiling. "What is this music?" She rubbed her eyes. "I can't believe . . . They jumped us! Girls!" Someone in the bathroom was smoking something. "What is that *smell*?"

Jake looked concerned. "It's so good to see you. Can I say that? I'm sorry you— This. This is my fault. I'm sorry."

"Say it."

"Thanks. It's so good to see you."

"I need a cab."

"Does it hurt? Your face?" He reached out and touched it.

"It's fine, but this music, it makes me want to—"

"What? Makes you want to what?"

"Curl up and die."

They rode in the Escalade back to Brooklyn.

"We didn't say good-bye," Ally said. "That was rude."

"Don't worry. I texted. He texted me back."

"I didn't get to—"

"I did," Jake reassured her. "We talked about it before you came. He said he would call her, Marty did, and talk her out of it."

Ally gazed at the twinkling lights on the East River. She pressed an ice cube against her jaw. "*Lizzie* wants it herself," she said sadly, wondering if it was only a phase. "Not Cybil. But maybe—maybe— if we make her wait. Just long enough. She'll change her mind. It's happened before." Like her obsession with eyeliner, black. That lasted only half of ninth grade. And Ally's obsession with Dave Matthews. That lasted only half of her twenties.

"She can only live the way people *expect*—for so long."

"What?"

"Before she settles back into default: her true self. And starts to do what she's meant to do . . ."

"And what's that?"

"I don't know."

Lizzie was gorgeous. Always. Tall. Lanky. Like Claire, she had an impossible figure: narrow shoulders, small waist and hips, full bust. And legs that started below her ribs and went on and on.

Friends, teachers, everyone, assumed she'd make her mark in front of a camera because she *could*.

But what would become of that pesky IQ? That 143? The Mensa invitation? The Johns Hopkins people, the giftedness researchers, nosing about?

"You know," Jake offered, "it's okay if Lizzie's not perfect."

Ally turned to him. "What do you mean?"

"She knows, you know, that she was an oops. She told me that."

"And?"

"I'm sure you don't agree, but—"

"I don't," Ally snapped. "She wasn't a mistake. I think *chance* plays a role in this life."

"That's not—"

"The universe—God, whatever—makes plans that sometimes have nothing to do with our own."

"Okay," Jake said, "but you don't have to *prove*—she doesn't have to be the most perfect person ever born to prove she wasn't a mistake."

She studied him a moment. She knew he was right. Her eyes grew cool and she pressed her lips together and then released them. She looked out the window. "I don't know what you're talking about."

"Yes, you do."

She gazed at the river, the Brooklyn skyline. "Someone sent gifts. Was it you?"

"Maybe. What if it was?"

Ally said nothing.

"How is your face?"

The Escalade pulled up to the brownstone. Ally climbed out and walked toward the stoop, fishing for her keys at the bottom of her purse.

Jake followed. "Are you okay?"

"Fine," she said.

"I only have two more days in town."

She climbed the stoop, tipsy, jaw aching, hardly hearing him. "Where are my—?"

Jake stood at the bottom and waited. "By the way. Your friend, Ted?"

Ally looked up. What about him?

"That toy company? I made some calls. It's pretty sketch."

She found her keys. "Sketch?"

"The guys who run it."

"How are they sketch?" She thought of what Weather had told her. "Like what?"

"I don't know. That's what I heard."

Ally turned and unlocked the door.

Jake stayed and watched. "If you need me, I'm at the St. Regis."

"Are you?" she said and turned again, before she went in. "I tried you there. They said you weren't."

"Try again, Ally," Jake said and smiled. "Please. Try again."

AT MIDNIGHT, A WEDDING party arrived, two dozen revelers, drunk, post-reception, including the bride. Ally and Jake joined them in singing "Don't Stop Believin'," a full-bar rendition, and Ally thought she might burst from joy. Jake excused himself to the restroom, and Ally wandered over to the dartboard to get a closer view of the bride.

The dress was magnificent, Ally thought. The perfect white. A cool ivory, to match the bride's pale freckled skin. The bodice was embroidered in pearl and lace. The waist was high, with a beaded sash, and the layered tulle skirt swept across the sawdust floor. "It's beautiful," Ally said breathlessly, feeling tipsy. "You look beautiful."

The bride smiled. "Thank you," she said and aimed her dart. As it flew from her fingers, the groom swept in, lifted her up, and carried her off to dance to the song playing on the jukebox. Eric Clapton, Ally thought. Wonderful.

She sighed and peered around the room. Where was Jake? Alone, she felt that feeling again, that sad-single-woman-at-the-wedding feeling, the one she'd endured twice a year for a decade; there it was again, the sinking moment of humiliation when everyone seated at the table rose, all but Ally; they all took flight, off to the dance floor, because the band had broken into "Brown Eyed Girl" or "Walk This Way" or "Play That Funky Music" . . . again.

Again.

And, again, Ally would reach for her clutch, push back, rise, and beeline to the bathroom, somewhere, anywhere, quiet, to call Claire and check on Lizzie. "Did she eat? How is she?" And Lizzie was fine. Always fine.

"Can I have this dance?" Jake said, breaking her reverie. Oh, right. She wasn't alone. Jake was back. "The bride is pretty." Ally nodded. "Pretty dress. You would look pretty in a dress like that." Ally rolled her eyes and sighed as he pulled her close and wrapped his arms around her waist. "You'd make a pretty, pretty bride." She wrapped her wrists around his neck, and they danced and danced, next to the darts.

"Hey, Yaz?"

"Hey what?"

"You have plans?"

"Not really."

At quarter past two, heavy limbed and happy, Ally made her way to the door. One step in front of the other, she thought, with Jake on her heels. Walk straight. Keep your head high. Look forward. He's right behind you.

The room was tilting. Then it was spinning.

That is the door, she reminded herself. Walk toward the door. It will take you outside.

"Drive me home?" Ally said, out in the lot. Jake was a few yards behind. "Want to? Want to, Yaz?"

"Yep," he said. "I do. Want to."

The night was black, streaked with patches of red and gold light. The air was warm and salty and fresh. The pebbles crunched under their shoes as they walked toward Jake's car in the corner of the lot.

"That's it there." She pointed to the Chevy. Jake caught up and wove his fingers through her fingers.

Quiet for a moment, they strolled and gazed at the stars.

At the Chevy, Ally stopped and searched for Jake's keys in the bottom of her purse. She found them finally, pulled them out, and lobbed them to him. The keys flew high and left and wide, but Jake jumped easily and caught them in midair.

"Nice catch," she said.

"Shitty throw."

"Sorry, Yaz," she said, not a bit sorry. She circled the bumper.

Jake smiled and unlocked the door. He held it open as she climbed in, and then he shut it carefully.

Inside the Chevy, Ally pulled on her seat belt, managed to insert it and lock it, ready. She sat there and waited, patient and demure, for Jake to take her home.

Jake climbed in, shut his door, and slipped his key in the ignition. He turned on the radio to some station's all-Zeppelin Saturday night, turned to Ally, and unclipped her belt. He caught the belt so it didn't snap back, then reached and returned it over her body and back to its starting place.

"What are you doing?" Ally asked.

He didn't answer. He locked the doors and killed the head-lights, and in one swift motion and before Ally knew it, they were madly kissing across the console, the Zeppelin blasting.

The tight quarters, protruding knobs, gearshift, and steering wheel forced them to squeeze, collapse, and meld, and quickly the windows were fogged and opaque.

After some minutes, Ally straddled him and pushed back his seat. Slowly she released him from his button-down shirt, kissing his neck and chest as she did. She wanted him to trust her, to let himself go, to own her for the moment, like he'd said. "Let's let tonight be about you," she whispered in his ear, grinding into him, pressing her elbows into his shoulders, kissing his forehead, pulling his hair. "You, you, you." She now knew his body the way he knew hers.

She pulled back, shimmied from her dress straps, moved her arms through them, and yanked the sundress down around her waist. Braless, she lifted her breasts toward his mouth. She plunged her hips into his, arched back, then pushed him back and found his bare chest. She sucked and gnawed and licked and bit as Jake let out a ravenous cry of pain and pleasure. "Shit!" he yelled above the music.

Then she leaned back, lifted herself, and unbuttoned his jeans. She pulled down his zipper between her legs and pulled down his jeans as Jake lifted up. She tugged down his briefs and left them at his shins, below his knees, restraining his movement.

Capturing him.

She reached for the condom in Jake's hand, then lifted him out from between his thighs, encircled her hands firmly around him, and pressed on the floor of the car with her feet.

With her teeth, she tore the wrapper, and quickly, in an instant, in a second in the dark, she unfurled and tugged the sheath over him tight.

Jake watched and placed his hands on Ally's waist.

Slowly he lowered her, down and toward him, into a deep, deep kiss. A kiss that felt like sex itself. He wrapped his arms around her, pulled her in tight, but she pulled out of his embrace. She held him erect, straight in the air and stood, legs apart, until her head reached the roof of the car.

As she did this, Jake mouthed her breasts, found her ass with his hands, shaped and worked it, plying and smacking and spreading her out and then back in.

Ally lowered herself to his tip. She touched him there quickly, then pulled up sharply, thrusting her breasts back into his face.

He gripped them with his hands and closed his mouth over them. Finding her nipples, back and forth, he sucked and chewed and pulled and sucked as Ally lowered toward him again. She allowed him entrance and then rescinded the invitation.

Up and down, they both endured this for an hour. An excruciating, innervating hour. Ally, in control, circling, taking Jake in, but only barely, then pulling up, pretending to change her mind, to tease him.

Jake was grabbing, gnawing, sucking, her shoulders, neck, nipples. He groaned and heaved and squirmed as she plundered him over and over, and soon he felt angry and hostile with desire.

Ally could sense he had let himself go. He was finally tense and gripping and pained. "Wait, wait!" she cried. "I want to be me!"

"What?" Jake said, looking into her eyes.

"I want to be me again! Please!" Ally begged.

"Ally! You are! You are you!" he said.

Ally looked down at him, realizing this, and kissed him and laughed.

Jake laughed too, and couldn't resist her anymore. He cried out, "Fuck!" and wrapped his forearms around her back. Reaching his hands up over her shoulders, he pulled Ally down with such savage force and thrust so hard, she thought she might burst.

Harder and harder, deeper and deeper, he thrust and gripped and held her in place as if he was a vise.

He pounded and struck and crashed into Ally with ferocious abandon.

In his grip, she lost her breath. She writhed and struggled as Jake fought and sealed her, airtight around him.

The car disappeared. The world disappeared as he pummeled her, greedy, awash in sweat, ravenous, and savage, and finally, his whole body seized and he came and came and came—he shook and shuddered and came into the condom, tense and thrilled and crying out.

Ally smiled, filled with joy, as he released her, and seconds later they both collapsed in a soaking-wet heap.

Jake looked up at her, into her eyes. He reached up and held the sides of her face. She held his. He peppered her with kisses as his whole body seemed to exhale with relief. They started to laugh and Jake then to cry, and Ally kissed him tenderly.

ON THURSDAY MORNING AT nine o'clock, Ally awoke with a throbbing head. She stayed in bed for half an hour and texted Ted. He didn't text back. She called him twice and twice he allowed her to roll to his voice mail.

She sat in the kitchen, sipping coffee, feeling laden by the actual cup. The coffee cup. It wasn't hers. It was Claire's. Claire's china. Her wedding china. The table was Claire's. Everything in the kitchen was Claire's.

Practically.

Maybe Ted was right, she thought, gazing at the mug.

Maybe she should go. On a trip. Get out of Brooklyn. Out of the brownstone. Maybe she'd sell it. And if she didn't, maybe she'd sell everything in it and start fresh. Rid the walls and floors of the smell, that mild stench of secondhand smoke. Peel off the wallpaper. Update the millwork. Repaint. Refurnish.

Claire had fallen apart in those rooms after all. When Ally was six. When Eugene died. Ally's dad.

For months and years, she'd stepped through the motions of daily life, body in, but heart out, of the real world.

For a year, she told Ally, she wondered if she'd been married at all. The marriage had felt like a dream, she said. Eugene himself felt like a dream.

Until Ally appeared again: home from school, or just woken up, her face his. She reminded Claire he had been real.

He had been real. He had been there. And then he wasn't.

Ally's face had his valentine shape. She'd grown his nose, and her large round eyes and smile were his.

Claire's genes had skipped Ally and taken root in Lizzie. Lizzie's height, figure, ringlets: Claire's. Claire's nose, elegant, pronounced. The nose of a queen, a real-live woman. Not the nose of a child or a doll.

She spoke to him daily, Ally recalled, sitting there by herself. "You can come home now," Claire said to the air. Ally would listen sometimes. "Gone long enough, Eugene. Now. It's time to come home."

"Who are you talking to?"

Claire denied it. I'm talking to myself, she'd said to Ally. It helped her think.

She drank and smoked and drank some more, and one day announced, "This is our fourth. August without him. Our fourth August first."

Every day was a new day without Eugene.

Week by week, month by month, his things, his effects, disappeared. Ally would look for his glasses, his hat, but Claire put everything into a bedroom on the fourth floor and locked it with a key.

First his papers, wallets, shoes. His books. Then scarves and winter coats, galoshes, gloves. His backgammon set, chess, records, even *Abbey Road*, which they all had listened to and loved.

The door was locked and never opened. Not, at least, in Ally's presence.

It had been her sitter, Setta, who'd left the tiny violin. At the ballet class. Inside the dressing room. Under the bench.

Claire had been annoyed, but Eugene had calmed her down on the phone. It was no problem at all, he said, to swing by ballet on his way back from work. Nothing, for Gene, merited a fuss. But, of course, if he'd driven home that day, from Broad Street to Broadway and over the bridge, he wouldn't have turned onto Tillary Street, to fetch the forgotten violin, Ally's, and the legally blind man wouldn't have struck him.

When they returned from California, Claire fired the sitter and bedtime vanished. Ally put herself to sleep when she wanted to sleep. Claire resigned from cooking breakfast: eggs, oatmeal, anything warm. She served only yogurt and glasses of milk. Or only milk.

Ally was welcome to pour herself cereal, Claire said. And so she did. She learned to contend with the cold gallon jug, heaved it and tipped it and kept it from spilling. She taught herself to cook and bake and wash.

"Well," Claire said, "our life will be perfect. Now. It can't get worse."

Ally watched her light a Parliament, inhale deeply, and exhale slowly, sending the secondhand smoke toward the sky, as if she were blowing it into God's face.

She never talked about Ally's dad. She never talked about marriage or love or sex at all.

Well, *once*, Ally thought. There was that once.

"I'll only say this," Claire said.

"Please don't. Here." Ally was standing in her cinder-block room in New South dorm on her first day of school. First hour. Georgetown.

Claire, legs crossed, sat on Ally's new dorm bed, tapping her knee with a cigarette lighter. "*One* thing. Come on. One thing."

"My *roommate* will be here *any*—"

"Sex is not love. Love is not sex."

Ally turned and carried her clothes from the bed to the drawers. "Great. Terrific."

"Love is what happens when sex ends."

"Thanks. Okay. I'll keep that in mind."

"If you ask me—"

"But I *didn't* ask."

"Do not have sex—until you make sure—you can love him without it."

"Now I know!"

"I knew I could. Love your dad. When the sex stopped. He was fun. If he's fun, then go right ahead. All right?"

"All right! I'm so glad we did this! Done?" The door opened wide. Thankfully. "Nanda!" Ally cried with too much relief.

"Hi," Nanda said with big, sad eyes, lifting her purse strap over her head. The anorexic, Ally said to Anna that night on the phone. From Bombay, she said. But better than Claire! Nanda's parents had entered too, jet-lagged, and when Claire rose to greet them, she stealthily switched her cigarette lighter to her left hand.

Ted was right, Ally thought, sitting there. It was the house. This house. She had to get out. Lizzie had. She checked her phone. He hadn't called back.

At three, another rainstorm rolled in. Ally could smell it when she left Brooklyn. The gray sky carried a soft, whipping wind. Thunder rumbled in the distance.

As the torrent discharged, she started to run along Canal. As she arrived, so did Mac, from Apartment 1 on the ground floor.

Mac had turned ninety the day before. A Korean War vet and consummate gentleman, he caught sight of Ally running toward the door and kindly held it open for her.

"Thank you," she said, slipping inside, looking drowned.

"Too late, I think," Mac said and smiled.

She dripped from her elbows, fingertips, nose. "Better late than never." She turned and climbed the fire stairs.

Breathless and upset, she pushed through the door on the fourth floor, turned a corner, and bumped into Teddy taking out the trash.

"Listen, Ally, I'm walking out. Got a meeting uptown in ten. I'm already late." He led her inside to dry off. "Stay right there. I'll get you a— Do you want clothes? Dry clothes?" He went to the bathroom to find her a towel.

"But why would Weather say that? Why?"

"The weird one? The fat girl?"

"She's not that fat, and she's Lizzie's best friend!"

"Maybe she's lying!"

"Why would she lie?"

He didn't answer. Ally stood there, looked around, and shivered. The AC was blasting. Seconds later, Ted returned, walking briskly. He handed her a towel. "She knows Lizzie hates me."

"Lizzie doesn't hate you."

"Yes, she does."

"No, she doesn't. She has—she has daddy issues. And she's *protective*."

"Of what?"

"Of me."

"That's true." He glanced at his watch. "I've got to go—you want to stay and dry off?"

"No." Ally dried her face with the towel and took a deep breath. "I just can't *believe* Lizzie would do this. Yuck, this is wet. This towel is wet." She handed it back. "It smells weird. Like puke."

Ted took the towel. "It's all I've got!" He chucked it behind him onto the couch.

"Why are you *yelling*?"

"Sorry! I'm stressed! I have to be at Fiftieth and Sixth in ten minutes. Team from Hong Kong." He took Ally's elbow and led her to the door. "I'll call you after? Want to get dinner? ABC? NoMad?"

"No," Ally said, peeling away from him toward the kitchen. "You understand she's my *child*?"

"She's not a *child*."

"I want to get to the bottom of this. I need paper towels."

"She's not a child. She's twenty years old." He glanced again nervously at his watch.

Ally moved from the sink to the cabinets. "I said *my* child. Not *a* child. She's ruining her life, and Weather said it was your idea." She couldn't find a paper product. "Do you have a napkin or dishcloth?"

"She's not ruining her—" He crossed to his desk. "Plenty of women pose for—*Playboy*—and do great."

"Like who?" Ally said, checking the cabinets for something absorbent.

"Singers. Actresses. That's what she wants." He locked his briefcase and grabbed his phone.

"Meryl Streep posed for *Playboy*?"

"I don't know, but I'm sure she's been naked. They *all* do it. Girls these days, they don't lead with the old-school thing. The man-hating thing. Like you." He headed toward her, briefcase in hand. "They lead—like Lizzie said at dinner—with sex. Sex sells."

Ally turned. "I don't hate men."

"What I mean is, she's not—conservative—like you. She's not a—prude." He looked around the kitchen. "I don't have napkins."

Ally recoiled. Affronted, her mouth fell open. "I'm not a *prude*."

He gave her a look. "I'm not saying it's not charming—can we go?"

"Just because I don't sleep with *you*—that doesn't make me a prude."

"Okay, wrong word. But we need to leave, Ally. Now." Again, he led her off, leaving behind a puddle of rain as if she'd peed. "You have to let her live her life." At the front door, he stepped into the closet and searched for a jacket to wear in the rain.

"Who says? Dr. Phil?"

He found a slicker and slipped into it. "She's out of school. She has her own place. You need to let go." He grabbed an umbrella. "You need an umbrella?"

Ally stood there, studying him. "That is—that is just some—solipsistic—*bullshit* truism." She felt defensive. "I don't have to let her go—or fly—or be free. In fact, I plan to stay in her face for the rest of her life. And if she doesn't thank me now, she will, because she will *know* that she was *loved*."

"Oh, really?" He slipped into loafers. "Fine."

"Fine? Oh, is it fine? I wasn't asking for your permission."

He opened the door. "Keep her in a tower the rest of her life."

Ally walked out into the hall. "Life is not some Sting song," she said, and as she did a pretty young woman stepped from the elevator.

The woman saw Ally and stopped in her tracks, looking trapped.

"Hello," said Ally.

The woman looked confused and gripped the lapel of her Burberry trench with her free hand. "Is Ted here?"

"Yeah. He's right—"

"I'm right here." Teddy stepped out and closed the door. "Simone, Ally. Ally, Simone."

"Hi," Ally said again and waved.

Simone turned and looked at the elevator. She pressed the down button a few times, as if she couldn't flee fast enough.

Ted locked his door. "Simone's an intern for Bunny this summer. Bunny Dunn? You know her, Ally? She did my loft?"

Ally nodded. "I know *of* her."

"We're doing the bathroom. You have the tile? Simone? Did you bring the tile?" He looked at Simone. She shook her head. "I'm leaving. I thought you were coming tomorrow."

"I was nearby," she said unsurely.

Ally walked toward her. She couldn't help it. She eyed Simone's suit—chic, pink—her tight pencil skirt and calf-print stilettos and thick lipstick. Her boobs, Ally thought, were impossibly high. She could model like Lizzie. Absolute stunner.

Ah, to be young.

In silence, they all rode the elevator down.

In silence they stepped out under the awning. Then Ted panicked. "Damn! I forgot a fucking—damn! Ally, money for a cab? I have to—run back in."

"No," Ally said. "I'll take the train."

"Simone? Money?"

"No."

"Back in the morning?"

"Sure," Simone said.

"Nine or so, and bring the tile."

Simone nodded.

"Ally," said Ted, stepping in close. "I want to finish— I got a house in South Hampton, all right? Six bedrooms. Not that we need them." She didn't respond. Then he whispered, "I'm sorry. I didn't mean *prude*. I meant uptight." He kissed her on the cheek and went back inside.

Ally turned toward the lobby for a moment. She watched him as he went up the stairs. She then turned around. It was still pouring.

Simone stood with her under the canopy, both deciding to wait out the rain.

They didn't speak.

Then Ally said, "I know you're with him. In some way. It's fine."

She stared straight ahead. "Dating. Whatever. We're not—exclusive."
She turned to Simone. "I saw your face. How panicked you looked.
Don't worry. Bunny Dunn? You're lucky. She's talented. Best of luck."

Simone said nothing.

Ally kept rambling. "My daughter's your age. Just out of Duke.
It's a hard time. After school." She looked at Simone. "Where do
you go?"

Simone looked at Ally. "I'm not a student."

"Oh, you're not? Did you graduate? The intern thing is such a
mess. They get you for free? It's so unfair."

"No, ma'am. I'm not an intern."

"Oh," Ally said, surprised. "What are you?"

"I'm a hooker."

"Oh!" Ally said, and her gaze moved high and fell on a streetlamp.
She didn't move. She stood there, feeling her heart gaining speed.
Then her right hand drifted to her face. She rubbed her eye, then
her cheek and smiled.

"You think it's funny?" Simone said.

"No," Ally said apologetically. "No, I don't." She ran her hand
through her wet hair.

"You won't say I told you?"

"No, no. It's our secret."

Simone nodded. "That kind of man, they don't change. I know
another girl, works for him, too. Three times a week. He's a no-condom
man. He's got the cash. I thought you should know."

"Yes," Ally said, blinking and stunned. "No, and he does. He has
the cash."

A no-condom man?

"The man is an addict," Simone continued. "And I'm telling you because . . . you seem like a nice lady. How could you know? Wives never know." She looked at the sky.

"I did," Ally said. "I knew." Then she turned to her. "Simone, honey. I teach. Gender Studies. Brooklyn College."

Simone nodded. "Yeah? So what?"

"I can help you—find a good job."

"I got one," said Simone. "And you're all wet, so what are you waiting for?"

Indeed, Ally was soaked through. She nodded.

"I just thought—between women. You know?"

Ally said, "Yes. Between women. Thank you." She then stepped out into the pouring rain.

A few blocks later, she started to jog. Then she ran, arms raised, fists clenched, cheering aloud and celebrating. Then she slowed down and caught her breath.

How do you ever know someone? All this deception. All these secrets. All these roles we play.

She wondered.

She'd never counted Ted's freckles. He'd never counted hers. He'd never even asked.

She hailed a cab at Houston and Bowery.

"Fifty-Fourth and Fifth, please," she said to the driver. "The St. Regis."

FOR MINUTES ALLY SAT with her legs splayed, Jake still inside her. She nuzzled his jaw, his cheeks, his nose. She felt as if she loved this man. At least she loved making love to this man.

Their faces were red and flushed with perspiration, their bodies coated as if they'd been dipped in warm oil and water. Skin slipped on skin, sweat trickled down between Ally's breasts and from Jake's hairline next to his temples.

Finally, she pushed off the seat back and lifted up slowly. He hadn't lost form and was still strong and hard as Ally rose off him, contracting around him.

Finally separate, she bent her right knee, pulled it between them, and managed to place her right foot on the passenger seat. With Jake supporting her waist with his hands, she moved there and spun on the balls of her feet.

Jake then rolled the condom off, toward the tip, where it was full.

Silent and fixated, Ally watched with a drunken, comic reverence as he carefully knotted the end of the sheath.

When he was finished he held it in the air, exhausted and smiling. "What should we do with it?"

Ally stared at it silently. The power—the potential—in that little sack was limitless, she thought in her tipsy stupor. The tiniest drop could initiate events. Important events. World-changing events. Little miracles. One little sperm made Gandhi, she thought. Marie Curie. Another made Bach. Another made Mozart. Vincent van Gogh. Amelia Earhart. Others made Einstein and Martin Luther King. Others made Pol Pot and Sacagawea. And Lizzie.

Sex was incredible, Ally thought, staring at the bulging condom. But sometimes, all that stood between sex—between sex and creating a person was this water balloon made from polymer particles, wrapped in foil the shape of a Triscuit.

"We should—give them a funeral," Ally whispered in a sympathetic voice, only half kidding. "They thought they had a journey ahead of them. They thought they were headed for big things." She smiled ruefully. "Didn't we all?" She reached out her hand. "Give them to me."

Jake handed the sack to her. She carefully placed it on the floor where her feet would have been if they weren't beneath her, as Jake rolled down his window to let in some air, lifted his ass, and pulled up his briefs. They were down around his shins, and his jeans were too. She had pinned him there, trussed him like a turkey or a bad little boy confined to his seat. "Hold on a sec. Hold on, Al," he said, with his shins freed, jeans pulled up.

He killed the ignition and took out the keys.

She watched him climb out into the night, circle the car, to the back, to the trunk.

When he returned, he stood at the door, wiping his face with a dry towel. He leaned in and handed another towel to Ally.

She wiped her face too, her neck, inner thighs, and when she was done, she handed the towel to Jake, who wiped down the back of the driver's seat with it. He then threw both towels over the seat into the back and climbed out again.

There on the gravel, he scooped up the bedding he'd grabbed from the trunk: sleeping bag, comforter, a pillow from his dorm. He was taking it home.

He climbed back inside and shoved the whole bundle over the console. "Make a little room."

"What are you doing?"

"Making you a bed . . ." He arranged the blankets, prodding and molding them until they formed a nest.

"You're a dream," Ally said as she nestled into it, closing her eyes, curling up into a fetal position.

Jake pulled on his shirt, closed the door, pulled on his seat belt, started the car, and rolled down the windows, all four. He killed the radio and backed from the lot.

The night was quiet and dark and still as he drove off, and Ally drifted to sleep.

All she could hear was the faint breezy hum, the wind of the drive, and the full-throated peeping, the comforting bleat of late-spring crickets. All she could feel, wrapped around her bare ankles, was Jake's strong hand.

THE DRIVER REGARDED HER in the rearview.

Ally gazed back at him through the reflection. Her chest was heaving, her nose was red, and her eyes were moist. She was wet through and through and elated and upset at the same time.

The driver turned and reached to his right, then reached back to Ally, over the divider, and handed her something.

The towel was pink and clean and dry. Bath size.

"Thank you," she whispered. She could barely speak. She dried her arms and wiped her face. The threads were soft and smelled like detergent. "Thank you so much," she said again.

The cabbie nodded and looked concerned. "You want heat?" he asked kindly, with some sort of accent she couldn't place.

"Thank you."

"NPR?"

"No, thanks. Thank you for asking."

The driver nodded and looked ahead to offer her privacy. The light turned green. Slowly and carefully, he headed uptown.

She dialed the St. Regis. When the operator answered, she asked for Jake Bean.

After placing her on hold, the operator said, "I'm sorry, ma'am. But no one is registered under that name."

"Oh, I'm sorry," Ally replied, remembering again. "Noah. Noah. Noah Bean. Like the legume. Or the vegetable. If it's a green bean." She took a breath and bit her lower lip. Why was she rambling? She felt so foolish for so many reasons.

"Hold on, ma'am." A moment passed. "I'm so sorry. There's no reservation under that name either."

Ally rubbed her forehead in frustration. Had Jake left? Changed hotels? She took a deep breath and thought about it. Where did he go? Would he have called to say he moved? Went back to LA?

Then she remembered. "Yastrzemski," Ally said. "Carl. Carl Yastrzemski."

"One moment, please," the operator said and connected Ally immediately.

JAKE PARKED THE CHEVY across from the house. He killed the headlights and then the engine, and Ally, dozing, opened her eyes.

"Home," he said.

She sat up slowly and looked left, gazing past him, out the window. "Oh no," she said, rubbing her eyes, blinking awake. "That was dumb."

"What?"

"I didn't turn . . . a lamp on inside . . . or the light on the porch."

Jake turned his head and looked at the house.

"Look. It's so dark." The streetlamps stood on the two outer sides of the neighboring houses, left and right, so Ally's, in fact, was shrouded in darkness. "I hate coming home to an empty house." The windows were black and the porch in shadow.

"You scared?" Jake asked and looked at her.

Ally inhaled a long, deep breath, sitting there still. "I'm always scared," she admitted to him. "I'm never not scared." Then they locked eyes. "I haven't slept through the night in ten years."

Jake studied her. "Come on. Let's go."

They went up the steps to the front porch, and Ally paused. She spotted a truck parked down the block. "That's never there," she whispered, alarmed.

"What?" said Jake.

"That truck down the street."

He craned his neck and gazed at it.

"They said the robbers were driving a pickup. They said maybe black."

"That's blue."

"It is?"

"Or gray. It's not black."

"It's not?"

"We're fine."

Ally looked down and fished through her purse to find her keys. "I'm so glad you're here. You're staying, right?"

"Right."

She was still tipsy.

"I don't want the smell," she explained to Jake, letting her dress fall down to the floor. Jake leaned in the doorway and watched. "Can you shower, too? Please?" she asked.

He took off his shirt. The bathroom was dark. They had left the lights off. He unzipped his jeans.

"Thirdhand smoke," Ally drawled on. "It's not widely known . . . but it mixes with stuff—the nicotine does—on your hair and your clothes, and forms, like, cancer-causing fumes." She pulled down her panties and kicked them away. "It affects kids. Delays development. Lowers IQs." Naked completely, she swept back the curtain and turned on the water. She reached out her hand, assessing the spray, as it grew hot. "Ever see *Psycho*?"

"Ally, come on. We're all locked up." Jake stood there naked and ready to shower.

"But this would be perfect. Us in the shower. Three men. Under five-two. They're all short. Did I tell you that?" She stepped into the tub. "You were too young, but . . . ," Ally continued, closing her eyes to the hot stream.

Jake stepped in and picked up the bottle of No More Tears. He squirted a dollop into his hand. "Too young for what?"

"The last movie I saw in a theater . . . ten years ago. I have this image of Rocky himself—Rocky the boxer?"

"Sylvester Stallone?"

"And the actress who showed her vagina?"

"Uh—"

"No. You wouldn't know. You were a baby."

"*Basic Instinct*? Sharon Stone?"

"Yes, her. They had a shower scene—they were both nude and I wanted to puke. Oh, that feels good." He shampooed her hair. She shampooed his.

An hour later, Jake fell asleep and Ally woke up and climbed from the bed. Something was keeping her mind on alert. Maybe the robbers. That was it. What was it?

She found her purse and dug for her phone to listen to the message Meer had left:

"*Elle*? October?" Meer said.

Ally's heart sank.

"*Cosmo*? May?"

Meer had found out. Meer knew. Ally had been writing for *Elle* and *Cosmo*, *Glamour* and *Redbook*, for years and years, to make ends meet. She used a fake name as she doled out advice on women and wealth. Basic economics. Home budgets. Retirement savings.

Someone had squealed. Yoko had squealed. She couldn't remember whom else she'd told. No one else knew.

She hung up the phone and powered it off and imagined Meer Monday: Her grades were late. Why was this? Meer would ask. Was this why? The magazine writing? On the side? How could she focus with two different jobs? Where was her focus? Glossy rags or research and scholarship? Why did she keep it a secret from Brown?

Ally collected her thousand-dollar checks, four hundred here, three hundred there, and put them all into one account, to be touched only for college tuition, namely, Lizzie's.

She was the dumb one. She had been stupid, trusting Yoko.

Eyelids heavy, she put down the phone with bone-weary dread.

She shouldn't have told a single soul. No one at all. She'd told Yoko and Yoko'd told Meer . . . and Ally had been protecting her!

She was the idiot. She should have kept her secret safe.

This time, she would.

She looked through the dark at Jake asleep.

Tomorrow had come. The week's end. Or was it the beginning? Ally had ignored her work for two days, and Lizzie was due at the station at one. She couldn't afford to fool around. Anymore.

AT THE ST. REGIS, a bellman met her as she climbed from the cab. He held an umbrella over her head, enormous and black, as she strode the red carpet and up the front steps.

In the lobby, rain dripped off her and puddled on the floor. She looked around for Jake.

Everything shined; everything glimmered: gold-framed chairs with red velvet seats, glistening mirrors, crystal chandeliers, and vases filled with towering lilies.

All the men looked dignified: The bellmen in white kid gloves, black suits. Guards in gray suits, speaking into their mikes. Businessmen in navy drifting through the lobby from the King Cole Bar. From the front desk, "May I help you, ma'am?"

Ally turned. "I'm waiting for a friend."

The handsome Italian nodded and smiled. Ally turned back toward the elevator bay. A few seconds later, he appeared with a stack of white paper towels.

"Thanks," she said.

He smiled and nodded as an elevator dinged and Jake stepped out. "Ally?" he said. He saw her first.

Ally turned toward him, and as he flew toward her, she burst into tears.

"Come up," he said sweetly.

"I can't."

"You can. Why are you here?"

"I don't know."

"Come up, Professor. Before we land on 'Page Six.'" He pulled his cap low and led her into the elevator nook.

In Jake's suite, Ally stood in front of a window, searching through the mist for Central Park. It was there somewhere, up Fifth Avenue. Past the Plaza. The view was shrouded in fog.

"Something warm?" Jake asked from across the room. He stood by the desk, holding the phone. "Room service?"

"That would be nice." She turned and looked around.

The room was scattered with tufted sofas and fringed ottomans, column lamps on ticking-striped tablecloths. Tasseled drapes framed the windows, and chandeliers hung from the ceiling.

Jake looked strange and wonderful in it: the formal spread, the chintz, the silk. "Pot of tea and chocolate cake. The molten one," she heard him say. It suited him somehow. "Thank you," he said. Hanging up, he turned to Ally. "There's a minibar we can bust open, but let's get you out of those clothes first."

Ally looked at him.

"I didn't mean that way." Then he smiled. "Unless you want to."

Ally turned toward the window again and looked for the trees. Some sign of trees, of Central Park.

Jake studied her. "Seriously. Go get dry. There's a robe in the bathroom, through the, uh, bedroom."

Ally didn't move. "It's beautiful," she said. "You *live* here?"

"You think this is cool? Check out the *bathroom*. There's a TV *inside* the mirror." Ally turned around and smiled. They locked eyes. "Seriously. You're on the john and the ladies from *The View* are staring out at you from inside the mirror. Whoopi, Barbara—"

Ally laughed.

"The only problem is, you get kind of spoiled." He looked at her with meaning. "It's hard to stay at Motel 6 once you've stayed here. It's hard to go back to Velveeta in a can once you've had, I don't know, French Brie."

"French Brie? That sounds so funny coming from you."

Jake smiled. "You know what I mean."

Ally did. They locked eyes. Once she'd had Jake, every man had paled in comparison. A moment passed. "Why did you find me? What do you want?"

He stared at her and thought about it. He looked at his hands and said, "Well, to start with . . . I wanted to see if you remembered me."

She shook her head. "Of course I did."

"I wanted to see if you ever thought . . . you made a mistake."

Ally nodded. "It wasn't. No. Maybe it was." She tried to explain. "You would've been *stuck*, and if I got fired . . . I'm sorry, Jake."

Jake considered her words. "I know there's no whining on the yacht, and I won't. Whine on the yacht. But . . . all this stuff . . .

money, fame . . . it's nothing if you don't love someone." He gathered his courage. "So here it is: I was in love with you back at school. And here I am now—and I haven't seen you in ten years—and I'm still in love with you."

Ally was stunned. She stood there blinking.

"That's a fact. And it's why—the dinner. To see if I was, and it turns out I am, and I want to know if you feel the same way."

Ally stood there, silent and still, for a long moment.

And then her phone rang.

She looked down, slipped it out of her pocket, and looked at the number. "Jake," she said and looked at him. "I know we're having a moment here . . ."

Jake smiled.

"I have to get this. It's my friend. We have a thing. An emergency thing. Three calls. This is her third."

"Sure," he said. "Go." He turned to the desk and picked up a script.

"*TMZ!*" Anna yelled after Ally picked up and said hi. "I saw you in a fight! A bar fight!"

"What?"

"A fight!"

"How?"

"On TV!"

"That was— Listen, I can't talk."

"Are you with him?"

"Yes," Ally said and glanced at Jake.

"Let me say hi!"

"No!"

"Please!"

"Anna, no. It's not a good time."

"Please!" Anna begged.

Ally paused and rolled her eyes. She turned around and looked at Jake. "My best friend—wants to say hi."

Jake rose and put down his script. "Sure."

She handed him the phone and whispered, "I'm sorry. Her name is Anna. With a short *A*. Like 'ant.' Not long. Not like 'ah-choo.' It makes her nuts."

Jake put the phone to his ear. "Anna?"

Ally, mortified, slipped from her Tretorns.

"Noah Bean?" Anna cried.

"Hi."

Barefoot, Ally headed toward the bathroom. She needed a minute. She needed a towel. A clean towel.

"I'm a huge fan! Huge! Huge!"

Jake turned and looked out the window. "Thanks."

"So is my husband. We *love* you. We *absolutely love* you. Love you."

"Thank you so much," he said again.

"But more important. Listen to me. Are you listening, Noah?"

"Yes."

"Good. *Ally* loves you."

Jake drew still and looked across the suite. Ally was gone.

"She might not show it. She might not admit it. Even to herself. But don't give up. She has—issues. I know this because I'm her best friend *and* an MD shrink. Do you know what that means? MD shrink? It means I'm smart."

"Okay."

"She *will* come around."

Jake looked down at the carpet and blinked.

"Noah? You there?"

"Yeah."

"Did you hear me?"

"You sure?" he asked, looking back up as Ally entered, shaking her head. She was embarrassed.

"She loved you. She still does."

"Thank you, Anna." Jake gazed at Ally. "That means a lot."

"Good," she said. "Good."

"Bye," he said, handing the phone back to Ally.

Ally took it. "There. Are you happy?"

"Yes," said Anna. "Elated. Thanks."

"I'll call you back."

"Bye, Als."

Jake sank slowly onto the sofa, looking refreshed. His eyes brightened.

"Sorry about that," Ally said.

He looked at her and smiled. That arresting smile. Sheepish and flushing, Ally stared at him, captivated. In her hand, the phone rang again. She looked at the number. "Lizzie's friend." She looked at him.

"Get it," he said. "I've got all night."

"I'm worried, Mrs. Hughes," Weather started. "She said she would be at my place at five. It's not like her to not show up. Do you know if her super's back?"

"I'm confused." Ally had moved to the window again. The fog was lifting. She saw the treetops of Central Park.

"She hasn't called me all day. She won't pick up. Nobody's seen her. Not from class. Not from Del's. Mrs. Hughes!"

"Weather, if we don't find her tonight—you have to—we have to go back to this place. Tomorrow, first thing."

"Okay, Mrs. Hughes, I can lead you from the train—where we got off—but I don't have the exact address."

"Tomorrow morning."

The doorbell rang. Ally looked up.

"Room service. Still want tea?" Jake got up and answered the door.

SHE ROLLED OVER AND Jake met her ear. "It's eight," he whispered.

"No!" Ally whined and bolted upright. Her head throbbed. She closed her eyes and thought about Meer. Meer's message. Meer's threat. Sober reality set in. "Jake?"

"Yeah?"

She opened her eyes. "There's no kind way to say this. I'm sorry . . ."

"I have to go."

"You have to go." She leaned in and kissed him, then rolled to get up. "I have to clean this whole house . . . in four hours."

"I'll help." He picked up a pillow and stripped off its case.

"She can't find a trace of us . . . I have to leave for the station at noon." She stood up slowly and held her head.

"Ally?" he said, looking at her as she swept back her hair. "If I were—if I were thirty-five, would you be rushing me out of here?"

"If you were *fifty*," Ally explained. "I decided—a long time ago—not to drag her into my dating."

"What dating?"

"Yes, that's right. There's a reason for that."

"How will you ever meet anyone?"

"I won't," she said and walked away, into the bathroom.

"I would marry you if you want," Jake called.

Ally caught herself on the sink. She took a deep breath and stood up straight. "You don't mean that," she called back, then looked at herself in the sink mirror. She looked afraid.

"I do," he said and appeared in the doorway, folding the blanket.

She turned on the water and splashed her face. She reached for a towel and wiped herself dry. Through the mirror, she looked at Jake.

"I would marry you if you want," he said again.

"And that would be a mistake for you." She put the towel back on the bar.

"Why?" he said.

She picked up her toothbrush. "Because," she said and grabbed the toothpaste. She squeezed a snake of it onto her brush and started to brush on the left as she spoke. "You're twenty-one . . . You're quitting school . . ." She brushed and brushed and then stopped and spit and started again on the right. "You don't know what kind of job you want . . . You're in debt . . . You're too young to be a dad." She spit again and returned the brush to the cup on the sink. "And we don't really know each other. Not from two days." She grabbed the cup and rinsed.

Jake watched her. "I know you."

She put the cup down, wiped her mouth, and turned to face him. "Jake, look. I have—inexplicable feelings—"

"Inexplicable?"

"Unexplainable."

"I know what it means. I just don't agree that your feelings are unexplainable."

"I'm totally delighted and overwhelmed by what happened here over the weekend, but—"

"But?"

"We don't know each other. Not truly."

"Ally," he said. "I've sat in your class and listened to you yammer—ninety minutes, twice a week—for three years. Six semesters. Two hundred sixteen total hours."

She looked at him. "Yammer?"

Jake smiled. "Did I say yammer? I meant lecture. I've read your papers, both your books, and you've read six hundred pages of me . . ."

Ally nodded and bit her lip.

"We've been talking, you and me—talking and flirting—for a while."

Ally turned. "It was your idea. And I thought we were— And now I sound like some old man with a beard and a hard-on, and that is—that is not what this was."

"What was it, then?"

"I make mistakes."

"Who told you that?"

"I make decisions, and—"

"No, I told you, it wasn't a fling. If I were a girl and you were a guy—"

"Jake. Please. If someone found out?" She turned, stepped toward him, and kissed him on the lips. "I'm sorry. Okay? *Marry* you?"

Tired, she thought, she must be tired. She sidestepped him and went into the bedroom and swallowed the knob of grief in her throat. Her knees felt weak and she started to tremble. She was hungover. She never drank. That's what this was.

In the doorway, Jake turned around and searched for his clothes. They were scattered across the bedroom floor.

In the kitchen, Ally made coffee.

"Thank you," he said as she gave him the mug. He was washing down the table. He stopped for a moment, put the sponge down, then crossed to the sink, where Ally was rinsing the last Stella bottle.

He leaned against the counter, studying her sadly, then turned his head and gazed out the window.

Ally turned off the water and watched him lift the mug to his lips. Like pillows, she thought, Jake's lips.

He hadn't shaved, and the dark wash of bristle, of five-o'clock shadow, the lack of sleep, and a certain sadness made him look ten years older that morning.

Ally studied him and thought of how beautifully he would age. Some men grow more handsome year after year, and Jake would be one of them. Lucky the lady who . . .

"Holy shit," Jake said and straightened up, startled. He focused out the window. "They're here." He placed his coffee mug down on the counter.

"Who?" Ally said and stepped toward him to see what he saw.

Beyond the front yard, beyond the front gate and across the

street, an extremely animated ten-year-old girl climbed from a cab, holding a toy gun in her hand.

"What are they doing?" Ally cried, panicked.

The driver helped Claire pull two tiny rollers from the trunk.

"Back, out the back!" Ally yelled.

"Good," Jake agreed, grabbing his duffel and his toolbox.

She took him by the arm and led him through the dining room toward the screened porch at the back of the house.

As they fled, she glanced through the window and saw Lizzie in the side yard, running toward the back, wielding her gun.

"I'm home! I'm home!" Lizzie yelled, her long blond braids bouncing off her back, gun in her hand.

"Where is she going? Shoot! Shoot!" Ally abandoned her route and doubled back, grabbing Jake and taking him with her. "The basement," she said. "It leads to the yard on the other side."

"Hello! We're home!" Claire called from the front hall. She had let herself in.

Ally opened the basement door and shoved Jake inside.

"Wait!" he said as she closed it.

"Ally?" called Claire. "We're home! Surprise!"

"Hello!" Ally yelled toward the kitchen. "I'll call you," she whispered to Jake through the door.

"You will?" he said. "Do you have my number?"

"No, I don't know. Sorry. I'm really sorry. I can't call you." She shut the door, turned, and ran down the hall. "Mom? Is that you?"

Claire was placing her purse on the counter, staring at two mugs of coffee. Two. "Surprise!" she said and looked up as Ally walked in.

"No kidding," Ally said.

"We took an early—"

"Where is she?" Ally pretended to look around.

In the sunny backyard, Lizzie climbed up onto her tire swing, happy to be home. She kicked off her shoes and pointed the toy gun high in the air at a bird flying by.

In the dark basement, Jake found the doors that led outside through a steep cellar egress. He unhitched the lock and tried to lift them, but they were stuck. Like a linebacker, he pounded on the steel with his shoulder and his back.

From the corner of the yard, Lizzie had a view of the red cellar doors. She grew still when she heard the noise, the thud-thud-thud, from the basement.

Her eyes grew wide as the doors began to give, and when one flew open and Jake popped out, she clutched the tire swing, pointed the gun at him, and let loose a terrified, ear-piercing scream.

Ally and Claire looked at each other and ran from the kitchen toward Lizzie's scream.

Through the porch, Ally could see her, clutching the swing rope, pointing the gun, mouth in an oval, eyes wide in horror, letting loose horrified scream after scream. "A man! A man!"

"What? What? What's in your hand?" Ally cried as she flew from the porch and down the steps.

"A man! A man!" Lizzie screamed, pointing at Jake.

Ally and Claire turned and saw Jake standing in the egress, half-in, half-out, covered in cobwebs.

Claire screamed and Lizzie screamed again and Ally bellowed

over them, "Stop! Stop! Put down that toy! He's the handyman! Stop!"

"What?" Claire said, looking at Ally.

"He is the *handyman*!"

Lizzie fell silent, dropped the toy gun, threw her head back, and laughed. Claire inhaled and smiled tightly.

"You bought the gun?" Ally cried, looking at Claire.

"It's what she wanted!"

Ally, fuming, turned to Jake. "Come, Jake! Come meet my mother and Lizzie. Come."

IN RED HOOK, THEY walked for about a mile, block to block, before Weather saw it. "There! That!" She pointed to the warehouse two blocks down. "That one there. Under the bridge."

"The one on the left?" Ally asked. "Across the street?"

"The far corner there!"

"Wait," said Jake. "Is that on Bushman? Bushman and Court?" He had insisted on joining them. Weather insisted they walk all the way from Borough Hall so she could retrace Lizzie's route.

They stopped on the corner as traffic sped past, blowing exhaust and kicking up dirt. "I think I know this building. I do. From all my research—1909—the Sugar Mill Fire!" Over their heads, the expressway roared.

"What?" Ally said.

"Ten girls died. Bushman and Court. Oh, man. This is perfect. See the relevance? This is—incredible. I can't *believe* it."

"Why?" Weather said.

"Can you?" said Jake. "Can you believe it?"

"I—I don't know. Yes," Ally said, looking around. "Maybe. I guess."

She was distracted. Next to the building, a crew from Con Ed ripped through the pavement.

"Two years before the Triangle fire. Or was it cotton? Vaseline? No. No, it was sugar. Sugar. It was. This was the building. Nothing has changed but the product! Man! Marty will love this!"

"Why is he freaking?"

"He has—a passion," Ally explained and stepped off the curb to cross the street.

"The irony, wow." Jake followed. "This guy runs a sugar mill, too . . ."

In secret, thought Ally. They're all tucked in. Hidden behind the grit and the noise.

"So what's the plan?" Jake stopped walking.

Ally turned to him. "I'm going in."

"Why? Are you sure? Who are these people? They could be armed. They could be dangerous."

"Were they? Weather?"

"No. He was tan. Polo, no socks."

"Really?" said Jake. "My sources said—"

"But I'm not a threat," Ally insisted. "I'll say—I'll say—it's an emergency. They'll understand."

"No. No." Jake shook his head. "If anyone goes, I go. I go inside."

"Yeah, Mrs. Hughes. Noah should go. They won't kill a star."

"No, Jake, thanks. I'm thrilled you're here. You make us feel safe. But, A, she's my child. And, B, I'm armed."

"Armed?" said Jake.

She crossed the street toward the construction.

"Armed with *what*?" Jake followed Ally. Weather followed Jake.

"Pepper spray," she said and patted her purse.

"What? Why?"

"Where did you get it?" Weather caught up. "Please, let me see!"

Keeping her stride, Ally took the canister out of her purse and gave it to Weather. "Careful. It can stop bears."

Weather brandished it. "'Hurry up, woman!'"

"It's not a toy." Ally reached out and took it back as they all heard a series of screeches and peels.

Four white vans, unmarked, raced by. One van, two, a third, and a fourth pulled up in front of Fishman's doors.

"What . . . what is this?" Two marked police cars followed behind, sirens swirling.

"Holy baloney. It's like a . . . raid," Weather said.

"What?" Ally said.

"I think she's right," Jake agreed.

Men in blue jackets and bulletproof vests, helmets and knee-pads, climbed from the vans, all of them carrying submachine guns.

"What is *happening*?" Ally said as one group gathered by the front doors and another spread out around the block. She realized then: A raid. Arrests. Seizures. Guns. She shot off toward the police.

"Ally!" Jake called.

She approached the FBI jackets. "Excuse me?" she said. "My daughter's inside." Weather had mentioned the ninth floor. Ally decided she'd go up and yell as loud as she could. "Excuse me," she said, approaching the agents.

One drew his gun. "Stop where you are!"

"What?" Ally stopped. "I just—"

"Hands up!"

In the middle of the street, Ally raised her hands. "Excuse me? May I just—"

"Shut up!" he said as she approached. "Put your hands behind your back!"

"This is a mistake. I have a question. My child—"

"Hands! Behind your back! Now!"

"Why are you yelling? Why is he yelling?"

Jake appeared next to her, hands in the air. "Do it, Ally."

"But—"

"Do it!"

Ally put her hands behind her back.

"Now turn and walk to me! Toward my voice now!"

Ally was confused. "Wait. What? Turn and walk backward?"

"Wait," said the agent, looking at Jake. "Aren't you that guy? Cooper? Bradley?"

"No. Not him."

"Bradley whatever?"

"No. Noah Bean."

"Yeah, you're the knight! Weapons? Any?"

"We were just walking—"

"I have some pepper spray."

"Get on the ground. Sorry, but do it."

Ally and Jake looked at each other. Jake rolled his eyes and fell to his knees. "Do what I do." He moved to his belly. Ally did too. The agent descended, lifted them up, and grabbed Ally's purse. "Work in this building?"

"No," Ally said.

"And you, sir?"

"No."

"But my daughter, she might. We were rescuing her."

Weather stayed crouched behind a car. She couldn't believe it.

On the ninth floor, Fishman yelled, "Wipe! Wipe! Wipe it all!" He glanced at Josh as he smashed his phone in one fell swoop. Pieces of plastic sailed through the air, hitting Josh in the face.

"What the fuck?" Josh said as Fishman collected the tiny pieces and threw them out the window.

He'd wiped the hard drive in five minutes flat. Fishman had hired him for this moment, for his kill skill.

The hallway was empty and strangely quiet as they jogged toward the stairwell that led to the furnace, that led to outside.

Up and down the halls, the models were oblivious behind closed doors, all except Lizzie, who stood in the pantry and gazed out the window. "Shit," she said, turning to Sasha. "We should get down. Under the table." They both ducked. "Kill you, Weather. I will kill," Lizzie muttered.

"What? What it is?" Sasha said.

"Cops out front, and my *mother* is here."

Twenty minutes later, FBI agents led Fishman and Josh around the corner of Bushman and Court. Both men were handcuffed.

Ally and Jake were further explaining themselves to the agents when Ally saw Lizzie and gasped.

She watched as an agent placed Lizzie and Sasha into the back of an unmarked car.

Ally just stared as the agent released her. Twenty feet away, Con Ed resumed. Jackhammers flew. Cement soot and particles whirled around her, choking her throat. The sidewalk screamed from the deafening drills as they drove up and down and struck their bits, exploding in ashy, smelly exhaust. The moment became unbearable. Ally turned and walked away without looking back.

Swiftly, Jake caught up. "What she did was legal, Ally." He walked beside her. "They can't arrest her. She's twenty. She did nothing wrong."

"Pepper spray," she said to herself. "The cops show up with automatic rifles . . . I bring Mace . . ."

"So?"

"I don't know who I am anymore." She said nothing else, and when she hit Clinton, she knew where she was. She took a right and walked herself home.

Jake followed, and Weather followed Jake, for blocks and blocks, an hour walk, all the way back to Cranberry Street.

"HE'S THE HANDYMAN! CALM down!" Suddenly Ally was perfectly composed and in command, the arbiter of reason and common sense. She turned to Lizzie. "Give me the BB gun. Now. Please."

Lizzie did so as Jake walked toward them in the backyard. "Sorry. I didn't mean to scare you."

Ally turned. "Lizzie, down off the swing, please."

Lizzie jumped off and onto the grass. "Hi, Mom."

"Hi, honey."

"Early! Surprise!"

"Surprise!" Ally said as Jake walked up. She tucked the toy gun into her pocket. "Jake," she said, shaking her head in exasperation. "This is my mom. Mom, Jake."

"Hello," said Claire.

"Lizzie, this is Jake."

"Hi," said Lizzie.

"Hi," said Jake and smiled at Lizzie.

"Lizzie, you have a surprise in your room and you can thank Jake," Ally said.

"Thank you. What surprise?" Lizzie said.

"He can't tell you," Ally said. "It's secret. And there's a second surprise too. For your report."

"A secret surprise and a second surprise!" She ran toward the back porch.

Ally looked at Claire and said quietly, "Jake put the bunk bed together."

"How nice—to have a man around the house."

"Yes, it was," Ally said and turned to Jake. "Let's get you paid."

Jake nodded. "I'll wait out front."

"I'll grab a check," Ally pretended.

Jake looked at Claire. "Nice to meet you."

"You too," she said and watched him walk off. "Handsome," she whispered.

"You think?" Ally said and turned toward the house. "The BBs go back."

"Why? Why?" Claire followed. "You're the feminist."

"What are you saying?"

"So? What's wrong with boy toys?"

Minutes later, out front, Ally held out a yellow bank check.

"Your mom's at the window," Jake said as she approached. He stood by his car.

"Of course she is," Ally said, handing him the check and extending her hand, businesslike. "This is horrible. Please forgive me."

He took the check and shook her hand. He held it a moment, then let go and folded the check in halves, then quarters. "Faking this, right?"

"Of course," she said.

Then he said, "I want to see you."

Ally said nothing.

"I want to date you from Boston."

"No." She looked at her feet. She could feel herself starting to tremble again.

"Or I can move. Down here."

"What would you do?"

"I don't know. Figure it out."

"For work," Ally said.

"Find odd jobs."

She glanced at the house, at her shoes. She took a deep breath and studied Jake. "You're young. Go explore."

"Explore what?"

"Everything. Go and travel while you can." Ally was concerned. He'd lived between only two states. He'd never been anywhere, seen anything, or met anyone outside New England.

"I don't want to—"

"Not Timbuktu. Go see New York. See the West Coast. Get out of Boston. Get out of Providence."

"Why? I want to—see if this works. Give it a shot."

"No." She wouldn't let him do it. Stay to date her. Despite all the life he had lived already, Jake was still twenty-one.

Twenty-one.

The same age as Ally when she made a choice that changed the course of her life forever.

"Please," she said. "It's hard to see now. But this is the time—to *become* who you are."

"I'm not asking for your advice."

"You have potential."

"I can't play ball."

"So it's not baseball. It's something else. But you're not a handyman, Jake. Not that there's anything wrong with that. If it were you. You're smart and sweet, and so—hot. That's—a *rare* combination, you know?"

"Let me—hold on—get this straight." Jake studied her, biting his lip. "You don't want to take this further? Ever? At all? Just like that?"

"I can't. I'm in enough trouble already."

"Why?"

"My *job*," Ally said.

"I don't—?"

"I am hanging on by a *string*. Meer's calls? She found out—I write these articles—on the side. *Cosmo. Elle. Redbook. Vogue.* A dollar a word. Using a name—a fake name—my mother's name."

"So?"

"Serious scholars don't write for *Vogue*! According to Meer!"

"What does that have to do with us?"

"She is looking for *any* reason—any excuse— I could get fired for dating you. I could get fired for this—this weekend—and you don't have work, so what would we do?"

"So it's the money?"

"I have a *child*." She was near tears. "Please, don't make this . . . harder than it is!"

"I'm glad it's hard!" Jake stared at her, mouth closed, lips pressed together. He didn't understand. Not fully.

Ally looked down. "I can't do it. I can't date you. That's final."

Jake looked away. Ally looked up. She watched him as he glanced at the check, then at his car. The bedding was still bundled in the front. He looked at Ally. "You're a coward." He swiftly circled the front of the Chevy.

"Yes, I am!" Ally said. "And I have every reason to be!" He opened the door and climbed in. She looked away as he started the engine. Then she circled too, in front of him, and crossed the street, her chest tight with panic, heart beating fast, choking back tears.

She thought she might faint as she walked up the steps. She wasn't cruel. She'd never been cruel to a person before.

What had she done?

She turned around.

She watched as Jake pulled onto the road. He rolled down the window and fast-pitched the condom, full, like a ball, across the street and into a hedge. Then he released the yellow confetti—the torn-up check.

A breeze caught and held the pieces in midair, carried them aloft till they all floated down to rest on the road in a scattered puddle.

Ally stood there and watched the Chevy, Jake inside it, grow smaller and smaller.

Then he turned a corner and disappeared.

At the table in the kitchen, Claire dunked a tea bag. "He started *early* to do all that."

Ally paused before she spoke. "He did the ACs—yesterday. He came back this morning to finish the bed." She stood in the pantry, flour in one hand, sugar in the other. She was starting to make a birthday cake.

"What was he doing in the basement?"

"A wall. Mold. He washed it down. Shoot. I'm out of vanilla."

Lizzie appeared. "I found a sock and a shirt." She held up one of Jake's socks and his Sox shirt.

"Honey, I have to run to the store. Want to come?" Ally put the sugar on the counter.

"Where did you find them?" Claire asked Lizzie.

"Under the bed. Mommy's bed."

"Why were you under my bed?" Ally asked.

"The second surprise. That's where you hide my Christmas presents."

Ally smiled. "Lizzie Hughes: the best girl detective in the world!"

"I didn't—"

"Dining room."

"Yay!" Lizzie ran out.

"Paper bag!" Ally called. She smiled at Claire. "Little soldiers. For her report. Diorama due Tuesday."

"You look exhausted."

"I am. I am. Thank goodness this year is *over*." She picked up her purse.

"How is your TA?"

"I don't know. I'm headed to the store. Need anything?"

By that afternoon, the cake had cooled. Lizzie sat in the screened-in porch, gluing together a shoebox tavern.

In the yard Ally stood in the cool grass, gazing up at her dogwood tree.

Claire sidled up. "Beautiful weekend."

"It was."

"Too bad you were all holed up."

Ally studied the dogwood flowers, open and white. She reached up and touched one. The four petals were soft and wrinkled.

"Meg Moran called last night. Remember her?"

"Do I?" said Ally, rubbing a petal between her fingertips.

"They had a place on Remsen Street. Sold five years ago. Moved to New London."

"Where?"

"New London. A few miles from Mystic. Mystic Seaport? Mystic, Connecticut?"

Ally's stomach did a flip-flop. Her gaze moved from the beautiful tree to the white billowed clouds in the bright-blue sky. "What did she want?"

"She swore she saw you in Mystic this weekend. Holding hands with a handsome young man."

Ally smiled. "I wish."

"She said she was happy to see you so happy. So in love."

"In love?" Ally scoffed. "Too bad it wasn't me."

Claire nodded and eyed her daughter. "I told her that. I said you were home, grading papers. She said she was absolutely sure it was you."

Ally gazed again at the tree. "I guess she needs new glasses then." She reached up and snapped off a dogwood bloom. "Isn't it early for this to be—or is it late?"

Claire looked up at the tree. "Late. Couple weeks late. Which is odd, with the winter we had."

"So if it's cold, the trees bloom early? I don't get it."

Claire ignored her. "You can't afford another mistake." Her voice dropped in pitch.

Ally waited.

"All my money is in the brownstone. I cannot support you if something else happens. Are you on the pill?"

"That is none—"

"You cannot afford to be casual!"

"She didn't see me!"

"I wasn't born yesterday!" Claire yelled. She caught herself and looked toward the porch. Then she whispered. "Maybe you fool a ten-year-old girl, but not me—"

Ally turned and strode away, back to the house. She chucked the dogwood bud to the ground.

Claire followed. "Your chances of finding a man now are zero to none. No decent man wants used goods. No man wants another man's child—or two, God forbid!"

"Enough," Ally said. She'd heard it before. Many times.

"Your focus is tenure. Lizzie and tenure and—"

"I know how you feel." She skipped steps up to the porch. At the door, she turned. "I'm not getting it. Meer is after me. What are we even talking about?"

"I am discussing what happened this weekend!"

"And I am *not!*" She opened the door, slipped inside, and let it bang shut.

Inside the porch, Lizzie looked up from her diorama.

"Elizabeth. Please. Go upstairs."

"Why?"

"So I can talk to Grandma. Alone. Come back down in five or ten minutes."

Lizzie stood up and left the room, taking her Nathan Hale with her.

Ally doubled back, opened the door, and stood there again, staring at her mother. Claire stood her ground in the same spot.

"You're right," she admitted. "I had a weekend of meaningless sex."

Claire's eyes grew wide.

"I didn't plan it. I planned to grade papers. But it happened and it was great and amazing. Do you want the details?"

Claire fumed. "Tell me that boy does not go to Brown."

"No. But he did." Ally's eyes brimmed with tears. "A week ago, he was in my class, and that made the whole thing naughty and dangerous and stupid—and better than any sex I've had. Which, face it, Mother, has not been much." She took a breath. Her tears spilled. "I have been focused. I have been good. I have been sexless. For years. *Years.* And he was fantastic. He was— It was fantastic fucking sex for two days straight, and now he's gone. He offered to *marry* me, and I kicked him out. I didn't want to, but I did. So it's done. So what do you want to do about it? *Ground* me? Give me a big time-out? Send me to my room? What? What?"

Claire was frozen with anger.

"I love you, Mother, but I'm *thirty-one.* At some point you have to—*back off.*"

The two women stared at each other and seethed. Ally then let the door go and went back inside.

She flew through the porch to the front hall. She climbed the stairs and walked down the hall toward Lizzie's room.

She peeked through the crack Lizzie left in the door. "Okay, I'm done," she said calmly. "You can go down."

Lizzie sat on her new top bunk and flipped through a book. "Are you in a fight?"

"Sort of."

"With Grandma?"

"A little."

Lizzie nodded. "I love my bed. Thank you so much. I was so surprised."

"Good."

"Tuesday's my birthday."

"I know. I can't wait. I'm baking your cake."

"Where is she now?"

"Still out back. Let's give her a sec. I'll see you downstairs and we'll frost the cake."

"Can I help?"

"Of course." Ally then moved away from the door, went down the hall, and entered her room. She reached across the bed, picked up the phone, and took it with her into the bathroom. Safe inside, she shut the door, locked it.

"I need a favor," she said weakly, on the phone.

"Everything okay?" Anna asked. She had just moved to Denver.

"UTI. Call something in? So I don't die?"

"Of course."

"Thank you," Ally said softly.

"Ally?"

"Yes?"

"Sit in a bathing suit for too long?" Anna laughed. "Something I should know?"

Ally told Anna about the weekend, about Jake.

"Why did you send him *away*?" Anna asked when she had finished.

"He's *twenty-one*," Ally said, anguished. "Broke, unemployed, in debt. *Twenty-one*."

"You sound like your mom."

"I have a job—a child—"

"Please. You aren't holding out for some, you know, *conventional* life?"

Ally was silent for a moment. Then she said, "What?"

"The fairy-tale life. You know what I mean. Milestone shit: Good college. Grad school sweetheart. Perfect wedding?"

"Anna, please. You don't understand."

"Hot-climate honeymoon. Short-lived career. Two perfect kids, fish, dog."

Ally rolled her eyes.

"Two houses, two cars: big one for hockey gear, sleek one for date night."

"You need to stop. I could get fired."

"He stays rich. You stay skinny. It all works out?"

"I can't risk my job."

"But *twenty-one* might have been perfect for you. Picking up where you—"

"Enough, Anna, please!" Ally said, interrupting her best friend, the newly licensed psychiatrist.

Anna went on: "All I'm saying is, look at the world. What do you want? A suicide bomber to take you out?"

"No. What? What do you mean?"

"To die of a disease? Like SARS or something?"

"No."

"Then why can't you try for a happy ending, like everyone else?"

Ally looked at the ceiling in tears. "No one's ending is happy, Anna. We all die."

"You can die happy. You can die *loved*. Didn't you read *The Notebook*?"

"No."

"They made a movie. It's coming out soon. I'll fly to Rhode Island and take you to see it."

"Stop. Please stop." She started to cry.

"I'm sorry," Anna said. "I'll send you a plague of locusts instead. Will that be better?"

Ally thought locusts might be better. "Locusts and Cipro, please, tonight. Before my kidneys explode."

Anna promised to order the Cipro.

They both hung up.

After the call, Ally felt dizzy. She sat on the side of the tub and breathed. Deeply, slowly. Then she started to weep and weep. She wept into a washcloth for twenty minutes and then went downstairs to frost Lizzie's cake.

At six thirty, the doorbell rang.

Her heart leapt as she ran downstairs and through the front hall to answer it. Could it be Jake? No mail Sunday. Who could it be? No one had ordered a pizza, no. He had left his T-shirt, after all, and a sock. Maybe he left his hammer, a tool? "Coming!" she called as she opened the door, hoping, dreading, and there he was:

Harry Goodman.

Harry the handyman.

Harry, who'd canceled on Ally three times.

"Hi, Harry," Ally said, swallowing her disappointment.

"Hi, Miss Hughes," Harry mumbled. "Still need help?"

Ally smiled and shook her head. "No, Harry. Got someone else."

Harry nodded. "I'm going through stuff. You know how it is."

"I do," she said kindly.

"Okay," said Harry, turning around and heading down the steps. "If it doesn't work out, you know who to call. And they caught the guys. The robber guys. By the way."

"They did?" Ally said, surprised and relieved.

He stopped and turned on the bottom step. "Over at the Chad Brown housing project. Guy was selling an old lady's meds, from Slater Ave. My brother's a cop. I tell you that?"

"Are you sure?"

"Oh yeah." Harry looked sure. "Last night. All three. Cousins. All short. Runs in families, some stuff does."

"Right," Ally said. "Some stuff does. Well, that's a relief." Harry nodded. Closing the door, she said, "Take care, Harry."

"You, too, Miss Hughes."

She locked the lock and went back upstairs to draw Lizzie's bath.

Later, in bed, she arranged the pillows, settled back, knees knocked together, bare feet splayed under the blanket. She read and graded a twelve-page paper on the hour from eleven that night until the next day.

Her muscles ached. Her vision blurred, but she blinked the words back into focus.

During Lizzie's birthday week, Ally pulled off the road to sob twice. For five days she slept in Lizzie's room, on the bottom bunk, until she had time to strip down her own bed and wash the sheets, which smelled like sex.

The pillowcases smelled like Jake.

She left those till the following week.

The next month, too, felt eerily familiar, with frantic to-do lists on top of nausea. The nausea of grief.

"Have you lost weight?" Claire asked with profound approval.

Ally nodded. Twelve pounds. In under four weeks. She couldn't help it. "I haven't been feeling well."

"Well, whatever—*however*—you're feeling," Claire said, "you *look* terrific."

IN ALLY'S KITCHEN, WEATHER sat on the table. She rested her feet on a chair and ate a yogurt from Ally's fridge. She had helped herself. "Mrs. Hughes? What's with the boxes? At the front door?"

Jake looked at Ally. He stood at the sink, hand washing dishes.

Ally was mixing the batter for a cake, absorbed in thought and staring at a photo sitting on the windowsill:

Claire and Lizzie in a silver frame. Lizzie, four, in a light-pink dress with a Peter Pan collar, with a basket of eggs, and Claire so pretty in her early fifties before the lung cancer wasted her away. Easter weekend at Pierrepont Playground. A freezing-cold Saturday, Ally remembered. Lizzie was smiling but shivering, too.

Next to it sat a gold frame: Lizzie, on her birthday, blowing out candles. On the buffet sat a shoebox tavern.

The heart holds tight, Ally thought, looking at the photo, thinking of the weekend ten years before.

A friend moves away. A lover leaves. A child grows up. A mother dies. But the heart holds on. "Oh no," she said to herself out loud. "What am I doing?"

At the sink, Jake turned.

"What've I been doing?" She looked up, and then at Jake, and then at Weather. "I can't keep her . . . from . . ." She looked at the ceiling, her face contorted, and her eyes brimmed with tears. "I have to . . . let her . . . I have to . . . back off."

No one replied for a few moments, and then Weather nodded. "I bet your mother felt the same way. When you were twenty. Isn't that when you got knocked up?"

Jake and Ally looked at Weather. Ally rolled her eyes. "Weather, go home. I love you and thank you, but you need to go. Right now."

"Fine, Mrs. Hughes. Say how you *really* feel."

"That's how I feel. And please call me Ally, or Lizzie's mom, like you used to. Mrs. Hughes was my mother. And I am not . . . her."

Weather put the yogurt and spoon down and slid off the table. "Spoon in the sink," Ally said.

Weather picked up the spoon and handed it to Jake. "Good-bye, Noah Bean."

"Good-bye, Weather."

"Good-bye, Lizzie's Mom," Weather said, walking out.

Once she was gone, Ally waited. She counted to twenty and then looked at Jake. She waited some more, drew on her courage; and then she admitted, "I loved you. I did."

Jake smiled with a quiet knowing, but neither one moved.

"I fell in love with you. That weekend." She paused. "But it happened so fast, and our ages, my job . . ." Her voice cracked. "I'm so sorry. I didn't *want* to send you away."

Jake let his head fall in comic relief. "Finally!" he said. "I've been waiting to hear that for ten years!"

Ten years. All that time.

Ally walked toward him and stopped at his feet. She gazed at his shoes and they both waited. Then she looked up and Jake looked down, and they kissed.

Sweet and tender, surprisingly familiar, it was as if they'd been apart for a short time.

In Jake's embrace, Ally was transported a decade back to the weekend in May, to Mystic, to the Cape, to the Providence campus, to the house on Grotto.

Claire's concern, all her disappointment, had died with her. The constant calls, punishing lectures, her fears, were now buried and gone, and Ally felt the relief of that weight for the first time in Jake's arms.

"She's home!" Weather cried from down the hall, interrupting the moment. Ally and Jake pulled apart as Weather appeared, back in the doorway. "You guys were kissing!"

"She's home?" Ally said.

"Ally and Jake! Sitting in a tree! K-I-S-S—"

"Weather, stop! She called you from home?"

"She called! She's fine! She's back at her place! They didn't arrest her. She's safe and sound, and I came back to tell you! Yay, me!"

"She called *you* before she called—?" Ally grimaced, frustrated.

"That is correct," Weather said, nodding. Then she turned and left again. "Please pick up from where you left off."

Ally didn't move. She looked at Jake.

"You want to go see her?"

"No. She's a grown-up. She'll call when she's ready." She exhaled, relieved.

Jake turned his head and glanced at the clock. "You *know*," he said softly. "You know, Ally, I'm leaving tonight. I have to head back and pack and—"

"What?" Her face fell. "You are?"

"I was trying to tell you . . . all week. My flight's at nine."

"Where are you going?"

He thought about it. "*Everywhere.*"

"When are you back?"

"Not till December."

"*December?*"

He nodded. "A junket."

"Please stay longer. Can you? The weekend?"

"Maybe I can. Maybe till Sunday. I have to make a call."

Ally was hopeful. "Please make a call."

The brownstone, in ways, reminded Ally of the Providence house: high ceilings, crown molding, small, scattered rooms shredding at the seams, carpet and wallpaper peeling and fraying.

She stopped at the stairs and gazed at the boxes piled on the floor. The dozen boxes, all from Jake.

Jake, behind her, pressed in close. He kissed her on the neck, stretched his arm over hers, and curled his other arm around her waist. Ally exhaled. He flattened his palm across her belly, pressing her firmly backward and into him.

It was exactly what Weather had said. Picking up right where they had left off.

She went up a step and faced him. Their mouths, now level,

came together. She wrapped her elbows around his neck. They kissed and kissed. Jake enveloped her. His hands found their way under her shirt and up her back.

"Jake," she whispered as his lips brushed her neck. "Can I just say—"

"You haven't had sex in years?"

"Years."

"Shocking. But you had a—"

"I did, but I never . . ." Jake pulled back and looked at her. Ally inhaled. "I haven't been . . . like, the actual thing . . . I haven't actually, truly done it since—"

"Hurry up, woman! There's no time to waste!" Jake ran around her and raced up the stairs. In his best British accent, he called back again, "No time to waste!"

Ally entered a few steps behind. Jake stood there, staring at the map. The map of the world from the Providence house. There were now little holes where the pushpins had been. She had taken them out and never replaced them. He turned and moved toward her.

"Wait," she said and walked to the closet. "I have something—to show you." Ally disappeared into the closet, fetching Jake's navy-blue Red Sox shirt. She stepped back out, holding it up. "Remember this?"

Jake smiled. Yes, he did. "I wondered what happened—"

"I kept it," she said. "They won that year."

"I know. I was there. In the stands."

Ally's eyes brimmed with tears. "I was *so* happy for you . . ."

Jake drew near, took the T-shirt, and laid it on top of Ally's bureau. Then he turned, cupped her face with his hands, looked into her eyes, and kissed her deeply. He pulled back and said: "I have to have you. I don't mean to sound— Could you be ready? Ready to go?" He was almost pleading.

"Yes!" she said.

Then he yelled, "Hands up!" Imitating the FBI agent.

"Oh my goodness!" Ally laughed and threw her hands high.

"Up! Keep them up!" Jake yanked her shirt up and over her head. He threw it aside. "Don't move!" He yanked down her bra straps, her bra, and leaned in, mouthing her breasts, back and forth, lifting them skyward.

Nothing mattered then but the desperate grabbing, kneading and pulling, both of them feeling for and finding each other. "I think there's been a—mistake," she said. "I have a gun!"

"Keep your mouth shut!" Jake's teeth found her neck as Ally raked her hands through his hair. She grabbed and culled it, pulling it hard, but not too hard, remembering how it made him wild. He scooped the back of her standing leg up and bent her knee. He seated her there, around his waist.

They kissed and kissed and he found her shorts. He dug inside and found her ass and spread her apart and back together, fingertips grubbing and rooting from behind, searching for heat, for sluice, a way in. "Down on the ground!" He climbed on the bed and placed her down and fell on her body hard and fast, finding her mouth deep in a kiss.

She tasted his breath, his tongue, his teeth. She pulled back and looked at his lines and shapes.

Jake then lifted back onto his knees. With nothing said and in mutual agreement and desperation, he unzipped his jeans and pulled them down. Ally did the same with her shorts and panties. She yanked them down over her knees and kicked them off at her ankles hard.

In an instant he was back on top, poised to enter, and Ally relished the weight of his legs, the pressure of his hips pressing against hers, his lack of restraint. She felt that urge and instinct, again, to be with him forever, in bed or anywhere, to hold him forever and never let go.

"Mom!" Lizzie yelled from down in the foyer.

Ally bolted upright and almost threw Jake clear off the bed.

"Mom! Are you home?"

"I'm here!" Ally called. "Be right down!"

Lizzie had let herself inside. Her super was back. She had her keys. She shoved her suitcase against the wall at the base of the stairs. The wig was gone. Her face was washed. She had changed into flip-flops and a white cotton sundress. She had pulled her hair loosely up off her neck. "What's with the boxes?"

Ally didn't answer.

She scanned the labels: Barneys, Dior, Louis Vuitton. "*Some-one* went shopping," she said to herself and moved toward the kitchen for something to eat. She smelled something baking.

Upstairs, Ally scrambled, pulling on clothes. "What do I look like? How do I look? Do I look like I've been kissing?"

"You look great," Jake said, watching her.

"That's not what I mean," Ally whispered. "I'll keep her in the kitchen. Sneak out the front and I'll see you later? At the hotel?"

"What?" Jake said.

She crawled across the bed. "You'll stay in New York for the weekend? Please?" She kissed him quickly.

"You just—asked me to miss my flight."

"Yes and that's great. And I'm happy you will, but she can't know we're up here—*doing* this."

Jake blinked slowly. "Why not?"

"Because." She climbed off the bed, zipped up her shorts, and tucked in her shirt. "Because I'm her mother."

"Ally?"

"What?"

"Lizzie knows that you've had sex. She knows she didn't come from a stork."

Ally rolled her eyes. "Sneak out the front. Please, Jake."

"Sneak out? Again?" He didn't move.

"I can't explain it right this second."

"Why don't you tell her . . . that you love me and I love you?"

"She knows I haven't seen you in ten years." Ally stepped into the hall, then stopped and turned. In the doorway, she said, "I'm sorry. I don't—know how to handle this."

"Clearly."

She nodded. "Thank you. For your patience."

In the kitchen, Lizzie made tea. "Do you want tea? I'm making tea." She turned the heat up under the kettle.

Ally stood in the doorway, relieved. "I'm sorry for camping out at your house."

"Are you baking cake?"

"I'm sorry for the calls."

"Are you baking cake?"

"I'm sorry I stalked you."

"Olive oil cake?"

"Yes. It's baking."

"For me?"

"For you in *jail*," Ally said. "Do you want to talk? If you don't, that's okay. It's your life."

"Yes, of course I want to talk." Lizzie took mugs down from the cabinet.

"If you do, great. If not, fine. I won't press."

"I said I do." Lizzie laughed. "Why are you acting so oddly calm? You're freaking me out."

"I'm not— I haven't been calm."

"What tea do you want?"

"We have a deal. You should've called back."

"I know," Lizzie said guiltily. "I know. I'm sorry. They stole my phone and I didn't want you to mess up my plan. What tea do you want?"

"Ah, the plan. Weather told me. Get naked to buy a new nose? That plan?"

"No." Lizzie studied her. "Is that—do you have a hickey on your neck?"

"What?" Ally said. She covered her neck with her hands. "No, no. I must be—breaking out from this heat—it's over one hundred degrees—"

"*Outside*," Lizzie said suspiciously.

"What are you looking at?"

"Nothing. You look like . . . you just had sex."

"What? Me?"

"Whatever. Forget it. Can you please sit down and let me explain?"

"You don't have to."

"I want to."

"Okay, but I don't want to sit. I want you to know . . . there's nothing you can do to make me not love you."

Lizzie rolled her eyes. "Thanks. That's nice. *What tea do you want?* I hate it when you don't listen to me."

"Fine. Earl Grey."

The kettle sang. Lizzie grabbed it and switched off the burner. She reached for the tea bags.

Ally didn't move. "I'm only saying, I love you, honey. Porn or not. I may not approve, but you're a grown-up."

"I don't feel like a grown-up right now." She poured the water into the mugs, put the kettle on the burner, and added the tea bags. Then she explained:

On Wednesday night, Lizzie had used Weather's phone to call Jones. They met at ten on Bleecker at John's.

The greasy pizza with oven-charred crust sat above the table on a raised tray. One slice was missing.

"Help yourself," Jones offered, chewing, smiling, happy to see her.

"I can't eat dairy. I can't eat gluten or meat or fruit. Tomato is a fruit. I can't eat anything on that plate." Lizzie stared at the pizza a moment, then looked away and took a deep breath. "You know how you guys have 'Wanted' posters?"

Jones nodded and sipped his Coke.

"And on your website, I saw the rewards you give for tips—the FBI."

"Yes," Jones confirmed, taking a bite of the succulent slice. A drop of grease dripped down his chin. He picked up a napkin and wiped it off.

Lizzie took a breath. "My question is: If there's no poster and someone like me gives you a tip that leads to an arrest—a big arrest—can I get money?"

"For the tip?"

"Or does there need to be a poster first?"

Jones smiled and swallowed. He put his slice down and leaned back. He took his napkin from his lap and wiped his mouth again. "Doesn't—doesn't work that way, hon. Money has to be in place. It's chain of command." He turned and waved the waiter over.

"Chain of command?"

"Something to drink?" the waiter asked Lizzie.

Lizzie glanced at the pizza for a moment. Steam was rising off the cheese, fogging the window. She looked at the waiter. "Coffee, please."

Jones took his slice, this time with two hands, and held it in front of his mouth, poised to eat. "If I want a criminal and I want to offer cash for tips, I have to write an EC memo—and send it up the chain of command. The guys above me have to sign off. The ASA. The SSA. The ASAC and the Special SAC, agent in charge, at my office. They approve it. Then I make a poster." He finally took a bite.

Lizzie considered this as he chewed. "Shit," she said and leaned forward. She placed her elbows on the table and ran her fingers through her long blond hair.

Jones studied her. "Why? Is it big?"

"It's big. It's huge."

"How do you know?" Jones put down his slice and moved the pizza from in between them toward the window.

"I know," Lizzie said as the waiter set down a cup of coffee. She leaned in and smelled it. There was nothing better than diner coffee on a hot, rainy night in New York City. Except pizza. Lizzie regarded him.

Jones leaned in and lowered his voice. "Now, Lizzie. A tip is from the public. You're in Cancún. You see a fugitive. You call me. That's a tip."

She said, "I know."

"But then there's a source."

"A source is inside, like on *Homeland*," she said. "The hooker from Iowa dating the Saudi in season one. The one with the necklace."

"The one who got shot," Jones said. "Shot and killed. It's dangerous work."

Lizzie looked away.

"And sometimes a source is paid for years and sometimes she gets paid once."

"That's it. I want to be a onetime source."

"But it still goes up the chain of command. So what are we talking about here, honey?"

"How long does it take? To go up the chain? Like how long until you could get a warrant?"

"I can call a judge for a warrant in an hour."

Lizzie gazed out the window at Bleecker. She looked back at Jones. "Eighteen thousand. That's what I need."

Jones paused and eyed Lizzie. "I can't promise and you can't extort me. What do you got?"

Lizzie took a breath and looked at the pizza. "Ah, fuck it. Give me a slice." She reached toward it and pulled out a hot, dripping slice covered with rings of pepperoni. She took a bite, and as she ate she said, "Tax evasion, pimping, and tampering. False imprisonment, sex trade with minors. Possession and production and distribution of child pornography and Internet crimes against kids." She swallowed. "No one can live without pizza!"

Jones leaned back and looked at her. He whistled through his teeth.

"That's what I got." She took another bite and spoke while she chewed. "But not little kids. A couple of mouthy under-eighteens and one Crimean who wants to go home and can't until she pays off her *debt*."

Jones studied her. This girl was good. He had had this same funny feeling before, a couple of times, when big cases and bigger convictions fell from the sky into his lap.

He pulled out his phone and dialed the office.

Two days later, after the raid, he dropped Lizzie in front of her building. She found her super, went inside, packed a suitcase, her vacation suitcase, and returned to the curb to hail a cab to go to her mother's, where she'd feel safe.

She had never done anything like this before.

This wasn't Nancy Drew or Marty's movie.

This was real.

The Screamer was real. Sasha was real. Josh and Fishman and Ted were real, and she was scared.

———

Ally was stunned. She could hardly speak. "Are you kidding me?"

"No," said Lizzie, gazing at the vapor rising from her tea.

"Lizzie! I thought—"

"Teddy funds it. He sent me. I thought you should know."

"Weather told me," Ally said.

They stared at each other. Lizzie then gazed at her tea on the counter. "It wasn't just me. Jones said they had a case open . . . They had been tracking Fishman for months . . . He's connected to stuff. Bigger stuff. They're going to flip him."

"What does that mean?"

"They're after the bad guys behind him." Lizzie looked up at Ally and swallowed. "I'm scared, Mom. I'm so scared."

"Come here, sweetie," Ally said. Lizzie fell easily into her arms, and Ally's eyes welled as she held her girl. "You're so brave."

"Please don't cry," Lizzie begged and pulled back.

"I won't, I won't." Ally leaned in and squeezed her again for good measure. The oven timer buzzed. "Sit, sit down, and I'll get the cake."

Lizzie took her mug and sat at the table.

Ally leaned over and opened the oven. She straightened up again, pulled on an oven mitt, and took out the cake.

"I wasn't supposed to be there today," Lizzie admitted, stirring her tea. It was too hot to drink. In a few minutes it would be perfect, the sting off its boil.

"Then why were you? What do you mean?" Ally asked, cutting the cake.

"They called to say the case was concluding. That I should stay away."

Ally slid a slice to a plate, turned, and placed it in front of Lizzie. "Why did you go?"

"I made a friend. I wanted to warn her."

"So dangerous! Lizzie!"

"I know. I know it was dumb."

Ally turned and drew her tea bag out of her mug. She dropped it steaming into the sink, turned back, and pulled out a chair.

Lizzie straightened and uncrossed her legs. She picked up her fork and took a bite of the olive oil cake, chewing it slowly. Relishing it. "I love this cake. It's so unique."

"It has flour."

"I don't care."

Ally smiled and studied her daughter. "I'm proud of you, Bug."

Lizzie smiled. "It was the best feeling—ever. Mom?" she continued, looking up from her cake. "Jones said I should apply for a thing—down in Virginia. FBI thing. He's making a call. It would start in a month."

Ally's mouth dropped open. Her hand floated to her chest in shock.

"They give you housing. Arlington, I think, or maybe DC. He asked for my grades. I faxed them my transcripts."

"Do you want to do it? Do you want to go?"

Lizzie smiled broadly, as surprised as Ally. "I kind of do. If I get in."

"If you get in? Of course you'll get in!"

"Please," Lizzie said in a rare modest moment. She was spent from the rush of the last few days. Tired, fragile, still frightened.

Behind Ally, Jake entered, freshly showered, tucking his shirt into his jeans. "Ladies," he said.

Lizzie looked up, eyes wide. She looked at Ally as Ally seemed to die a small death. "Hi, Noah. What are you doing here?"

"I was upstairs. In the bedroom. With your mom."

Lizzie smiled and tried not to laugh. Ally closed her eyes.

Jake took a seat. "Glad you're home safe," he said to Lizzie, then turned to Ally. "This is good-bye. I'm headed to London."

"What?" Ally opened her eyes. "But I thought—"

"I can't. My car is outside. I have to be on a nine o'clock flight."

"Oh." She studied him. Was he upset? She couldn't tell.

He placed a letter on the table. Five pages, folded in thirds. "I wrote this last night. It's a letter for you."

"For me?" She reached to pick it up.

"Wait," he said, "until I leave."

"Of course," Ally said and rose. "I'll walk you out."

Jake rose too. "Bye, Lizzie."

"Bye, Noah. Best of, you know, luck on your junket."

"Thanks," he said.

At the front door, he kissed Ally coolly. She was concerned. "Are you mad?"

Jake shook his head. "I'll be in Boston the twenty-first. See you then?"

"December?"

He nodded.

"Okay," she said. "Thank you . . . for loving me and almost, you know, having sex."

He laughed, leaned in, and squeezed her tight. When he pulled back, Ally felt woozy. Was he leaving again? Had she sent him off again?

He slipped his knuckle under her chin, lifted her head, and kissed her on the lips one last time. He turned and sauntered down the stoop toward the SUV.

Ally watched as he climbed in. She watched as the Escalade, Jake inside it, took off east toward the Brooklyn Bridge, toward Manhattan, toward London, toward everywhere but Cranberry Street.

"I love him," she said in the kitchen doorway. "So you know. Upstairs? It wasn't just fun."

"I *hope* it was fun," Lizzie said. "And I don't care if you love him or not. That's your problem."

"It's not a *problem*." Ally walked in. "Choose what you want from the boxes up there. The rest goes back."

"Why?" Lizzie said. "Is it all from Jake?"

"I don't want him spending money on me. Not like that. It's not right."

"Mom!"

"What? I'm not the type. I don't need gifts. I have everything I want right now. You're safe. I'll see Jake at Christmas. I guess. I hope . . ." Her voice trailed off, cracking and uncertain. She looked at her cake. "Tea and cake. I have it all." She tried to smile and picked up her fork, but she didn't feel hungry.

Lizzie studied her. "Mom, read the pages."

Ally looked at her. Looked at the letter.

"Now," Lizzie said and slid it across the table.

"You read it?"

"I was born nosy."

"You were," Ally said and opened the letter, five pages long. She loved this man. "This isn't a letter. What is this?" She was confused. She looked at Lizzie.

"It's tickets," said Lizzie.

"What? No, it's not. It's pieces of paper."

"No, it's tickets. You can print them now."

"On paper?"

"Yes." Lizzie laughed. "Welcome to the twenty-first century, Mom."

Ally read the tickets and gasped. "This is to London!"

Lizzie smiled.

"Tomorrow morning!"

"The second page is your limo confirmation." She leaned in as Ally flipped the pages. "Mom, it's yours. Your itinerary for *three* months!"

"*Three* months?"

"On his press tour! He's inviting you!"

She took a breath. "Three months?"

"How can you not?" Lizzie said. "You don't have to teach. You only have to write. You're off for the year. He'll pay the way. The whole thing. I'm moving in, for a few weeks. I'll water the plants."

Ally read it. "London. Paris. Vienna. Rome. *Sydney? Tokyo?*" She looked up, stunned. "This is . . . This is . . ."

"Happening." Lizzie took the pages and put them aside. She took Ally's hands into her own and swallowed the lump that had formed in her throat. "I know what you're thinking."

"You do?"

"Yes. How can I possibly pack for three months? All in one night? How can I get on a flight to *Europe* tomorrow morning when—?"

"No," Ally said, "I was thinking . . . well—if you're okay—I'd like to go. If you're okay."

"I'm better than okay! You have to, Mom!"

"Are you sure?"

"Yes!"

"But you're scared?"

"Please. I'll be fine. I'm always fine. Better than fine."

"With Jake!"

"With Jake! As long as your passport hasn't expired. Do you even have one?"

Ally's face dropped. "It might have!" she cried.

After a desperate one-hour search, Ally found her passport. It hadn't expired. Then she packed as best as she could for three whole months.

Lizzie brought up a box from downstairs. The smallest one. "Return the rest but open this. I insist." It was from La Perla. Italian lingerie.

Ally opened it.

The baby-doll nightie and underwear set was wrapped in tissue and hung on a hanger, complete with tags. Ally held it up in the air. They were both entranced.

The mint-green lace, pale, almost white, was delicate and detailed with openwork diamonds, daisy patterns, and rosebud straps. The silk was so thin and so feather soft, it almost felt as if it didn't exist. It felt like a breeze.

The plane flew out from JFK at seven fifteen the next morning.

Ally climbed from the back of the town car at Whitehall Place at eight forty-five and breathed in the humid London night.

Pink and white orchids brightened the grand Corinthia lobby. An enormous Baccarat crystal chandelier hung from the ceiling, round and shimmering like the sun.

Upstairs the penthouse sprawled and wound across parquet floors and paneled walls, with terraces that fell onto twinkling London.

The butler rang and brought up dinner. "Mr. Yastrzemski called ahead," he said to her kindly. He presented a tray of lemon sole, avocado salad, and elderflower jelly with Chantilly cream and cherries for dessert.

"You'll be joining the cooking class tomorrow?"

"I will? I don't know," Ally said with surprise.

"Mr. Yastrzemski signed you up. With our master chef."

Minutes later, Ally froze when she entered the bedroom. A single box sat in the center of the bed. It was robin's-egg blue with a white satin ribbon.

She recognized the signature gift wrap. Tiffany.

She crossed to the bed, crawled up on it, and sat for a moment, gazing at the gift. She took the box and pulled the ribbon. The bow unfurled and fell away, and she carefully lifted the tiny top.

Inside the box she found another. She'd thought she might. The second was smaller, dark blue, and velvet.

She lifted its lid, and indeed, inside it, there was a ring: a simple, sparkling, one-carat solitaire, raised on its yellow-gold band on six classic prongs to let the light through, to look lit from within.

Ally stared at it, eyes wide, and pulled it from the box.

She tried it on.

She held out her hand, awed and moved, too tired to protest.

Then she collapsed. She sat up again and pulled down the bedspread, crawled between the sheets, and burrowed under, feeling the heft and weight of the duvet, the crisp, cool sheets, soft and smooth, and the weight of the strange new ring on her hand.

If she had stayed, if she had let it, the bedding itself would have lulled her to sleep, so she climbed out again. She wanted to be refreshed and awake when Jake came back.

A shower might help, she told herself.

The bathroom was a palace of white and gray marble and polished chrome, gleaming and smooth. The shower stall smelled of spicy soaps and the shower jets drained the fatigue from her muscles.

Half an hour later, she wrapped herself up in a plush towel, impossibly plush, and dried off her wet, naked body.

She slipped herself into the baby-doll nightie, replacing the thong with white cotton briefs.

She wanted to be Ally for real.

Ally in London. Engaged to be married to Jake Bean. Not Noah Bean, but Jake.

And Ally Hughes did not wear a thong after a twelve-hour day of travel.

Wrapped in a robe and under a throw, she settled into a chaise on the terrace.

Sipping tea, she gazed out at the river Thames, the Waterloo Bridge and Big Ben, which shone like the moon from Elizabeth Tower.

She thought of her own Elizabeth at home. Her grown-up Lizzie. She thought of how the years had flown and not flown. She thought of Claire, and of Jake, and how much she loved them and missed them both at different times.

Where was he now?

She hadn't called to say she was coming. But she knew he knew. He'd ordered dinner! She wasn't worried. She watched the minute hand circle around, around, and around, clockwise, forward, never back, and fell asleep.

At quarter past twelve, Jake woke her up.

ACKNOWLEDGMENTS

Thank you to my hilarious and brilliant agent, Alexandra Machinist, for opening her spam folder at midnight, for her stellar advice, and for endlessly cracking me up. And to Sheila Crowley and Sophie Baker and the lovely Laura Regan, and everyone on the powerhouse teams at ICM and Curtis Brown.

This book would not be what it is today without Denise Roy, its editor at Dutton. My heartfelt thanks to Denise for tying Ally's shoelaces, for patiently walking me through this thing called getting a novel published, for her steadfast, astounding graciousness. This experience was an absolute pleasure. My thanks extend to Darren Booth, for his beautiful book cover, LeeAnn, Matthew, Katie, and everyone at Dutton and Penguin Random House.

Thanks, as well, to the following friends, lovers, scholars: Julia Rabig, Breanne Fahs, Barbara Winslow, Philip Shelley, Wendy Chapkis, Joannie Wooters-Reisin, Andrew Powers, and Isabel Jolly; to Bill and Mylin, for asking how the book was going; to Mary-Margaret Kunze, for taking Sundays; to Victor Constantino, for arguing over commas with me; and to my dear friend Elizabeth Barondes, for reading it first.

And last but not least, thanks to Doc Hog and DJ, my mom and dad.